Find Me~ Book Three

She Walked a Different Path

H.H. Rune

Heartfinder Media LLC

Find Me, Book Three~ She walked a different path.

The third in the Extraordinary Life Seeker series by H.H. Rune

While this work contains shimmers from the autobiographical record of the author, it is brought forth as a work of fiction. If anyone, by chance, "sees" themself in the pages of this work, I encourage them to feel touched that their presence has made enough of a difference in one person's life to be written about and remembered forever.

No real names have been mentioned for the privacy of all. This series is written from one person's perspective - with her often imperfect memory - and no harm is intended. Imparted wisdom is shared only to be a "potential" teaching moment that may help others in navigating their own lives; however, it is not intended to be taken as any sort of "therapy" or an answer to their own problems as such. The author recommends professional therapy to everyone all along their personal journey, as she has found it invaluable herself. Thank you, M.H.

There are some actual places mentioned in this book that may or may not have been visited by the author; they were included to introduce random places to readers to invite them to explore more. Resources are listed in the back.

Copyright exceptions:

"We don't know each other, you see. We are two strangers, but we both have someone we want to get rid of. No one would put it together, there would be absolutely no way to tie either of us to each other's crime- it just makes sense. Get it? We swap murders. Criss Cross." Strangers on a Train (1951) Book by Patricia Highsmith, Film Directed by Alfred Hitchcock

"Please die on your own sword, not somebody else's. If you're gonna lose, it's much more fun to lose based on what you thought. Do you know how many of you are gonna lose on somebody else's thesis? It's gonna kill at you, it's gonna eat at you, it's going to be the worst fucking feeling, so please fuckin' pause this video right now and ask yourself, *am I doing my shit because of me?* Then you're good, whether you're winning or losing. *Or am I doing it because somebody else is telling me it's the right way?* Or I'm subconsciously pandering to please somebody or something because of the short term stability? Figure that the fuck out." *~Gary Vaynerchuk*

Original cover by the author utilizing her Canva Pro account and original art on stamp was done by Scott Poole- scottpoole.com

Dedication and Thanks

I dedicate this volume to the kids I never planned on having. *M*y bonus* kids. *Definition of Bonus: something welcome and often unexpected that accompanies and enhances something that is itself good.*

You have shown me in real time how much growth is possible from where we come from. That empathy is prominent in our innocent hearts until it is talked or taught out of us. That you heard me even while acting like you weren't listening. I have been gifted the opportunity to watch you both, first up close and then from afar. Witnessing your successes, your challenges and what came your way. My wish for you is a sovereign life, one where you call the shots and remember who you are anytime you feel questioned. I am here for you, until death do us part.
Love, Your bonus Mom

Many thanks* to: To my editor R.C. and sensitivity reader R.R.
To my brilliant Beta readers ~A.N. & C.B~ I could not have put this together without you.
A heartfelt thanks to fellow Indie Author- A.S.
for all of the body-doubling hours of working together towards our dreams.
<3 H

*All of the initials left here in thanks and in my other books will be revealed in Book Five

Triggers & Style

Trigger Warnings:

Contains topics such as Foster Care, Death of Mother, Grief, Pornography Addiction, Religious Differences, Marital Discord, Sexually transmitted Disease, Murder Ideation, Russia.

Some of these triggers are only touched on, while others are shown more in depth. Some resources are listed at the end of the book.

Out of respect to one's life experiences, H.H. Rune

***

Stylistic Choices: With Indie publishing comes a freedom I wasn't expecting or maybe even wanted. Even with an editor, I have my own thoughts as to how some sentences should read. It is here that I ask for your understanding of all the quirks or stylistic choices you may see in this book. As a diagnosed neuro-divergent- (diagnosed at fifty-two,) I have a certain way of thinking and speaking. When I add a comma in a place that some feel is unwarranted, it is because I want the reader to experience a pause.

Cheat code for the Reader

This book uses three different type sets to show the varied viewpoints:

Bolded text shows the author's notes and memories in the traveling books themselves.

Italicized font portrays the author's journal entries over time.

Standard text is to signify the travels of Book Three

***

The "3" at the top of the excerpts is to show the change of scene to the traveling books' movements.
Other books will use ~1~, ~2~, ~4~, and ~5~.

***

The books in the Find Me, Extraordinary Life Seeker series are best read in order.

Find Me

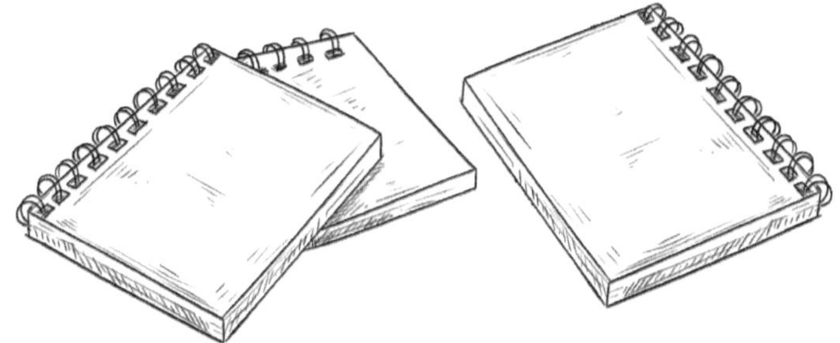

Book Three

D ear Reader,

This traveling book is my secret mission to live a more extraordinary life from within the confines of an ordinary one.

Only five copies of this book exist and this has made its way to you; you are now and forever a part of this story.

Inside you will find moments captured from one person's life. Each passage starts with the set of initials of the person with whom I share the connection.

We are all connected on some level; every person you meet leaves a mark on you whether good or bad. Often it is the worst people who *gift* us the best lessons.

It is my hope that this idea spurs you into living in a more extraordinary way; to think bigger and reach beyond what you currently see.

The memories inside may remind you of a time or a person in your own life; may you think of those people today for the good or the lessons you learned from them.

Please read this book then write your name and location in the back before giving it to someone else. Leave it on a bus, give it to a friend, it will only take a few minutes for you to participate and it is wonderful to think of the adventures it may have.

Let's see how small our world really is.

If you, by chance, recognize yourself in here, please bring the book and,

Find me...

~

How It All Started, Me, 2005-2009

*O*nce upon a time a woman was unsatisfied with her life as it was. As is common, those around her tried to convince her that everything was good and typical. Even though from the outside looking in- she had everything her little child and teenage heart had dreamed of— somehow when she had gained all of those pieces she had craved, it still wasn't enough.

As if a fairy godmother had landed in her kitchen and bonked her on the head with a magic wand, a new mission was placed in her heart, but this one felt much different than the ideas that came and fell away. This one she had to follow through on. It promised a way to expand her life in the most monumental way and potentially others— along the lines of six degrees of separation theory, yet personalized.

Five little books, drafted, with no names or a way to track them back to the author other than the short little anecdotes about her and those who impacted her life that she shared. She, a single link in the chain of humanity, hoping to connect with thousands, via the books and back again.

I had tried to be as scientific as possible with this little experiment of mine, sending the little books out from different locations and all. The first one had been launched from my childhood town, the second while crossing the border into Canada on a family trip. For the third, I had to get a little more creative. It was a reach and a gamble sent with trust, but I did it anyway. Through another friend, I asked an old acquaintance for a favor.

I remember that day, whirling my mental Rolodex to the person whom I knew lived as far away from me as I could think of. R.R. He may just be up for it.

I bundled up Book Three in a separate box, all tight and secure. The wrapped parcel inside was addressed already and I put the cash to ship it in a separate envelope inside with a note of thanks and instructions. I made it real easy for him. A box inside a box, all ready to go.

He never asked what it was, or why I wanted to send it. Maybe as a lawyer he thought it was better not to know. Days later I received an email saying it was done.

Book Three was on its way to Maine. Soon after it would be in the hands of someone. A true stranger to me. What will they think? What will they do with this little objective of mine?

Would the giftee help?

The idea had come from out of nowhere. I'd been deep in a rut. Trying to figure out what I could do or who I could be in my next phase, with both kids in school. I had spent one day writing and assembling the memory books with the intro page that implored that the books be passed along until someone who had been written about inside found one and could bring it back to me. A circle finally completed.

That is how I pictured it, one or more of the books eventually finding me. Once I started looking at exactly how many people there were in the U.S.A, I suddenly felt like the crazy person my husband tried to tell me I was back then by pinning my hopes on this gigantic request.

I guess I will have to just be okay if it doesn't work out, relegating myself to the idea that I had taken a damn chance instead of wondering about it forever. I still hold out hope that maybe it could work.

I did it for me, and maybe a little bit because he didn't think it was a good idea. He said that strangers wouldn't help another person like that. He imagined my volumes ending up in the trash. I frown at the thought.

I worked really hard on them. Thinking about all the people that I wrote about. Remembering what each person meant to me. Pain comes through when I think of them. Things didn't happen the way I wanted them to. Sometimes with some lovers, I thought forever was a possibility, but then it wasn't. The books are a part of me now, journeying beyond me, the same as my own children will someday.

Each volume, made in the same design as the book I had received from my first writing mentor, A.G. Blue cover, simple gold lettering I had placed myself. Light on pages but big on mission.

Meeting her in my writers group so many years ago, she gathered me under her wing and told me to keep writing no matter what anyone said. Maybe it was her courage beside mine that made me send them out like I did, despite the lack of support.

~

Mom

One of my friends stated that you were probably the weirdest person she had ever come across. I see that as a perk. You were not the ordinary June Cleaver type of mom, you are one of a kind. You grew up in a medium-sized family, with an alcoholic dad and a loving and extroverted mom.

Born in the South, you developed asthma and the whole family moved to Southern California so you could breathe better. I think you arrived around age seven. A lover of horses and animals, your upbringing as the third child in the family had you following after your older siblings and also looking out for your little brother.

Your father was an inventor type whose pride wouldn't let your mother work, which made you worry how everything would get paid for. Your mother loved to entertain and had grown up in a rich household.

Not wanting to fall into the same trap as your penny-pinching childhood home, you picked a lucrative and safe career to best help support a family one day, a role you thought you would enjoy for the long run, but it was not to be.

When we moved from California, we ventured North. A part-time position in a home decor store piqued an interest that was hidden away inside you. Suddenly seeing a new and exciting path- one in design, architecture and construction, you took the job and started back to school. You fell in love with the process of turning lackluster spaces into chaos first— then beauty.

Forever curious, you were always fascinated by something-a new hobby, a new goal. I watched and learned from you. Pottery and throwing dishes, designing wallpaper or t-shirts for a charity. That Easter you spent hours and hours making Czechoslovakian hand-waxed and dyed eggs. When we couldn't find the last one hid and had it explode months later stinking up the house. You won a Halloween costume contest as Snoopy the dog where literally no one at the party knew who you were because you didn't speak a word. You took your award and left to keep up the caper.

You were the different mom in the neighborhood, working long hours and spending time off at the art museum or going to art galleries to see what people were creating. You'd watch foreign films on the TV, and take us to plays to expand our world. You signed us up for summer camps to learn about art, nature, whatever was offered since you weren't given those options as a kid. You read like a crazy person— there's always something new to learn, to understand, a new perspective to help make something make sense.

In the romance department, I watched your marriage with my father falter and die, and later you entered into a relationship that emotionally tore you apart. It tore me apart to watch you hurt so badly. You tried for so long with him. Afterward you hardly dated anyone, and when you did, things didn't tend to work out.

You made your own way without a lot of financial backing, but you still traveled all over the world meeting people from many cultures. You wanted to make a difference for the planet long before it was cool, and came back from one of your trips, telling me to get some ducks to help eat the slugs in my garden. At the time I lived on a suburban cul-de-sac with CC&Rs and couldn't even contemplate having any farm animals, but it was a good idea.

From you, I grew my own love of design and the process of taking a space from ugliness into the very best version of itself. My love of all things art came from you, too, as I painted and sculpted whatever came to me.

You were all about fostering our imagination, pulling what was possible out of ourselves. Even when we might have needed more structure, you didn't want to crush our childlike wonder, so you often let us get away with things.

Or maybe you were tired — I'm not sure.

From you, I got my never-ending curiosity for everything. As you read new books, sought understanding of new technologies, or contemplated the universe, your brain never stopped, and neither does mine.

Along with your massive belief that anything was possible, came a forgetfulness of the old beliefs in exchange. Juggling the mundane while your brain danced along with the sprites of newness, your gaps come off as an absent mindedness, a failure of sorts, one you were criticized for. Maybe even by me.

But as my brain veers towards a familiar path, *I think differently.*

There are way too many cool things to learn about and that no matter how long one would live, there would never be enough time.

You have lived an extraordinary life without naming it, without claiming it.

Maybe that is where I got the idea from originally?

~

~3~

Isaac Oliver in Camden, Maine, sprinted the final five hundred yards of his daily run and whipped open his black metal mailbox front, fishing out a small, simply wrapped package along with his Visa bill.

He wondered if his daughter Eliza had ordered something, but it was addressed to him: I. Oliver.

Isaac was a virile, but desperately shy forty-five year old man. His eyes, a slate blue, showed the moody clouds that have been flying within him for some time now. They are in stark contrast to his olive skin which reflects an unknown heritage of which he feels no connection.

He runs— mostly away from his feelings. He jets out of the house daily, sprinting miles and miles away from home. This time away is one of the only reasons he is able to function in life.

Isaac pulled the key from under his shoelaces and unlocked the front door. Kicking off his shoes, he grabbed a hand towel from the powder bath to wipe the sweat from his brow and plunked down on a roomy chair in the living room before opening up the package. It was a book.

He looked for an author, or some indication of who might have sent it to him. Running his fingers over the title on the front cover he opened to the first page. A heartfelt request from someone with unfinished business. It felt like the words came from a woman. He looked at the pages in the back for signatures of people who had received the book, and saw none. He was the first one to read it. Why would anyone send it to him? Very strange. He could count his friends on one hand. He wasn't much for being social.

"What is this thing," he thought to himself before skimming the pages. "Wow, this person had a few loves, unlike me."

Abby had been the only love he should have ever needed. He felt sorry for the woman expressing her words on the pages of the mysterious book. She had loved and lost many times. Pain must be her middle name. Yet, somehow she found the courage to write it all down and send it off in such a vulnerable way to strangers, *seemingly just for the hell of it*. Did this crazy idea really have a chance with how big and disconnected the world is?

As the pages fell away, his mind wafted to Abby. If only he could have shown it to her.

Once promised a lifetime of love and companionship, Isaac lies awake each night, feeling lost. His wife of fifteen years, the love of his entire world, Abby, died of breast cancer two years ago. The biggest reminder of her that remains is their daughter Eliza who is growing to look more like her mother every day.

The day after Abby passed, Isaac removed all the photos of their family together and put them in a box in the closet, as just seeing them was all too much for him. Painful moments in still life, he couldn't catch a breath, and his eyes remained blurred with tears for months.

He had battled brutally hard just to continue on living since she died, but he had to. Eliza needed him. He had forced aside the grief of losing Abby enough to be there for Eliza's everyday needs. Picking up the tasks that Abby had done for her, he'd made sure Eliza had a counselor to talk to, he'd taken her shopping for new clothes and tried to keep her somewhat sheltered from the hard stuff of all there was to fear in the world. Even with the memories, he had decided to keep them in the same house, she in her same room, in her same neighborhood, so she'd experience as few changes as possible, except for that one thing. Her mother.

His wife. Abby had been his missing piece. He walked through his early life feeling like he was half a person, forever hoping that someone would come along and complete him.

Even with that wish, he hadn't let anyone get close to him in all those years; only Coach Barrett and Abby. Maybe that was the problem.

Abby had seen through the façade that he kept in front of him; she had drawn him out. She had forced her way into his view in college, and thank God she did or he would never have seen her. She found him. Needled her way into his locked up and protective potential and into his soul. No one had ever made that kind of effort with him before.

Growing up in foster care made him feel that he wasn't really a part of a family or had anything concrete. He never knew how long he would be staying in the same house or when he might have to switch schools again. Everything was always in flux for as long as he could remember.

Isaac had always fended for himself. Even the suitcase that he carried from foster home to foster home had been purchased by him from a second hand shop with the money he should have been spending on his school lunches. He wanted at least one thing to call his own. Something that they couldn't take away from him.

Isaac was moved around a lot, but not because he was a troublemaker.

No, not at all. Mostly he fell into families who had their own drama or they believed he wasn't happy with them because he kept to himself all the time. That feeling of rejection from his own family transferred to every foster family he came to live with. He didn't bother trying to connect with anyone since he didn't have faith they'd stick around. His foster parents struggled to connect with him. They became tired of trying to reach him, and soon he was on the move again. In a cruel twist, his birth family never let go of their right to claim him, but they never did come back.

Isaac felt like a ghost, walking the halls of his many foster homes, watching in quiet envy the members of the real families love and being there for each other. For him everything was temporary. The only thing he could control was how well he did in school. In every school he attended, he achieved high marks.

It wasn't until high school that Isaac found any purpose for his being at all. He was running to class and the track coach saw him while in full bolt to get to Language Arts. The coach sped to catch up with him just before he dashed into class. He made a mental note of the door number and came back just before class ended and waited outside to talk to him.

Surprised to have someone's attention, he was talked into joining the track team. Coach took Isaac under his wing, helping him train, and when senior year came around, Coach assisted him in applying for a scholarship to the nearby university.

Isaac hadn't thought of going to college at all. He imagined his future would consist of aging out of the state foster care system and being thrust fully into being responsible for himself. Coach Barrett kept in touch with Isaac through his first year of college before having a heart attack and passing away. Isaac felt on his own yet again.

He set his mind on a business degree and worked summers for UPS delivering packages. He was successful because of his speed, and worked long weekend hours while going to school. He lived on campus in a dingy dorm, as cheaply as he could, buying cheap frozen meals and ramen noodles at the nearby grocery bargain store instead of paying for the cafeteria meal plans. He just managed.

He wasn't picky about food, and had a good metabolism, so whatever he ate got him to where he needed to go. He kept in athletic shape running to each of his classes every day and outrunning the dogs that tried to bite him on his weekend runs. Running felt better than walking to him, because when his pace slowed, he'd be forced to watch the other students on campus relating to each other. If he ran, he didn't have to experience the familiar and painful exclusion.

Girls were just walking works of art to him back then. He hadn't even spoken to a girl until that day in college when Abby yelled out to him.

"Geez you are fast!" she bellowed. "Do you ever stop?!"

He looked around to see if someone was talking to him. She was staring him down and looking so cute with her hands on her hips. He stalled then, almost falling over his feet, his backpack flinging forward onto the ground due to pent-up inertia.

This beauty beyond beauties was speaking to him, her eyes expecting a response.

"Um, thanks," he managed to say when his breath caught up with him.

She had chestnut hair with a little curl to it, mostly on the ends. It feathered away from her face on one side and she tucked it behind her ear on the other. He liked that. Her lips were pink and her eyes a light brown rimmed in green. Freckles accented her button nose. Her beauty was natural, not all completely made up like the other girls he had seen around campus.

Obviously still needing to go to class, he began walking at a quickened pace and she galloped alongside him for a while, before needing to break away to get to her geology class.

"Maybe I'll see you around sometime, Speedy," she winked.

"Yeah, maybe." He smiled at her with his slightly crooked teeth then bowed his head to hide them again out of his life-long self consciousness.

She touched his arm, "I'd like that," her eyes grew obvious with the invitation.

Isaac felt warm at the thought of Abby's touch, even all these years later. Her surprising arrival in his life had made his life so much bigger, and more colorful.

They stole minutes together before splitting off. Abby made him feel at ease and she would seek him out after class together. They ate lunch the following week, and as Isaac munched on his peanut butter and jelly sandwich she enjoyed a beefy Italian sub.

This went on a few times until Abby finally asked him for a coffee one Saturday and a study date at the campus library. It was Isaac's first real date. Ever.

She was sweet and would laugh when he blushed at her compliments. Over time, their friendship grew into something more.

Their first kiss was in the rotunda. He had stumbled into her, tripping over his feet in his new and slightly more stylish shoes. She caught and steadied him and smiled. Somehow Isaac's animal instincts kicked in and he bent lower and met her lips with his.

Over the next two years, they built something sustaining and beautiful. She added to his life all of those missing ingredients. With her, he felt smart, inspired, and important. It was with her that he found out what love was and he was finally able to trust in it.

Now that she was gone, it was just him and Eliza. Could he have the courage to step out from behind his walls again? He couldn't believe that there could be anyone for him in this whole world, except Abby. The woman in the book had found love more than once. Maybe it *was* possible to fall in love again.

How was he going to watch his own daughter love and lose, help her through heartbreak since he'd hardly any experience in romantic love at all? Eliza was such a good daughter. She needed guidance and security from him, as well as love, but Isaac had unknowingly pulled away. He had become a grown ghost of his younger self, walking the hallways of their house, just watching and spiriting along.

Eliza had also loved and lost. She'd navigated her mother's death, practically on her own. For the first time since his wife had died, Isaac thought of someone else potentially hurting more than he was. She'd lost her mother. He had never known his own mother, but he had missed the idea of her just the same.

She had lost the person who gave her life and loved her every step of the way. Her first word had been "mama." They cooked together in the kitchen making experimental recipes and pretending to host their own cooking show, happily serving up whatever concoction they had made with pride.

They'd sit together and read their individual books snuggled up side by side in the window seat in the living room, especially on those cold rainy days in the fall. Abby was there when Eliza broke her arm and had to go to the hospital to get a cast. When her friends all made fun of her braces, Abby was there to share her own crooked smile story to soften the blow.

He had been the spectator to it all, but he'd always let Abby do the heavy lifting of parenting because he felt he lacked experience.

Isaac only skimmed the book because he kept getting pulled into his own recollections. In the end he thought that maybe the book could help Eliza with some of the things that would be coming for her.

Isaac signed in the back of the book and set it down on the table next to him. His eyes misted up. "I still have time," he said to himself.

"Eliza?!"

"Yeah, Dad?" she called from her bedroom. "I'm in here." Eliza snuggled deeper into her pile of stuffed animals on her bed. She'd been reading.

Isaac walked in and plopped into her pillows with her. He hugged her intently for the first time in a long time. Eliza squirmed a little to move her nose away from his still sweaty armpits, before finally deciding she didn't care.

"What's up, Dad? You okay?" she asked after coming up for air.

"I was just missing Mom; I was wondering if you were, too."

"I do, Dad, all the time."

"Yeah, me, too."

They looked at each other and cried. Even though it was just the two of them, they were *still* a family. It was damn time Isaac remembered that.

He stood up. "Hey, let's go see Mom and tell her how we are and what we've been up to."

Eliza jumped up ready to go. Isaac put his arm around his daughter's shoulder. Wow, she was getting tall.

"First I'm going to shower; I gotta look my best."

Eliza plopped back down on her bed to wait for her father for their trip to the cemetery. They didn't go very often, mostly on holidays lately. She wasn't sure what had brought her dad into her room at that moment, as he was pretty much in his own world most of the time. Her counselor had said that her dad was on his own path in grieving. As much as she had wanted to pull her dad out of his head, she didn't know how. Mom had always been the key to Dad, and she couldn't find a way to pick the lock, let alone open the door.

"Okay, I'm ready." Her dad had on one of her mom's favorite shirts and he ran his hand through his still wet hair.

"Great!"

They grabbed their coats and went first to the corner floral boutique to buy flowers to take with them. They laid out a small colorful blanket and sat together on the cool grass near Abby's resting place. They all had a lot to talk about. But together they had time.

~

Gotta Go Through It, Me 2009

I am here. I have made my way through the forested highway to the coast. There are few people here today as the weather is dismal. It is often gray, but all the rain we get means the landscape is forever green, so I'll take it. Traffic was light coming over the pass, and with uncertain conditions expected, I imagine most people stayed home.

I wander down to the sand, and then sit bundled up. I'm the only one here for miles, it seems. I am glad. A sailboat bounces along the horizon as two fishing boats bob along to my left. The waves soothe me more with every minute that passes. I pause and take off my shoes. I want to feel the sand on my toes even though it's cold and damp, to feel something other than the uncertainty that plagues me.

A small caravan of horses with riders come from behind the beach grass, and head down closer to the surf. Their hooves splash water up almost to the rider's legs; they will all be wet soon enough.

I am very isolated with my thoughts here. I came to let things sink in. To process, to pray.

I pinch the sand between my toes. It grounds me. Even the seagulls are quieter than usual. I could sit here forever.

I sit on my jacket just below the grass line that spills into the open beach. I have found the perfect spot. My eyes still hurt from crying. I feel the tears coming again.

It feels wrong to cry when I am facing one of the most beautiful of all the world's views: the Pacific Ocean.

I close my eyes and take in the rhythm of the waves. I wish I had brought my dog to keep me company. He would lie beside me, I know, and just be here. Or he would walk with me for miles, just listening to me go on and on about it all.

I flatten the sand with my palm and write "love" and then erase it.

My most recent love did not serve me. Unless it was meant to show me what I do not want, and if that is the case, then it totally hit its mark.

The drizzle starts, and the real rain clouds are moving over me fast. In my wisdom this morning I brought an umbrella. I pop it open and sit under it like a fort. My own little hideaway. The wind pulls aggressively at the dome but I hold on for dear life.

Now to be grateful. I am grateful for my beautiful-inside-and-out daughters who light up my life. Grateful for their different personalities, their energy, and their amazing spirits.

I am grateful for my family and friends who still love me.

I have a fulfilling job at my own company (for as long as I can hold onto it), and a nice place to live (also for as long as I can hold onto it). I really do have so much.

It's the remembering of the good stuff sprinkled amongst the bad, sometimes, that is hard; but it's the only way to make it better, and to keep going.

I write "LOVE" in the sand again, only bigger. I leave it there to let the rain remove it in its own time. The grass around me sways to the rhythm of my heartbeat, and I sit wishing for things to be different, but not knowing how to get there.

To have the beach to oneself rarely happens and I drink it in. More time here is what I need, I imagine living nearby, to have this centering everyday.

Alas there is an interruption in the scenery and my solitude. A young couple, obviously in love, laugh and splash in the surf. It must be freezing, but they cannot feel the chill in their play.

An older couple walk their two dogs along the shoreline, glancing at each other, then at the younger couple, sharing a wink of remembrance of their own beach frolics over the years.

Another caravan of horses appear and then disappear back into the tall grasses toward the stable. Suddenly hundreds of gulls fly by, squawking and breaking my introspection.

There is a whole lot of living out there, and things still left to do. I will make it through.

Happy almost birthday to me. I hope I get just what I asked for.

~

Nearing Forty, Me, 2009

I was biking with a friend, L.C., and she said she couldn't imagine me as a stay-at-home mom- a suburban housewife. The idea to her was ludicrous. It didn't feel right.

Because I live in the city, in a little old house with two dogs and two cats and two daughters. It is a busy household, and I bike to work at my very own business. I have come quite a span from my days on the cul de sac.

I am looking forward to more adventures. A friend of mine wants to set me up with someone new. We will see what's in store for forty. Here we go.

***

Well, here I am. The evening of my fortieth birthday. Yesterday, I threw a potluck birthday party for myself. A wonderful room full of women, some from my previous life as a stay-at-home mom, and some from this new life that I have made since.

After opening my birthday cards, I looked out over the crowd and said, "Thank you all for coming. If I was gay, I'd want to sleep with every single one of you, I love you so much."

To some my statement was nuts, but it made many of them laugh and I wanted them to know how much it meant to me that they were here with me. It felt like a new beginning.

Ages zero to forty have been a hell of a ride so far. Work has seemed good lately, and things are moving right along. I am finally free of Mr. Fun in both my personal life and in the business. I have been pulled through the knothole, at last.

I think the lack of touch and having someone to talk to each day often makes me question if it was for the best, but I notice I am less jumpy, and worried about things, on my own.

I always believed that when you turn forty, you could stop apologizing for who you once were, and start appreciating how far you've come. But there is so much more that I want to do, and I just don't know where to start.

I have decided again to say yes more, and tonight on my actual birthday I got that chance. A friend called and asked if I would consider telling a story up in front of an audience. Something I wouldn't have agreed to do five years ago despite my commitment to live an extraordinary life. No way.

But now? Why the hell not?

I got up on stage with my hair in silly-for-my-age Princess Leia buns and I told a story about the worst date I had been on thus far, in this go-round of dating. And it was a doozy.

Here's what I shared:

We had started communicating online on a dating site, and when we talked on the phone, I noticed that he was very talkative. I believed it was nerves. The online messages that he left me were long, saying he said he was quite excited to meet me.

I set a time and a place: a nearby brew pub where we could get dinner and enjoy a stroll along the river. I got there early and waited for him out front, seeing him pull into the parking lot in a purple PT Cruiser with faux wood paneling, the car I hate most on the road today.

Somehow, I let it go, and we said hi. The brew pub I picked was too crowded so instead we walked along the water to the Mexican restaurant down a little further on, hoping to find a spot. We walked along and he talked almost the whole time about himself and how he had just gotten through a prostate cancer scare and how it left him somewhat impotent but he would love to try to work that out with me. Sometimes it accidentally made him pee. (Hello, is this really a first date conversation?)

I tried not to grimace as he spoke, as I am also a stress pee-er since having kids, aren't we all? But I just listened and was empathetic to his plight. He went on and on until we got to the restaurant and sat down.

We ordered. He kept talking. The food came. He kept talking and talking.

Then, he shared how he had really wanted to be a cop but he hadn't passed the psyche test. My ears perked up as I continued to gobble up the enchiladas in front of me, as his food got colder and colder, sitting mostly untouched.

He went on to say how, during his police academy interview, he went into very specific detail of how he would deal with a perp who had messed with someone in his family, which I understood and would also be majorly protective of mine. However, he also shared all the bodily harmful descriptions with me— a near stranger.

His detailed plan for the mutilation of the perpetrator, his relief to feel the protection of the badge, made me feel suddenly unsafe in his presence so I excused myself to use the restroom.

Reaching into my database of anyone I knew that had a car and may be able to pick me up on a Friday night, I landed on a good friend J.R. She said she would be right over and she could drop me back at my car, no problem.

Walking along the waterfront in the dark with a man I didn't know at all, who had thought very intently about how he would mangle another human being was a no-go.

As we were about to leave, I explained that I wasn't going to walk back to the car with him. He steamed as he left, but I didn't care. I wasn't going to be a crime victim for picking the wrong dude.

My friend arrived with backup. Her husband and her teen son had decided to tag along, maybe as bodyguards, but it felt humiliating. I would be a little more selective with anyone I was going to date from then on, or at least I hoped I would.

So I guess that made for quite a bad date already but the next day I got myself the meanest, most vengeful email from this man, and I was blown away.

Another friend, a psychology student at the time said, "Dear, you have just run into a textbook clinical narcissist. They go on the attack after being called out on their shit."

Thankfully, he managed to lose my number and I never heard from him again. Thankfully also, I would never, ever have to ride in that piece of shit-purple PT Cruiser.

The audience clapped and laughed on cue, and I was addicted. If they ever asked me to do that again the answer would be a resounding YES! It cemented even more, my love of storytelling.

In person or on the page, it is such a huge part of me. A love I hope I never lose; one I must keep alive. The words come regularly if I am to live my best life. Even if it is just stuff from my own head that I write down. I love it.

~

L or C w/ the last name of C

My experience was with only one of you. One of a set of identical twins in my neighborhood. Our exchange was brief yet left a big mark on me. Damn near literally.

I was aware of you and your sister, both living up the street from my house growing up. You were each tan, blondish and athletic. You appeared popular and always into one or more sports.

From what my mom told me later, you had just received your driver's license, and a cute little VW Bug for your sixteenth birthday. Our meeting was an accident.

I was walking home from school at the ripe old age of eight when our lives collided. One split second of utter stupidity on my part: I saw your car as it rounded the corner of the street but I foolishly believed I was fast enough to get across before you got down to where I was. There was no walk signal. I doubt you even saw me as I took off running, and your car naturally accelerated because of the steepness of the hill.

Wham! I slammed into the passenger door of your Bug and bounced off, landing on the ground, a bit crumpled.

You stopped immediately and knelt down to see if I was okay. I was stunned as I imagine you must have been as well. My body hurt, and I remember asking you, a stranger, for a ride home. We lived only seven houses away from each other. I was mere minutes from home, and you were just ten seconds away from yours. We had both almost made it, but not quite- that day.

You dropped me off at my house and my mom took me to the doctor where I had an X-ray and found out that I had a broken collar bone.

I am unsure about whether you came to visit or check on me after, or if you just kept your distance, wanting to forget the whole thing. You must have been traumatized as well.

So it is here that I wanted to share that I healed up nicely, after a month spent watching cartoons in a hard plaster, full-trunk body cast. Missing school the entire time was more than fine with me. Other than the cast being itchy, I was hardly bothered by the whole ordeal, and would forever have a story to tell.

This note is just to say that the little kid who ran into your car turned out okay and went on to have a pretty regular life. I often think back and know that some sort of angel or protector was present in that moment for the both of us.

It was lucky that my little body hadn't been pinned *under* your car that day or that I hadn't *died* in the accident- that would have been a tragedy for you to carry on forever after. In the spirit's infinite wisdom I have been able to go on to tell that story and many, many more.

Sorry for the dent.

~

The Last Few Years Have Mostly Sucked, Me, 2009

L ooking back is as much of a drag as it is a blur. Luckily my brain doesn't allow me to harp in on the details. The stupid affair, the divorce, getting into a crappy relationship. Finally getting out of it. Events punctuate if I grind in on them. I'm losing the house, the business is faltering, everything is going to shit. My impending bankruptcy. Oddly, I manage to keep going.

I somehow still believe that I will be okay and things will turn out for the best. Things have sucked for a lot of people, not just me. The mortgage crisis affected my brother, and a few more people I know. I am thankful that I have had options. Every time I thought I was a lost cause, an answer or path came. Some way out of the mess.

Even with the chaos, it would be nice to share my life with someone again. I miss the closeness of a lover, someone to talk to, to grow with, to love. I told the girls that whoever might come into our lives would have to be totally awesome to get in with us. I am feeling a little sorry for myself in that most of my friends have moved on with their lives, as I have left some behind as well.

At dinner with a friend in a bar, the older single men circled us like vultures and asked us to dance. I felt too young to be dancing to swing music in a bar with sixty year-old men. We politely refused their invitations. My friend sat across from me and asked me what I wanted next.

"I think I would like to get married again."

I had been imagining and delighting myself in all of the movies that Colin Firth has starred in. So asking for Colin Firth from the Universe seemed reasonable.

<u>He</u> was the dream. Tall, dark and handsome and oh, please, can you throw in an accent? My own little personal, dreamy Mr. Darcy?

I wanted everything I wanted in the first marriage plus. So stable, and a good dad, but also a fun world traveler. Was it possible?

With my life still in shambles, why would anyone want to be with me? Talk *about a fixer- upper. Do men even go to the bother of trying to fix women, or is it only the other way around?*

How dare I dream of someone new, when my life is a total mess.
Again.

~

~3~

Isaac got up early and made a hearty breakfast. It was Eliza's sixteenth birthday. He had a surprise used car parked in the neighbor's driveway for her. He was so excited he could barely keep himself from waking her up. Teenagers need to sleep, he told himself. She'd be getting the car plus the little blue book he had read all those months ago that had helped pull him out of his internal stuckness and brought him back to life.

He had saved the book for her, hoping there might be some wisdom in there for her to read and use for any of her own romantic entanglements that may come up, from a women's perspective.

Isaac had been happier lately. He and Eliza were closer, a new ease in the house had taken hold. Photos of the three of them -he, Eliza and Abby- were again scattered happily around the house. There were some new photos of just the two of them: on hikes from their camping trips, and their jaunts to the State Fair where they each held baby pigs until one pooped on Isaac and made Eliza nearly drop her pig from laughing.

They were both looking forward to their first international trip next month: a week in France where they would be staying in the countryside and learning to cook together in a Le Cordon Bleu style of cuisine. They talked about it nonstop.

Eliza had blossomed into a beautiful young woman. She resembled her mother, and Isaac was grateful for that. There were also some attributes she had that he could not call his or Abby's, that he assumed came from his side of the family.

A new notion of finding some of his birth family members hit. Maybe he had brothers or sisters who longed for family and felt a similarly lonely life as he had. It might be time to try and search them out. Even if it was a no, at least he could stop wondering. When his mother passed, he was able to obtain the records and names of his siblings from an old file from his last social worker, but he hadn't attempted a search.

Today was all about Eliza. He had cooked up her favorite blueberry pancakes, with his homemade blueberry syrup with orange zest. He had whipped the fresh cream with a whisk while tucked away in the walk-in pantry so as not to wake her up, and would do his best to blob some into a smiley face on top before adding the required sixteen candles to her thick stack.

Isaac was grateful for the new view of life that the book had given him. He'd taken care to wrap the book in pink and white-striped tissue paper, then added a Park Abbey rose from the garden to his uneven but made-with-love bow. Even though the spelling was different than his departed wife, he had bought a few shrubs of them for the yard in remembrance.

Eliza was a woman now, with womanly tastes, he figured. He loved her so much, and was so very thankful, that he felt alive again. He would forever have a part of Abby in Eliza.

A sleepy teenager appeared at the top of the stairs, she smelled something. Her sleepy amble grew urgent at the stair landing when she realized it was blueberry pancakes that were waiting for her.

"Yay! Thanks, Dad!"

The two of them were doing so much better, and she had a great summer planned. Eliza knew her friends wanted to take her to the mall for her birthday that day, but Dad said he got to keep her until noon.

Eliza was fine with that. She loved hanging with her dad.

"Happy Birthday, sweetheart," Isaac said.

"Hi, Dad. Looks Yummy."

"I have a couple of surprises for you."

"Okay, but I'm eating first. Famished."

Eliza devoured the top layer of her pancake stack, and looked over at her dad. He was staring at her.

"Dad, quit watching me eat."

"I was just thinking about how much you look like your mom, especially when you have blueberry syrup on your chin."

Her napkinned-hand shot to her face, "Gross, Dad, why didn't you tell me?"

Isaac laughed. "Don't worry, I won't tell anyone."

"How embarrassing," she said, rolling her eyes. "Okay, I'm ready for my surprises!"

"Well, Eliza, do you remember after Mom died and I basically tuned out, even with you?"

Eliza didn't like to think about that time, because it was so lonely for her.

"*Yes, I remember.*"

"This arrived in the mail one day, and it inspired me to pay more attention to the people I still had in my life. It reminded me of how important some have been to me, especially you. That was the day that we sat and talked and then went to see Mom. Well, I want you to have it."

"What is it?'

"You'll see. Open it up."

Eliza wiped her fingers on the napkin and picked up the beautifully wrapped gift.

"Dad, it's so pretty, did you do that?

"Yeah, *I can do a couple of things*," he said with a laugh.

Eliza pulled the ribbon off and stuck the rose into her bed-worn ponytail. She pulled the book from the nest of tissue.

"Read it when you get a chance. It was written by a woman who's had a few life experiences. She's sharing her life and her big dream with us. I was thinking you could maybe keep it and use it as a guidebook on life from a female perspective. It's not your mom, but someone else."

"Looks cool, Dad. But can I read it when I get home? The girls are coming to pick me up for our trip to the mall in an hour and I haven't even showered yet."

"Sure, but one more thing," Isaac tossed a shiny key chain down the table towards her."

"Dad, no way! Are you serious?!"

"Go look in Mrs. Smith's driveway."

Eliza ran to the front window. "Oh, my GOSH, a Volkswagen Bug! Awesome! Dad, thank you, thank you, thank you! WOW!" Eliza jumped at her father and planted a big kiss on his cheek. He gave her a big squeeze before she went squealing up the steps.

"This is the best day ever!" she shouted.

Eliza set the book down on the white painted bench at the end of her bed. She put the keys on top of the book. The car was great, but the book is what gave her dad back to her, so that present was even better.

~

Needing Something to Be Excited About Again, Me 2009

*T*he Colin Firth-like guy I was supposed to meet up with - the blind date planned by a friend- didn't happen as I'd hoped. In my frustration, I signed up for eHarmony to bide my time and wade into the dating pool in my forties. The site sent many possibilities to me. Many of them were very similar to my ex-husband including characteristics, even the same job that he had; so obviously there must have been some alignment there.

Today I broke down and cried at the thought that maybe I had been with the right guy all along. If we could have just figured out how to communicate our needs better, if we would have tried just one more counselor, maybe our marriage could have worked after all.

If I hadn't cheated, that is. He and I really did have some good times and often we were a good team together. He was a kind and understanding teacher, too, always showing me how to do something around the house if I wanted to update something. He showed me how to use the circular saw and the tile saw. How to measure things although that talent never stuck.

He even taught me how to calculate pi for a job bid that I needed to figure out the added square footage of a radius. Never judgy, never "why don't you know this already," he just showed me.

But why couldn't he wear colored underwear in the bedroom, or just some damn jeans instead of droopy Dockers every day? He changed after I left. Maybe as revenge, or maybe because it was a stupid thing for him to die on a hill about. I never bothered to ask.

After perusing my daily gentleman options, I almost called my ex, but didn't.

I just wanted to talk to him about the day that I decided I couldn't live the constrained life anymore. It was before the guy, before the affair. It was before all the chaos.

It was a day that he said no to what I thought was a simple, fun excursion with friends that I had been excited to do with him, all of us together. A rafting trip.

That conversation had become the final nail on the coffin of a long list of things he said he wouldn't try with me. We'd never have another cat, we wouldn't ever own a truck. He had done small towns already and would never move to one again.

All of that was before the affair, before I sought attention elsewhere. He said no to so many things and I stopped asking. Hearing him say no to everything that might come down the road, and it felt like a resounding no to us.

What's sad is that now, as the girls have gotten older, this might have been our time. To build our future, to figure out what was next for us, to have the time to be closer.

I ate dinner over there Tuesday night, and saw him yesterday. We talked for an hour on Sunday. I miss talking to him. Seems like every year or so I ask him to think about trying us again, each time he refuses. I need to remember he said no, he didn't want to try to be with me again. I have to let it go.

It's a little hard to do sometimes when every time I open up my computer, eHarmony sends me another one of him as "my perfect match".

~

E liza Oliver picked up the book that was waiting for her. After a busy trip to the mall, she flopped down on her bed to further examine the thoughtful gift.

A soft navy blue cover, FIND ME, 3 of 5, was printed on the front in gold lettering.

"Weird."

Eliza moved her stuffed animals around on her bed and settled into a really cozy spot. She ran her fingers down the spiral making a funny sound before opening to the first page. She read the request and was fascinated immediately. Sure, she would help if she could; why not?

Eliza read the excerpts with the initials atop each one. She remembered liking a boy and wanting him to like her back. A certain boy she had admired since sixth grade, even though boys had always been a puzzle to her. She had watched her friends gather and herd the boys together at a party once, watching them pair up two by two by the end of the night. Somehow she was always left alone.

The nerd in her had a few theories about that, in fact her imagination had been very active on the subject. Maybe it was her brainiac ways that held them at bay. Her straight A's must have earned her a rep. She considered letting her grades drop, just a little, to appeal to them, as a test. But in the end, she just couldn't do less than her very best.

For a long time, after Mom died, getting good grades was the only way her father would pay any attention to her, and now she did it for herself. Because she could. She loved to learn.

Her father would say how proud of her he was and how she was shaping her future with those building blocks of a good education. It felt good to achieve. Someday someone would appreciate her brains. Wouldn't it be great if he had brains, too?

She read the pages, skimming over some and re-reading others. She read into the night as the moon rose outside her window. Dad came in to wish her a goodnight, and he kissed her forehead.

"Try to get some sleep, you've got school tomorrow."

"I will. Thanks Dad, for everything. What a fun birthday."

Isaac turned and rested his shoulder in her doorway as he was leaving, "I love you, kiddo."

"Love you too, Dad." she looked up from the book and smiled.

She slouched down, and reached over to adjust her lamp to be able to see better. She pulled off her blue jeans and tucked herself under the covers.

This woman had seen some action and she wanted to take it all in. All those experiences hadn't seemed to sour her on love, they only fueled the pursuit. A pursuit Eliza decided it was time to try her hand at.

In the movies she had seen girls wink at boys when they were interested, or they would giggle nervously around them. She rolled her eyes at the ridiculousness of it. She had never winked at a boy, except that time when she had this annoying tick right before finals two years ago. She hadn't been sleeping much because she was studying so hard for Mr. Britsch's geometry test. She couldn't imagine laughing at a stupid joke just to make someone feel funny. She wished there was a class on love. "Why isn't there?" she asked helplessly.

I guess that's what mothers are good for. Sharing their experiences and helping their kids through the rough stuff. She didn't have her mother anymore and it didn't look like she would be getting a new one anytime soon.

"You will be my travel guide as I enter the romantic realm," she said to the book.

Perhaps she would have similar experiences as this woman and she could write about the people she had met, or how she reacted in their presence. Use it as a log, a diary she could learn from. This worked with this guy, this worked with that guy. A study of boys and men.

First things first though: she would have to start *talking* to Trevor more and see what happened. Eliza felt like she had a plan now, a plan to start maybe thinking about having a love life someday.

~

Working On Getting It Right Next Time, Me
2009

*M*om recommended a class. One that might help me understand men more, and understand women and myself in the process. It was a weekend seminar and my mother deemed it so important that she paid for my tuition, which was good, because I was broke.

It was called "Understanding Men, Celebrating Women", and taught by Alison Armstrong, the co-founder of an organization named PAX.

It seemed like a pretty important topic and may just help me in my search for my new love. He would be more adventurous than Mr. Stability, and more reliable than Mr. Fun. — A Mr. In Between? He was out there somewhere— I knew it.

I sat with maybe a hundred other women in a hotel ballroom in the big city closest to my town. There would be a morning session, then lunch and then an afternoon session with group chats sprinkled in.

The first day was about how men come into themselves, and growing through stages she described using ranks borrowed from the monarchical system:

Knight, prince, king and elder.

The knight phase is a male from puberty to his late twenties or early thirties. The knights are all about adventure and fun and being in the moment. They rarely get married at this time, but if they do, they are considering the marriage to be an adventure. They are especially interested in kitting out their cars or of showing off how good they are at something.

The prince section hits in the late twenties or early thirties to forties, and lasts well into the forties. It is the stage where men start to look around and put their head down to build up their kingdom. They are all about what they want, and what they hope to accomplish. They are painfully-aware that they are not kings. This is when they determine what is important to them and where they collect both things and people, often getting married and starting *a family if that is determined to be of importance to them.*

There is a dark tunnel between the stages of prince and king, as this is a time of great soul searching. This is often where they experience their "Mid-Life Crisis." Sometimes they take on a mistress in an effort to plump their ego.

Kings are men who know who they are and what they want. They have accomplished much of what they had planned and are very particular about what they will provide and to whom. They are decided and content and rarely falter or feel inadequate. They have a huge capacity to give, and they love to teach others what they have learned in some hope of leaving a mark. This is a time when they have reached sovereignty in themselves.

The elder is beyond the king. He is like the king but is even more dedicated to downloading his wisdom or advice to others. Leaving a legacy is paramount, as well as taking care of others.

The best descriptor that the speaker used that I will never forget about these stages was that you can usually see most in play, quite literally, if you walk into a Home Depot.

The knights are the young ones, goofing around with the flags while using the forklift, racing each other up aisles or competing with each other about how many boxes they can lift.

The princes are heading into management, and taking their career and trajectory more seriously.

The kings are the older men, often adorned with white beards, who may be retired from another field but work there to stay busy and be an advisor to others. They are the helpful ones that will spend all the time necessary to explain how to fix the pipe rather than just telling you what aisle to look in.

The elders sometimes work there, too, but I hadn't seen any in my time working there. Alison Armstrong's description made it easy to see and determine which stage each man might fit into.

I knew that I wasn't looking for a prince anymore; any man who would be appealing to me would already be a king or somewhere close. I didn't want to have to help him figure it out.

Another wisdom nugget that came from the class was that men have what she calls, "Outposts." These are things or people or places that mean a great deal to them. These "Outposts" could range from their loyalty to a sports team or time spent working on a hobby, or anything that they overwhelmingly prioritize or see as part of who they are.

The critical nugget she shared was that poking fun at these particular things, even in jest works to undermine their love of their "Outpost." Ribbing them on that topic is not a good route to being happy together in the long run. While a partner doesn't have to always participate with them in their "things" all of the time, she suggested that one should refrain from being critical about the topic or make their partner "feel wrong" for enjoying it either. They will often sport whatever is associated with it.

Another great take-away from the class I continue to ruminate over is when a group of men in different age ranges came on stage and answered questions we had submitted to the leader beforehand.

There was one twentysomething, ie: a prince, another couple of kings and one elder.

The question that stuck with me the most was answered most eloquently by the one I found most attractive. He was of a similar age to my own, a quite handsome and salt-and-pepper bearded king.

"What is something women do in relationships that you wish they wouldn't?"

He stood in thought for a moment then began, "I think the one thing that I wish women wouldn't do is the thing I have seen happen over and over again. That as soon as we get together, they just kind of fold in behind us and cease being themselves. They unconsciously get rid of or lose the amazing woman we fell in love with in the first place."

Talk about jaw-dropping.

This was all written to the best of my memory, post class, I wish every woman would take her class. So much more was shared.

~

~3~

E liza brought the book downstairs with her when she came down the next morning. She'd been up late the night before, reading.

"Dad, I don't think I can keep this book."

"Why not, hon?"

"This lady asked for it to be passed around so she could get it back someday."

"Yeah, you're right. Who would you like to give it to?"

"How about Mary Smith next door? She helped us and looked after us when Mom got sick. I think she might be in a book club."

"That sounds good. Do you want me to give it to her?"

"No, I will."

"Okay, sounds good," he said with the muffle of an egg sandwich in his mouth.

"I'll be right back." Eliza checked her hair in the mirror by the front door, things were good: her father was his old self again, a new car, her sweet sixteen.

Every Monday, Mary had friends over to talk about whatever book they were reading. If she had a book club, she must like books.

She slipped on her shoes and danced outside leaning over and hugging the hood of her new car in the driveway on her way. Eliza rapped at the door, and it was answered quickly. The woman standing in the doorway was tall, sturdy but not fat, and had smile lines that seemed to crisscross her entire face. Eliza thought the lines might reach all the way to her toes. Her dress was colorful with poppies, red and orange, and a yellow kerchief held back her long gray curly hair.

"Hello, Eliza, I hope you had a happy birthday." She reached out and gave Eliza a hug.

Eliza squeezed Mary and said "Thank you, and thanks for keeping the car a secret; I just love it."

"I thought you might,"

"I have something for you; it's a book."

"Honey, it's your birthday week, not mine."

"I know, I just want you to have it."

Eliza told Mary about how the book had affected her dad when he received it in the mail months ago.

"We've had it too long already."

"Hmm, let's have a look."

Eliza handed her the book bundled with the same ribbon her dad had used. A navy blue hard paper cover with a spiral binding. "Find Me" was hand-embossed onto the front cover, almost a plea in itself.

She opened the cover and read the first page, "Someone needs help."

"Yes, I know. Do you think you can?"

"Eliza, this is a wonderful gift. I will be sure to share it with my book club; maybe someone will know something or catch a clue about the person who wrote it."

Eliza smiled. "I thought you would know what to do."

"It's quite a rare book; you and your dad must feel very special. It looks like you were the first people to receive it."

Eliza knew it was true. They *were* special, and once again they were seeing each other. If she couldn't have her mom back, at least she still had her dad.

"Yes, kind of amazing. I think it helped me and Dad get closer by talking about some of the stories inside and he told me more about how he grew up. It made him start thinking about some of the people who helped him through some hard times and those who made an effort to get to know him, especially his old track coach that helped him get into college. It was where he met Mom. Honestly, I never knew what questions to ask, as Dad has always been so quiet. The idea of people helping this woman, and that strangers can make a difference in someone's life seemed to get Dad to open up. It's been really good."

"That's wonderful honey," Mary put her arms around Eliza. She was almost grown now, fully as tall as Abby was.

Eliza said goodbye and Mary closed the door behind her. "Time for a tea and a read."

Mary walked to the front window and watched as Eliza walked home. She remembered seeing Eliza's first steps in the driveway when the family first moved in and watching her draw with chalk often all day with her mother in the summers. She had watched that family grow and change, then suffer a huge loss and now come together again.

To think that this little almost one-of-a-kind book had helped bring them together made Mary tear up.

She walked to the kitchen and flipped the electric kettle on. Ruffling through her large box of tea flavors, she settled on a lemon twist version with a touch of caffeine. The kettle roiled and clicked off and she poured the water over the tea bag into her favorite Royal Doulton *Old Country Roses* tea cup, setting it on one of the matching saucers. Tucking the book under one arm, she walked slowly into the sunroom at the back of the house. She set the cup on the matching wicker table and settled into her down cushioned wicker chair.

Reaching for one of her hand-crocheted throws, she covered her legs with it before pulling the tea bag out of the cup and pinching the water out as much as she could without burning her fingers. She wrapped the string around the bag before setting it down on the saucer.

She pulled the book into her lap and opened the cover again, flipping to the back to see the names of her two wonderful neighbors. She was thankful that the Olivers had shared the book with her, but mostly she was thankful that the author had somehow sent the book to them. It connected them as a family again. That was what they needed most.

~

A Bit of Peace for the Moment, Me 2010

Today I woke up feeling great. It feels like the calm before the storm. The kids are enjoying their last summer days, still in bed. I sit with a coffee on my front porch, reading Anne Morrow Lindbergh's **A Gift from the Sea.**

The sun is shining, the morning is abuzz with squirrels hiding their nuts in my lawn in preparation for winter. I watched them for a while. It is quiet, save for the freeway nearby my little house for which the sounds soothe me like the waves crashing in at the beach.

I am settled for the moment. It is dangerous to open my eyes wide and look around, as I will see many things that must be done. My Shasta daisies need deadheading, the dog needs a bath. I could get up and make French toast this morning for my two favorite people in my life- my girls. But instead, I sit, sipping and watching a lone skateboarder ride past my house.

In the book, Lindbergh talks about how women need some solitude to replenish themselves. How we often give in excess and end up resentful of the giving. It is in our nature to nurture and give. To take care of others.

But we must make a conscious effort to continue to feed our own souls, in order to have enough left over.

Why is it so hard to ask for what we need? Why is it so hard to claim time for ourselves? It seems like we are genetically engineered to be caretakers in every relationship, regardless if it is with children, spouses or parents. Our role goes on forever, or until the woman says, "Hey! This isn't working for me."

I sit and think about all the ways this tug-of-war presents in our daily lives.

Divorce, abandonment, insanity, depression. All because no one taught us that it's okay to say, "I need a vacation from my life and the day-to-day pressures it might contain once in a damn while."

Oftentimes we get a moment of peace. With a cup of coffee and a book, or a stolen moment in time for inwardly thinking and appreciating all that we have. That can feel like a getaway.

I look at some of my friends who are so committed to "helping others" that they are running around like chickens with their heads cut off, trying to reach some sort of Mother Teresa, Saint-like status, and all the while, their kids cannot even pop some microwave popcorn for themselves, let alone actually cook a meal or fend for themselves into their teens.

Their kids' responsibilities can be written on a Post-it note, and their mom gradually becomes so resentful of the whole thing, she loses it.

I may be a little ahead as I have already been through this once or twice. My married life was easier in some regards, and sometimes harder.

"Harder" being on a relative scale now that I have even more information about "hard." Being a single parent, and trying to provide for all of us, is completely different altogether.

Time is one's greatest asset. It is scarce. It can be very hard to find.

I look around the yard again: the smoke bush needs trimming; the lawn needs to be watered; my front porch is a mess.

But my kids are sleeping, my coffee cup is full, and this time is for me— so, I'm taking it.

~

K.O.

My sister-in-law. For the first chunk of my knowing you, you lived in Alaska, far away from view. You had a young son, the only grandchild in the family, until we added our oldest daughter to the mix. It was rare to get together so I didn't know your children very well, let alone you.

Once you had your second son, you wanted to move your family to the lower forty-eight and settle in a nearby state. We heard about you more often but still rarely saw you except holidays. You had a troublesome partner; he wasn't all there. I will leave it at that.

Snippets of family togetherness happened here and there. Once we came to your house and the boys were watching Spongebob Squarepants. You asked if our daughter liked the show.

"We haven't watched it," I heard myself say condescendingly. "I mean it's too ridiculous- a character that looks like a kitchen sponge lives in a pineapple house under the sea and works in a restaurant?" By the end of that trip, it was not only one of our daughter's favorites but mine, too.

When your boys were a little older you planned a trip to come and see us. I was pregnant with my youngest and we all planned a trip downtown to the children's science museum. One of the interactive displays you could experience there was to tour a parked and partially submerged submarine. I wasn't interested (claustrophobic) so I offered to take the other kids into the water play area while everyone else went.

As my daughter tried the different water toys, your son sat quietly underneath a table with one plaything, seemingly content. At one point, my daughter came over to ask me to put an apron on her and when I looked up again my little nephew was nowhere to be seen.

Frantic, I rushed around, looking all over for him. I grabbed my daughter and ran up to the person working at the counter, "My nephew is missing! Can you please help me?"

"Yes, what was he wearing? We can send out an alert."

I described his outfit, tears streaming down my face. I was never so scared in my entire life. Within minutes they had the entire facility on lock down with all exit doors manned and countless people roaming looking for him. More minutes passed and the person at the counter said, "We found him. He made it all the way into the restaurant kitchen. Someone is with him now; I'll take you there."

The kitchen! I thought, how in the world could he have gotten out the door of the water area and all the way across the building to the restaurant?

When we were all together again, and the group was done with the submarine tour, I confessed to you that I had lost your son. I was crying, bawling- and begged for your forgiveness.

"Oh," you said quite calmly, "I should have told you he does that."

Yeah—that would have been nice to know.

~

~3~

M ary sat in her sunroom as it started to rain on the semi-clean glass panels overhead. The drops first came as a sprinkle and as the sky darkened, she felt the promise of a real storm coming. Soon, sheets of water were streaming down the glass walls. The sound was calming and she knew the windows were storm-worthy, as her husband Grant had installed them himself.

It was nice that she didn't have any demands on her today, after waking up feeling a little out of sorts. She had turned over and ran her hand over her husband's side of the bed, begging him to be there. It was her husband Grant's heavenly birthday. He would have been seventy-one, and they would have been celebrating their thirty-fifth wedding anniversary this December if he hadn't passed away. She sure missed him.

She'd spent three years in architecture school before quitting after getting pregnant with her previous husband's child at twenty-two. She had tried to make the marriage work to no avail. Her husband hadn't wanted children, and they had found themselves at odds about it most of the time at home. When Eliot was only a year old, Mary came to believe that her husband's outward resentment towards their son was more harmful than growing up without a father at all. He paid child support each month for the first two years of Eliot's life, but never came around or even asked about him.

Mary wanted nothing to do with Eliot's real father. After starting the position at the county office, and with more than a few paychecks in the bank, she relieved her ex of the monthly support bill and any pretense as well.

She and Eliot would make it on their own. Mary hadn't counted on finding love again, believing no man could care about another man's child. How wrong she was.

Not even close to looking for love, she met Grant at her job at the county building office, and was struck with how thorough and professional he was at first, so strict about having his paperwork in order. He schmoozed the inspectors to commit to his promised construction schedule prior to him starting each job. He was a planner. He wanted things his way.

She had been there about a year, and she knew how unorganized the office was. How the inspectors worked out their own schedules and would often be late to job sites or even push out an appointment if something else came up that got them closer to home at the end of the day. They'd check into the office in the morning and were handed their files, often trading with each other if they didn't care for that builder or were anticipating any pushback or excuses from the contractor.

Mary greeted Grant at the counter and looked over his permits and plans before handing him off to the engineer if needed, or she'd stamp them herself if everything looked okay. Of course, Grant was nice to her since she was in essence the gatekeeper of each job's success. She didn't think any more about it.

She'd smirk as he left, noticing his well worn jeans that hung slightly on his frame; *he needed to tighten up his toolbelt.* He was on the thinner side, too, but muscular in all the right places. She imagined him swinging a beam over his shoulder, no problem. Maybe he just needed some good, old fashioned, home-cooked meals?

Mary watched him find his groove in the business. His insistence to have his jobs run smoothly was his way of trying to make his own way in the world. She found out later that he had turned his father down when he asked him to join the family's construction company in the city. Instead Grant started his own business. He wanted to learn from the ground up, rather than be handed some golden key to success and ride on the coattails of his already successful dad. It was one of the things she grew to love about him.

Mary took another sip of her tea and realized that she had been daydreaming. She sighed and took in the water streaming down the windows, and smiled. Adjusting her glasses, she started back into the book again. The author recounted moments with her grandmother and friends of all sorts, as well as time with men with whom things hadn't worked out. Each person had helped shape her somehow, leaving some kind of imprint, no doubt.

She was happy that things hadn't worked out with her first husband Allen. That everything aligned for her to find Grant. She set the book down, and took the last sip of tea while listening to the rain. She closed her eyes, remembering her own love story: the day she realized she felt more than a professional interest in the handsome, strong minded contractor, who would soon show her exactly how big his heart really was.

That morning at home had been rough and when she finally got to work, her desk was decorated with balloons for her birthday. She was twenty-five. It was nine thirty when she arrived, much later than usual because her little Eliot was home sick with a fever. She'd left him lying on his sitter Gladys' couch with a stuffed elephant tucked under his tiny arm. He was three. She kissed him lightly on his forehead, feeling the heat as she pursed her lips. Guilt set in hard. She whispered a promise to be back just as soon as she could. Eliot squeezed his elephant harder and squirmed away from her words.

Mary went about her day as best she could, smiling as each of the customers came in and wished her a happy birthday upon noticing the decorations. She *wasn't* having a happy birthday with her little boy sick at home. She begged for the day to pass.

Grant was at the counter, they were working out final details on a small bathroom project he was doing. She was offering advice to make it easier for someone with a walker. At about eleven o'clock she got a call from the sitter.

"Hello?"

Gladys was frantic. "Eliot is missing; I can't find him anywhere. He must have hidden while I was heating up some soup for him. I've torn apart the whole house looking for him. Please come home now!"

Mary's face showed panic as she slammed down the receiver.

Grant begged, "What!? What!?"

Mary grabbed her purse, "I'm sorry, I have to leave. My son is missing. I need to find him."

"God, let me drive you; you can't drive in this state. Let's go, my truck is right out front."

Mary was grateful that Grant drove, as she sat shaking in his passenger seat and Grant reached over to put his hand on hers in support.

"It'll be okay; we'll find him."

Together they ran up the stairs of the apartment building to the fourth floor. Gladys stood in the open doorway and Grant made a mad dash past her to look in all the rooms, even the closets, not caring about the woman's privacy or even knowing what the child looked like.

"He's not here," he shouted as Mary spoke to Gladys about the last place she had seen him.

"He was lying on the couch watching TV, almost asleep. I gave him a cool towel for his forehead and a baby aspirin like you told me, then I went into the kitchen to make him some chicken soup. I was only away from him for about ten minutes."

"Let's check your place," Grant said, "Could he have gone over there?"

"He doesn't have a key or anything, but let's." The three of them bolted to the door down the hall and found it slightly ajar.

"Eliot?" Mary half shouted and half whispered. If he wasn't there she didn't know what she would do.

It was quiet, and little Eliot didn't answer. Grant checked the bathroom, and the kitchen before checking the boy's room. Nothing. Mary walked into her bedroom, the last room that he might be in. He wasn't on her bed, or sitting in the reading chair that the two of them snuggled in each night for story time. She breathed in a big breath and opened her closet door, the very last place he could be.

There he was, fast asleep in a pile of his mother's clothing. Softly snoring because of his runny nose, with his elephant was still tucked under his arm. His left thumb was plunked squarely in his mouth. Mary picked him up and felt his limp little body tuck into the crease of her shoulder. He was okay. He just missed his mama, her smell, and wanted to feel her with him.

Mary and Gladys cried with relief as Grant put his arm around Mary and brushed through the boy's hair.

"That was the scariest thing I think I have ever gone through," he said.

"You?!" Mary said half laughing, before her face settled into a relieved smile.

"Thank you for being here. I don't know how I would have driven home in that state. I don't think I was even breathing the whole way."

"I'm sorry, I should have checked your apartment; it didn't occur to me at all," said Gladys through her own relieved tears.

"No, you did everything right, I usually lock the door. He wouldn't have been able to get in here if I would have locked it. I must have forgotten to do it today. For some reason he found his way over here."

"I'm not going back to work. Grant, will you tell them for me? I just want to sit here and be with my boy. He needs me a lot more than that place does today."

"Want me to stay?" Grant had asked. She did but she wasn't sure how to ask him or even what that might mean.

"No, it's okay. We will be okay now. It's just me and my little man against the world."

Grant patted her spare shoulder and he and Gladys walked together into the hallway.

"*Mighty nice of you* to bring her home. I didn't know what to do. I just knew that she needed to get home right away. I didn't think about her driving in that state." Gladys shared.

"Everything worked out for the best. I am going to give you my phone number, Ma'am. If Eliot is better and Mary needs a ride to work tomorrow, could you call me? Her car is still at the office. I can come early and give her a ride."

Grant pulled a flat pencil from his toolbelt and wrote his phone number on the back of a bill that Gladys had on her entry table. *Gladys would be passing that number on to Mary when the time came.* She hadn't seen a spark that bright between two people for a long time.

In the morning, Eliot was back to his own self, and once Mary realized that her car was still at work, she asked Gladys for the bus schedule, only to hear, "Your ride is waiting for you downstairs." There was a glint in her eye.

Grant was there on that scary day, and came around a lot after. Within a month, they said their "I do's" at the county courthouse, just one building over from where they met.

Grant wanted the entire package: her *and* Eliot.

~

Washing My Hands in Cold Water, Me
2010

My shop is in an old building, and my unit has never had hot water running to it. All day, every day, I am washing my hands in freezing cold water. It makes me feel poor and pathetic. It is simply a limitation of the building but it feels like so much more to me, I am not sure why.

Maybe it's a constant reminder that something isn't right, or that I am not good enough. If I was more successful I would be in a fancier shop with actual hot water. This bathroom is also what my customers use, so they get to experience that feeling of inferiority, too.

I think if it was once in a while it wouldn't leave as much of an impression but the day-in and day- out of it tears away at my belief of being able to take care of myself.

I often delve deeper into things than I probably should. Can't help it really— I just can't.

~

It is Crumbling, Me 2010

The house is quiet. When you live alone and you leave a room and come back, it is exactly the same as when you left it. The lights are still on if you left them on. The couch cushion is crunched in the same way. The glass you left orphaned is still there; the water inside sits stagnant.

I can't sleep. Not sure why. My eyes fling open and remain like that for hours. My mind twists around scenarios, and settles in the not so good.

I went to the bathroom, and discovered that I had worn my underwear backwards all day. It's too early for senility, right? I leave them on backwards. No point changing them now. Maybe I don't deserve right-way-round underwear?

I grab a spoonful of peanut butter to calm my hunger pangs until morning, and climb the stairs back to bed. I flip on the lamp, and pick up the book I am trying to read to better myself. Hopefully I will drift off.

The money problems are at a critical stage now- my reserves are depleted and I've had to borrow money from my ex.

The business is not sustainable with the economy as it is; the house is on the edge of repossession.

One more punch in the face and I'm done.

I cannot see my way through the muck.

~

D.M.

I remember my first impressions of you. You came barreling into the room at bunco, wearing shorts and a t-shirt in the middle of winter, your pregnant belly about to burst. You lived across the street and were the most helpful person I had ever met- doing for others before you were ever asked.

You said you were so hot because of the baby. It was your second child, a daughter. You were from the south and retained some of your southern drawl in your move to the Pacific Northwest. You taught me the difference between "y'all" and "all y'all." A trained nurse, you were married to a doctor, but you had dedicated yourself to being a stay- at-home mother while the kids were small.

You were a *baby buff*, loving any infants that came into view. If anyone was pregnant, you were there with maternity clothes to lend, tips to offer, and boy, oh, boy, when that baby finally arrived, you were there with hands outstretched. Gimme, gimme. Your mama was the same way. There was no holding one's own baby when you or your mama were around.

I remember when you saved me. I was always so miserable with my morning sickness, upchucking daily up until birth- both times. It was my eldest's birthday. At four, she had overindulged in sweets and pizza and was red from running around. We got her to the powder room downstairs before she spilled her guts, however it was not inside the commode where it splatted.

Projectile one could say. It wouldn't take much for my chunks to join her chunks as a new wallpaper of sorts, so I closed the door and phoned my husband, leaving a message that we would need to move. And I meant it.

You came over and cleaned up that bathroom- it was no sweat for you. You'd cleaned up worse. I was forever grateful and knew that you were one of those once in a lifetime champions who care more for others than they care for themselves.

Whatever people were going through, you placed yourself in between them and the hardship. A balancing buffer to help in the cause. A death, a cancer diagnosis: you were always on top of the news and gave the rest of us updates. You were always the initiator of a meal-train campaign to help out whoever needed it.

The nursing profession pulls the very best people of humanity, and those who sign up are selfless to the core. I hope the universe puts plenty of babies into your loving arms. Even if it's just for a nuzzle.

~

~3~

Mary Smith handed out decaf coffee to her book club guests. They were abuzz with neighborhood gossip, and had to be shushed to start the meeting. Mary was beyond excited to share her new find.

"This is a new book; it's not even on the market yet. I have only just been given a sneak peek, and I wanted to bring it to you first."

"Wow." "Oh, my, Goodness." "How wonderful," all came from the crowd.

"Good. Let's begin."

Dear Reader,

This traveling book is my secret mission to live a more extraordinary life from within the confines of an ordinary one.

Only five copies of this book exist and this has made its way to you; you are now and forever a part of this story.

Inside you will find moments captured from one person's life. Each passage starts with the set of initials of the person with whom I share the connection.

We are all connected on some level; every person you meet leaves a mark on you whether good or bad. Often it is the worst people who *gift* us the best lessons.

It is my hope that this idea spurs you into living in a more extraordinary way; to think bigger and reach beyond what you currently see.

The memories inside may remind you of a time or a person in your own life; may you think of those people today for the good or the lessons you learned from them.

Please read this book then write your name and location in the back before giving it to someone else. Leave it on a bus, give it to a friend, it will only take a few minutes for you to participate and it is wonderful to think of the adventures it may have.

Let's see how small our world really is.

If you, by chance, recognize yourself in here, please bring the book

and,

> **Find me...**

It was as if a hole opened up in the floor and swallowed them all, *well-whole*. Then finally someone spoke.

"Read it, keep going..."

Mary smiled, "Are you sure you want to participate?"

"Of course!" They all shouted.

Mary read aloud the collective stories of the anonymous writer. She put the book down and rose to get the mini lemon tarts she had baked that afternoon. The women stirred in the gossip soup, each trying to figure out who the author might be. They took turns signing their names, until they had added twelve signatures in the near empty pages in the back.

"Now ladies, do any of these stories ring true for you? Do you know who the author might be?"

"Well, I can certainly relate to the one where the guy had fancied someone else but pursued me, but I don't know anyone that all of these might fit."

One by one they claimed the author was still a mystery. And one by one they relayed some of their similar but own stories, to the delight and sometimes astonishment of their fellow book lovers. This chatting went on until late that night, so late that they ordered three pizzas to eat.

"What should we do with it now?" asked Velda.

"Should we take it somewhere and just leave it?" asked someone else. "Who should be the one? Probably Mary since it came to her."

"What about the Senior Center?" voiced another.

Mary opened her mouth to speak. "This idea is the most random and romantic idea I have ever heard of. We need to do something worthy of its daring. Why don't we hang up a map and close our eyes and stick a pin in the place it should go next. There are used book stores all over the country, as we all know. Let's send it on an adventure! All those in favor?"

"Ayes" leapt from the room. Such passionate ladies, Mary thought of her friends. What spirit they all had.!

Mary retrieved a massive poster map of the United States from her late husband's study. She pinned it up on the wall by the front door. They had all agreed to let Mary do the picking, but she was surprised to be suddenly blindfolded and spun around five times before she was let free to stick the pin. There was chuckling as she veered over near the coat rack, then hit her toe on the entry chair that hadn't been moved in over thirty years.

"Geez, Mary, don't ya know your own house?" Giggles ensued.

Mary steadied herself and tried again. Finding the paper-feel of the poster, she pressed hard so that the tack would stick. She eased off the blindfold and took the magnifying glass from Velda.

"*Washington. Skamania*, in Washington State."

"Girls, I will find a home for this book just as close to this position as I can. Thanks to all of you for your input, your help and your participation."

And as they always did before they ended their night together, they said a prayer, a happy prayer that each of them and their families would remain safe from harm and in good health, but tonight they added another wish.

"We wish that the woman who is waiting to see her book again gets her wish and is granted this dream come true."

They gathered their coats and all took off in their respective cars. None of them would ever forget that night, and how close they felt to each other in this wild literary adventure.

~

I Tried Really Hard, Me 2010

When I think of how far I have come in the last five years since the divorce, I am in awe of what I have managed to do and learn.

I am also torn up at the thought of losing it all, any minute.

In my mid-twenties to early thirties, I had the perfect suburban mom life volunteering at my daughters' school, then in the local government scene. I had found my voice. People listened and I helped make change. Then the explosion of my marriage, and making of a new life from the ashes. Reinvention of myself at thirty-five.

After living most of my life in the suburbs, I moved to the city. A place where I never thought I would end up. I'd ride my bike down to the river, and watch the world from a different perspective and seeing my daughters grow more worldly, too. This is just the beginning.

Things to do in the next forty years.

1. Write more

2. Get healthy

3. Go to Italy

4. Say yes.

5. Have a romantic & magical partner

6. I don't want to limit my life to a list.

~

~3~

The next day, Mary Smith got on the web to find a used bookstore close to Skamania County, Washington- some unsuspecting bookseller to send the traveling book to. Her book buddies would be asking for an update soon. Several of them had already called offering to help. Several others had started their own little journals using people's initials, just like the author had. People that meant something to them, mini-autobiographies to share with their children if they saw fit. Maybe they would mail them out, too, to see if they could partake in the same goal.

"Hmm...how about this one?" Mary said aloud to no one. "*Words To Live By*"- a used book shop. It's perfect!"

She wrote the telephone number down and called the owner for the address. After hearing it and writing it down, the employee asked what it was concerning. Mary quickly hung up, *it was better to surprise them.*

She found a small cardboard box, and padded it with some of her stash of Christmas tissue paper and tucked the book inside, adding a bit more tissue to cover. She carefully wrapped the box in an inside-out brown paper shopping bag and taped up the edges with duct tape. It was all she had. Using a thick black pen, she wrote the address nice and legibly on the front and skipped the return address.

She'd get dressed and take it to the post office this afternoon, and would tell Eliza and Isaac what happened to it, but only if they asked. She loved her role as the short-term caretaker of the book. It made her feel so sneaky, so much more adventurous than she did in her typical day. Quite the actress when young, she donned black sunglasses and a camel trench coat to step up the mystique.

Mary set the package on the counter and the postal worker slid it onto the scale.

"Book rate please," she said, tipping her glasses slightly to peer at the young woman.

"Yes, Ma'am, that will be $4.68."

Mary slid five dollar bills to the woman, watching her young but nimble fingers rub the wide stamp label over the corner of the package. They both said their thanks, and Mary turned to leave, looking back to see the package disappear down into the massive mail bin.

"Gone, but not likely forgotten."

~

A Glimmer of Hope, Me, 2010

*I*n the chaos of my everyday life, there was still hope. As each of the bad things piled up and festered and rotted away like layers of the most pungent onion, something surfaced that was unexpected and wonderful at the same time.

I went to work every day at my old place of employment. Luckily they needed me back. I was able to break my lease on my store with my very understanding landlord with some design work and by handing over many of the samples I had left in my showroom. I was grateful she let me out of it.

The bankruptcy hearing was scheduled and I had finished my classes to qualify. The house was on track to be auctioned off in two months, but until then I had a place to stay.

I had been imagining my next love and delighting myself in escape with the movies that Colin Firth starred in: *Love Actually*; *Bridget's Jones's Diary*; and *Nanny McFee*. I had basically asked the Universe for my own personal Colin Firth. If I was allowing myself to imagine and dream again, why not shoot for the stars?

He was still the dream. Tall, dark and handsome with an accent. Sigh...

A friend in a neighboring shop had told me over and over again that she had someone she wanted me to meet, but it had been months and months and still no progress. She somehow saw us together in her mind's eye. It was a friend of her husband's that she had met years previous at a work event.

The man in question had been married at the time and I had been involved with Mr. Fun at the time, so she hadn't worked to put anything together. When his relationship ended, he was working on rebuilding, too.

He hadn't wanted to break up his family, but his wife pulled the plug and he was suddenly forced into a life he had not planned. I first saw his picture on my friend's Facebook page. When I tried to friend him, his privacy settings were so tight I wasn't able to see his page so I had given up the idea of him and myself.

Busy with the constant fight to keep my home, I had plenty to do. I tried a short sale which was not successful. Then I tried to rent it out, but what I could get didn't cover the mortgage.

I had attempted a loan modification with the bank, and with one missed document that the third party coordinator said I hadn't needed, the bank rejected me and my attempt to keep my house. I had only two months to find a place for me, my daughters, and my mother to live. Mom moved into an available apartment next door to my house so it was easy to move her and she was stabilized for the moment.

Yes, my daughters could stay indefinitely with their father but I didn't want to lose them now, along with everything else so I had to figure it out.

Where would I be going?

And then my own personal Mr. Darcy arrived. The privacy barrier on his Facebook account was lifted and he wanted to meet me, too.

He was tall, dark and handsome, and being from South Africa he was gifted with the most beautiful accent. He had been alone for a while now; and he was sad. He knew I was up to my eyeballs in garbage but that I was trying to claw my way out. I didn't hide my circumstances.

Maybe he fancied being the hero, I will never know. He didn't treat me like the pathetic imp I felt I was at the moment– instead- he was open to the possibility. I am at the heart of it, a good woman. I am loving and kind and thoughtful, even if I am broke and almost homeless at the moment.

Suddenly there was the excitement of an email or message to come home to. The wild idea that I could fall in love again.

We tried to take it slow, but it just didn't happen that way.

He felt like the Mr. In Between of my Mr. Stability and Mr. Fun. He had a job, and took care of and loved his kids, AND he was a world traveler who spoke different languages. He was dashing and exciting and kind.

We fell hard for each other and after only a month of dating, he proposed.

I was still trying to get it all worked out, working two jobs, reaching for any option that may help me out of the hole I was in.

But I was also exhausted and my health was suffering as well. I had little left for anyone. I was the one to help everyone else. I didn't know how to ask for help. It wasn't a comfortable place for me. I was always the one who gave. I never knew any different.

I had no reserves in the bank, in my body, in my head or heart to keep fighting with.

He said, "I love you, let me help you."

"I love you, too," I said and I did.

It was on top of a mountain, in the dark with the blustery wind blasting at the windows. He asked me to be his and slipped a ring on my finger. We promised to start a life together with his kids and mine, and that whatever came we would conquer it together.

I hadn't meant for it to be that way- marrying him was not a way to free myself from my rancid finances and near hopeless situation- it felt like the absolute right thing.

A gift- exactly what I asked for- what I prayed for. I believed he was sent from the heavens to me.

Just in time.

~

~3~

A dented up *"Words to Live By"* sign lay next to a dumpster in rural Skamania County, Washington.

The run down bookstore; out of business just days before, the new tenants of the space assessed what to do with all of its abandoned junk. The bookstore owner had skipped out on the last month's rent and supposedly left town. After fifteen years the space was chock full of bookcases, some of which were still filled with books, not to mention layers of thick dust.

The new tenants imagined that many of the more valuable books had been sold before closing, but they were beyond annoyed to see so many left behind for them to deal with.

They were working to box up all the books to donate to the local bookmobile when a package addressed to the former tenant arrived. Only the name of the former biz and address was written on the roughed-up brown package. It was a bit of a risk opening it, in that it wasn't addressed to them, but the two new bridal shopkeepers, Sophie and Calli, couldn't be bothered to check with authorities.

They placed the package in with all of the other books going to the bookmobile. After hours of stacking and lifting books, the two girls decided to make the first run to the bookmobile drop off site. Sophie's boyfriend pulled up in his brand new truck. They loaded up seventeen grocery store fruit-sized boxes.

After their first run, they drove through the Boni Lynn Drive-in to get ice creams so they would have the energy to load up the truck again. The second bundle contained the newly delivered package that had mysteriously arrived today. There were thirty-two boxes in all.

The two shopkeepers reached for their donation slip at the same time, and Calli backed off to let Sophie slide it into her white denim jacket pocket.

They high-fived each other as they sauntered out of the building, *"A tax deduction before we even opened*!"

"Hell yeah!"

They all climbed back into the truck and took off down the road, blaring Rascal Flatts' version of the old Tom Cochrane favorite *Life is a Highway* on the radio. As the twenty- something's rolled through stop sign after stop sign, older pedestrians stared at them in disappointment. Many poked at their hearing aids to try to lull the loud music as they drove by.

Nothing else mattered to them that night. They had worked their butts off to get the shop ready to start painting tomorrow since their big grand opening was just a week away. Tonight they would be celebrating with the guys big time!

~

Details, Me 2010

The person I loved went away to see his father in another country far away. We didn't say goodbye properly because we weren't getting along. I'd spent the day before lying on my mother's couch, crying my eyes out from uncertainty. It felt like we had broken up, but we hadn't said the words. Everything was in shambles and as always, I wanted to control everything, and the outcome. I felt a huge desire to fix whatever it was and get back to us being okay again.

We were engaged but we hadn't worked out all the details. Where would we live? His kids lived mostly with their mom so the original idea was he would move to my town so my daughters would be closer to their schools and friends. We went and looked at houses, and imagined living in them together. The pillars of my life continued to shatter around me and the emotional earthquake of failure felt never-ending, but he attempted to help me in any way he could.

Once it started looking like I wouldn't have a house to sell to have money for our future together, any leverage of where we would live that I might have been able to muster, blew away like a dusty tumbleweed.

Unbeknownst to me, his daughter freaked out at the thought of her father selling her childhood home, he then promised her he would never leave it. It was a promise he made without me. So he retracted his willingness to move to our city, and doubled down on his place, drawing what I would count as the first line in the sand of our relationship. It felt like it should have at least been a talking point between us, so I was upset.

I guess I'd take the leftovers. Just like moving in with my first husband - living in another woman's pick for a house. A neighborhood that felt as if it had no soul. It would be us to move across the border into his house which was chosen by him and his ex. It would be my kids who had to get up ghastly early and drive across state lines to get to school if they chose to live with me during the week at all. Nothing would change for him other than with my presence he would get to have his children more.

This time I desperately wanted a team-like relationship. His unilateral decision was a hit to us, but I wasn't in a position to fight very hard against it. He was taking us in- what could I do?

Before we moved, his father fell ill and Mr. In Between decided to take his children to go and visit him for potentially the last time. They'd be out of the country and it would give him and me a break from talking about the hard stuff.

While he was away I did my best to keep busy, even attending a charity event hosted by a girlfriend. All who attended were asked to dress up in fancy dresses all within the same color. As we streamed in off the street, we could go upstairs to the ballroom or line up for a reading by a fortune teller to have our futures told. I began chatting with the women in front of and behind me. They were friendly and soon the three of us were gabbing and befriending each other on Facebook. Strangers to me beforehand, we had enough in common to want to connect and stay in touch. L.P and M.G.

Desperately wanting to know how my sweetie and I were going to navigate our issues, I waited to talk to the fortune teller, happy to hand her ten dollars for a little wisdom. Suddenly it was my turn and I sat down with the woman; she took my hands in hers and closed her eyes.

"You are struggling."

"Yes, there's this guy and we aren't getting along at the moment. I need to know if we are soulmates, if being with him is the right thing for me." (Not that I felt I had much choice at the moment.)

"I see. Yes, you are soulmates, but right now you are stressing each other out. You need to take some time and space away from each other to heal and make ready for the new."

Just hearing that we were soulmates made my heart soar. It was the confirmation I was looking for, a sign to rest my mind on my worried days. Soulmates! Joy! I had finally found him!

She went on, but I kept thinking back to what she said. We needed to take a break, and we were, but for how long and what does that look like? But we were soulmates- my heart soared.

I often find myself in a black-and-white thinking space. It is either or, with no gray space in between. We were on a break right now, whether we wanted to be or not, but I guess it was for the best.

He and I didn't speak every day but usually an email was exchanged. Every day felt more like an ending before we had really begun. I was still battered and off in a ditch, so maybe it was just me. Maybe things were fine, or would be fine once we got some things straightened out and were back in *the same country together.*

He sent me a novelty bottle with a note in it, from a nearby tourist trap they were visiting, saying he was thinking about me. His words spoke of love and a future together. I believed it all.

Our time apart was hard for us both and when he got back from his trip, we had a good talk. Both of us were deeply in love and saw a life together. The time apart felt like just what we needed. When my house went back to the bank, he took in me and my kids.

The bankruptcy hearing, the business shuttered, the house that I loved-gone.

I just tucked into a fetal position behind him. And he held my pieces together. I will forever be grateful. I did love him then, and I believed we would be happy together-eventually and forever.

My oldest drove herself and her little sister in rush hour traffic on the freeway daily and I could never thank her enough for being that kid. She was the one that made do, believing her mother was happy, and wanting to help in any way she could. It was an adjustment for all of us.

Just one of them. Over time, the one-sided "compromises" would become more common than I could ever have imagined.

~

~3~

Librarian Gail Kaster was shocked at the amount of boxes of books that had been donated. She stood in the parking lot outside the school yard. If she ever dreamed of having a fun old bookstore at the coast someday, this would have been enough to get it going. But it was not the right time, and she had no interest in all the other things associated with a business: the accounting; marketing; renting out a place and keeping it going. This batch promised to help them rock the library's smaller mission but not without a big fat headache first.

It was way too many books for their tiny bookmobile, even with sharing some with the small satellite branches she had been stocking. These would need to be edited down quickly as there was no storage for any leftovers. Gail would choose based on condition, appropriateness for the age groups she needed, and of course, the classics. The others would have to fight for their spot on board. Pity there weren't any children's books.

The children's section took up half of her little bus and she wouldn't be giving up any space on that. She had about two hours to get through all of the boxes, before heading out to the next library visit east; it would take her a full hour to get there so she had no time to spare.

Kari Gellar, college intern, wandered into the chaos seeing Gail fully hunched over the boxes, rifling through number nineteen of the thirty-two boxes that were just delivered.

"What's all this?"

"We just got a huge donation. That bookstore downtown went under. I'm drowning. Help me go through these," Gail said with a sigh. "I think we are going to have to get rid of most of these; it's such a shame."

Kari felt sad that a lot of the books would end up in a dumpster. She loved books, all genres. She always had, ever since she was little.

Kari took in the three separate piles of books on the floor. Gail motioned toward each pile with instruction. "This one is for inclusion on the bus, but we might have to decide what we are going to take off in order for them to be put on, so be selective. That pile is to donate to other bookmobiles, so make sure they are decent and not too racy or smelling of must, and the rest is to throw out. I have Gregory coming to pick those up in his truck. He'll be here within the hour."

Minute by minute the stacks grew into wonky pyramidal teetering shapes. Kari opened a box and came across a wrapped paper package that was addressed to the business but never opened.

"What should I do with this?" she asked Gail.

"Open it, it could be something good."

Kari carefully sliced the box open with a box cutter.

"It's a book, Find Me, 3 of 5. No author, looks self published somehow, some signatures in the back."

"It has a spiral binding that's too hard to show on a shelf and I've never heard of it, toss it." Gail said without pausing to look twice.

Kari flipped open the cover and found the enticing prologue. She quickly scanned a few pages and was interested. "Like in the trash? Uh. Mind if I take it home?"

"Help yourself," said Gail, continuing to barrel through her task.

Kari walked the blue book over to her backpack and slid it into the front zippered pocket.

"I could use a little reading material for after finals tomorrow," she mumbled to herself.

"That's what I like to hear," said Gail, with a big old grin on her frantic face.

'How did she hear that?' wondered Kari. *Gail must have bionic ears.*

~

P.T.

I remember interviewing for the job of looking after your kids. We hit it off immediately and laughed once we realized we were both Bluebirds when we were kids.

You were a working mom, even though you didn't have to work. You lived in a huge house, and had a blended family. Your husband had kids before meeting you and he jumped into having more children with you because he loved you so much. I was lucky enough to be a part of your family for a time as a nanny to your two little ones.

Your daughter, so cute, with her dark hair; she loved to wear dresses. Your son, a wee bit older than a toddler. He had a visible birthmark of a missing patch of hair near his baby soft spot location; that always caught my attention. He was such a little love.

I practiced being a mom as I took care of them. The neighborhood community was strong, and I wished, back then, that someday I would have that. Friends close by for my children to play with, fellow moms to talk to and hang out with. And I did have that eventually, most likely from being able to experience it firsthand.

I got your kiddos up for school, ran them around when needed, and then you would come home and make dinner. You ran 5K's and 10K's, always striving to be healthy and fed the kids well. *But you smoked, and hid it.* That one little vice waited like a drug dealer on the outskirts of your life for you to come play with in the midst of everything else. I do hope you stopped. I remember one time I was driving with your children, and we pulled up alongside you. We were excited and went to wave. I have never seen an arm move so fast as yours did to drop your cigarette below the visibility of the car window. The kids didn't see, but I did.

You made homemade pesto that was divine and it was in your house that I learned to like macaroni and cheese. It was a fave of your kids that I never had growing up.

You taught me how to pick the perfect orange. Navel always,

thinner skin when you squeeze it, heavy for its size- so you know it's juicy. I think of you every time I pick up an orange at the store. Frankly, they often don't make the cut and I leave them for the next poor sucker who doesn't know how to pick an orange.

With you, I got a class on what a successful marriage with two sane parents could be. The kids had schedules and even some responsibilities. It was a great place to view what a functional family and homelife looked like, to shoot for myself someday.

I remember bringing my fiancé over to meet you and your husband. Husband-to-be was much older than me and you wanted to *grill* him a bit. It was sweet that you cared so much. Your daughter was six and when she asked what he liked to do for fun, he explained that he loved belonging to the country club for "*the social aspect of it*". That was when I realized how green he was in relating to kids. Gave the rest of us a laugh.

I remember when you and your husband went out of town and left me with the kids for an entire week. By day two I thought I was losing it and I called you for support.

"I mean, you don't have to come home or anything." I said, hopeful they would get on a plane.

"Oh, *we are not* coming home. You are going to have to figure this out."

And I did and it was hard and good and showed me what the 24/7 life of having children would look like, up close and personal like.

Another time your whole family was out of town and I felt super creative so I painted a jungle animal mural in your playroom because I had a wild hair to do something since the room was too boring. Prior to my applying a masterpiece the walls held a few posters of the alphabet or other non-descript decor.

Maybe my artwork is still there? It was the last time I was over when I visited with my own two littles. Thanks for being another inspiring example of what being a mom could be.

~

~3~

Kari Gellar, student, part-time librarian intern, and full-time dreamer sat at her desk in her parents' rustic cabin home. Pulling the odd book out of her backpack, she shoved it under her other school books.

"When I finish studying for finals, *then I will read you*," she promised.

Kari had a history final to study for, an English paper to write, and an accounting test she hoped to pass. As much as she tried to concentrate on her studies, she found it difficult, as her curiosity for the mysterious little blue book— grew. Finally, after an hour, she punted her studies, grabbed the book and jumped onto her bed.

She could pull an all-nighter for school if she had to. But she deserved a break.

Kari read the pages curiously as the sun went down outside over the forested hill. Flipping on her lamp, she mused about what an odd thing she had come into possession of- a literary log of some random woman's experiences shared in such a vulnerable and interesting way.

The author had captured her moments with these people so vividly that Kari could imagine each scenario. Each interaction must have lain dormant in the author's psyche for years, possibly doing damage as it sat.

Kari could relate to some of the experiences; one in particular reminded her of Jake back in high school. It was two years ago. She had become enchanted with him in English class, attracted by his clean-cut looks and by listening to him tell his adventurous stories of hiking and camping among the sandy, clay colored plateaus of Utah. She would close her eyes and imagine herself and him hiking among the arches and of seeing all types of places together. Try as she did to get his attention with her flirting, he finally pulled her aside and told her it would not be.

"Hey, Kari, You are nice and all, but I'm Mormon, and I'm always going to be Mormon, so it just wouldn't work between us."

Kari was happy that he was so kind and upfront about things, as she'd read that unrequited love was one of the most painful experiences known to man *or woman*. She thought for a microsecond about converting to be with him, but was unsure that she wanted to commit to something that significant for the rest of her life when she still had so many unanswered questions about "God."

Any faith she felt, so far, seemed to be cobbled together from varied thoughts and principles of many of the religions she'd read about. She'd spent months on one thought, then was soon off to chase the next, picking and choosing, based on the moment, and what interested her-she was fine with that type of thinking for now.

With all of Kari's reading up about spirituality and experimenting by attending different churches, she finally decided that she felt closest to a higher power while in the woods or out near a natural body of water, than in some building.

Kari finished the last excerpt and wrote her name at the bottom of the list. Previous names were few. One man, and a number of women. Not that many to speak of. People needed to see this book. She held hope that people would help the author in her mission of being found again. While she couldn't promise it would happen, she had already done her part by saving it from the dumpster. The least she could do was take it to school and pass it around.

~

~3~

Kari Gellar arrived at the community college she had been attending for the last year. On track to start at the university in the fall, she was proud of herself. The internship with the bookmobile had led to something bigger; an opportunity to work at the university library which would pay her tuition and was a needed bump towards her future.

Kari stood in line at the coffee counter, desperately craving a café mocha. Her friend Shannon sidled up behind her and yanked her hair.

"Hey there. I've already had three cups of coffee this morning. Can you tell?" Shannon held her hand out, as it quivered. "I was up all night studying, were you?"

"Hey yourself. I studied for a while last night, then got into this crazy new book, then crashed. I figured if I hadn't learned it already, one night wasn't going to make that big of a difference."

Kari handed the blue book to Shannon, and grabbed her café mocha from the barista.

"Check it out after your last final, then give it to someone else."

"Somebody else? Don't you want it back?"

"Nope."

"Okay, weirdo. Good luck on your finals today!"

"You too."

~

An Opportunity for a New Way, Me, 2010

*I*t's as much of a drag as it is a blur. The last two years. Somehow this brain of mine doesn't let me dwell on the details and I'm grateful for it.

The words of the lawyer I sought trying to get rid of my business partner a year ago echoes back into my head. **It's a lesson, it's a lesson, it's a lesson.** Everything that has come my way is a lesson. I only beat myself up by looking back over my journal entries.

Landing my fiancé still felt like a Godsend- literally. Maybe God did send him to me, or maybe God sent me to him; I guess we will find out. Maybe it's time I give the religious way a chance since so many people feel supported. Maybe I **could** become a member of the flock?

~

~3~

S hannon Valdez stowed the book in the side pouch of her backpack and went to all of her classes that day, taking tests and hoping for decent grades. It was her last semester, and she had achieved enough credits to attain her associates degree. She was so excited to get out of school and move towards the next stage of her career path: the police academy.

With her parents on the force, it was all she ever wanted to be. Shannon had already been on a dozen ride-a-longs over the last five years, and with each run she felt more committed to her purpose. She liked helping others and especially liked puzzles. She hoped to eventually become a detective.

Rushing out of her last class, she held up a peace sign to the teacher that he didn't notice. She wouldn't be thinking about what she learned in that class ever again. Art history. *What a snooze.*

She couldn't wait to get started with self defense and firearms training classes that were taught the first year at the academy. A new apartment in the big city with her cousin who was also starting the academy at the same time. It was funny that both she and Joseph wanted to become police officers. He was two years older but had taken time off after high school and only finished up his Associates degree recently. He got his first taste for wearing a badge while working at the airport doing security but that was not cutting it. He wanted it all.

Shannon plopped down on a couch in the student union. Her brain was fried and the caffeine was wearing off. She had stayed up most of the night trying to memorize the artists that they had learned about this term: Cezanne; Renoir; Dali— that guy's stuff was especially weird. She should probably say *"creative"* instead. She closed her eyes for what felt like a second and woke up disoriented after nearly an hour.

"What happened?!" She yelped to herself, taking a jerking glance at her watch. The little blue book teetered perilously out of the edge of her backpack pocket, and fell with a light thump as Shannon sped through the doorway to catch the last bus back home.

Shannon would never know of the missed opportunity she might have been able to work on that summer. It could have been one of the biggest puzzles she'd ever come across in her early, pre-career life.

The book sat in the student commons for three more days, being read, looked at and signed over and over, but no one took any ownership of the book and the quest inside.

The traveling book wasn't getting very far.

~

Red Flags I Ignored, Me, 2011

"We are getting married so we should share everything. Your computer is old so you can use mine, perhaps we should share one email address."

It was true, my computer was old and I had used it for my business and my writing. His newer Apple device sat in a sunny area of the kitchen and had a massive display. I was excited to have a chance to use it. I sat down to learn how to log in. As he stood behind me, the screen suddenly lit and a litany of images appeared.

A bevy of naked and splayed women. Each seemed to have one finger in their mouth and the other somewhere else, if you know what I mean. They were all large-breasted with a perhaps surgical perkiness, a look I could never pull off since having kids.

He pressed buttons to escape the scene.

"I'm a very visual person. Some of my work friends started sending me things like that when I was going through the divorce; I'll tell them to stop," he promised.

My Dad had subscribed to Playboy ever since I was a kid and my friends and I would often sneak peeks at them when Dad wasn't home. In that, I was accustomed to the "needs" of men and their necessity for the visual. Personally, I mostly enjoyed the comics in those magazines.

Dad was Dad. As expected, his most loved issues were the ones with the blondes. Shrug. I guess I could understand my husband's penchant if he could let it go as promised.

With the computer sharing, he wanted full access to my emails as well. We weren't to keep anything separate. He put the tracker app on my phone (which he was paying for by then) and stated that we weren't to keep anything from each other. "Nothing."

I made a note to myself to stop writing. With our challenges, I couldn't risk him coming into the honest words about how I felt. Where we might have built trust and had a conversation, instead, I felt an urgency to hide my feelings away lest they be used against me.

When I did write, it was in journals when I was alone that I would tuck under my failed business papers in boxes that I stored in the bottom of his son's closet. He wouldn't bother to look in there. Mostly my words and the bigger part of myself— the writer, fell away to navigate each and every difficulty that came up for us.

A new, and uncomfortable aspect of control was now in force. I pushed much of myself deeper inside and waited to see how this would all pan out.

We weren't even married yet and already things felt different.

~

$$\sim3\sim$$

Professor Jeremy Cate zombied among the couches in the lounging area of the commons with a small stack of books. He liked to leave volumes from his personal collection around to help inspire others to read, and introduce the students to new genres secretly. His fascination for books was only matched by his fascination with wine. He has collections similar in size and worth of both.

Jeremy lives alone. His wife Natalia died two years ago of a heart aneurysm. Taken so suddenly, he couldn't breathe for weeks. He barely ate or bathed. His students would come to class but there was no teacher to teach. On days when he was there, he wasn't fully there.

After work, if he did go in, he would hunker into his chair and wait for his Talia to walk in through the door as if she was just getting back from a long day teaching. But she never came back.

Over time, the phone calls to ask about how he was doing lessened, as well as the spontaneous dinner invites from friends. People moved on with their own lives, and Jeremy wished he could too.

Slowly he made small goals for himself. Eat breakfast, something other than the frozen cooked-in-the-microwave kind. Speak to three people he didn't know. Ask them a question about themselves.

After a year he was able to be a proper teacher again, and was toying with the idea of moving to a new place; an idea he hoped would give him something big to look forward to. Somehow, that move hadn't come.

He had spent the last two years alone and lonely. Natalia had been everything to him. They didn't have children, a choice they had made early on in their relationship. Instead they had dreamed of far away places and great adventures yet to come. They had saved and waited for enough money so they could take a proper sabbatical from their positions at the college.

Without her and their shared plan, Jeremy had settled into a life of mere existence. He woke up, got ready for his classes, ate, slept, went through the most nagging of hygienic motions and days spent teaching the same books every year. Jeremy seemed to be just biding time before he could be with his precious Natalia again.

He plopped down on one of the hideous orange and brown couches. Resting his arm over the vinyl strap on the side, he tried to imagine how many people had sat where he was now. How many of those kids had also thought this was an ugly couch? Who in God's name would have purchased this couch in the first place?

Half sticking out from between the cushions to the left of him was a book. He pulled it free and adjusted his glasses to read the title in the after-hours student hall light.

Find Me 3 of 5. No author given.

He had seen thousands, maybe millions, of books in his lifetime and during his career, but none like this one. He opened the cover and read the first page, a request from an unknown author. He flipped through the pages and discovered what appeared to be almost a hundred signatures in the back.

He would need to get in better light to read the whole thing, but his interest was piqued. The book said it was meant to be moved around, so he took that as an invitation to take it home with him. Maybe he could help the author, maybe she was close-by? Maybe he was being watched on the sly. It might even make a great TV show or movie. He sat struck with the possibilities.

Packing up all of the final exam papers that the students had written, he was grateful for the two weeks he had until the start of the next session. To avoid thinking about his life, he had again volunteered to teach summer school.

Before, he and Natalia would take their summers off, either going abroad or spending weeks camping out with no destination in mind. They would just drive and see where they ended up. They would often visit his parents in Wyoming, or fly out to Toronto and spend time with her parents. Time alone was his toughest time.

Stacking the book on top of his file folders, he walked out the back door of the English rotunda. Walking through the vacant parking lot to the final row, he opened up the back of his Volvo Station Wagon XC70 and placed the papers down into the cavity below the panel used to cover the spare tire.

Once, Jeremy had test papers stolen out of his car and he learned to hide them to make sure they were safe. Because of his carelessness, all of his students had to come back to school that term and take a new abbreviated test. Who knew that English tests were actually worth money to cheating students? He gave each student one grade level higher to try to make things right for the hassle.

Climbing in behind the wheel, he stopped at the nearest Indian food place and ordered four veggie samosas and one order of chicken tikka masala with garlic naan. While he waited for them to cook it, he ran next door to the wine shop to buy a bottle of pinot gris to go with the dinner. Indian food had been one of their favorite meals to share together. That order had been enough for them to share, but with just him he was content to have leftovers. He didn't want to change his order.

He drove along Highway 43 on his way back to his condo. Opening up his trunk, his first trip inside was to set the papers on his desk to work on later. It had been a busy day and all he wanted was to relax. He made another trip to the car for the food, and the smells wafted into his nostrils as he pulled the bag off the seat. Yum.

He locked the car and went inside for the last time. He had enough to last him through the weekend; he didn't have to go anywhere if he didn't want to. He plated half of the meal and put the other half in the fridge for later.

Biting into the naan, he held it in his mouth as he walked, and ventured out onto the back deck in time to see the sun going down. He munched on food and drank the wine straight from the bottle. With no one to share it with, why not?

The back porch sat high with a view overlooking the water of the Willamette River. This was the spot that Natalia had fallen in love with when they moved here from Wyoming.

Hummingbirds still visited the bird feeders that she had set out, and Jeremy kept the sugar water filled. No need to abandon the little sprites just because Natalia was gone. The garden courtyard on the lower floor had a low fence and he could see the people walking along the trail just beyond the row of burning bushes. Sometimes he would wave and be friendly, depending on his mood. If he wasn't feeling super chipper, he would often get up and go inside, especially if he spied a couple who looked to be deeply in love.

A hummingbird flitted in front of him, then another joined in. He smiled and said, "*Hello*" before the two little birds flew off to their nests.

Alone again.

Sometimes out here he would think about the future, what he might do, or how to move beyond his current state. He liked what he did for a living for the most part, but it wasn't the total dream.

He finished his part of the dinner and put the cork back into the bottle of wine before placing it into the door of the fridge. He suddenly remem-bered the book he'd brought home. Going down to retrieve it from his office, he passed the large framed wedding photo of the two of them. He lightly touched the glass as he gazed at her face.

"My Love, what on earth will I do without you?" His head dropped as he entered the office. The piles of papers hadn't set right and the book had fallen to the floor.

Scooping it up under his arm, he walked back to the fridge and grabbed the wine again, deciding to drink it in bed. He had a new book to read tonight. Correcting his massive pile of finals could wait until tomorrow. He set the wine on the nightstand and pulled off his clothes and tossed them to the floor before climbing into bed in his underwear.

~

J.P.

You came into my life because of my woo-woo mother. In her own search for answers she sought and found a source that could reach beyond the known world. A medium. A large man with an almost Buddha-like appearance, you sat with your legs crossed on a pillow surrounded by sheaths of colorful saris.

As you greeted me for my first medium experience, you explained how it would go. You would be bringing forth Jubal, a long-time spirit who liked to come and speak to those who sought answers, by saying some kind of incantation. Then we could settle into any questions I may have.

At the time, I was three years deep in a high school relationship where we believed we would eventually get married. I had a big list of all the questions I had always wondered about. Some of my questions related to that romantic relationship, and some about other people I knew.

I was allowed to tape the conversation, however the actual tape went missing years ago. I wish beyond wishes I would have kept it safe to listen to later on.

The man with Jubal inside closed his eyes and said words in some other language. His voice changed from the initial effeminate tone of the *man* to a much deeper, soul grabbing voice of another. He added foreign words to the front of his greetings with English in the middle so I would understand.

I began, "What should I be when I grow up?"

More words and then a statement. "You have a gift. One that you will share with many."

"Is it my dancing?" my teenage self asked, thinking and hoping that the hours I had spent joyously boogying to disco music in the basement of our home might just turn into something.

"You have a gift with people. You will reach and impact many in your life."

Okay, I thought, not sure what to do with that, so I pushed on.

"Do I know the man I will marry?" I asked hoping for some confirmation that my current boyfriend and I were on the right path that we thought we were.

He hesitated.

"No, I don't think you know the man you are going to marry."

Shaken, I asked if I would have children someday.

"Yes, you will have children."

"Will I have boys or girls?"

"Do I have to answer? he asked.

I was curious but could have settled without an answer, then he reluctantly told me I would have two boys. Having been taking care of four boys on Wednesdays for the last two years, I was not phased. Whatever child I would have would be loved, welcomed and just fine with me.

I mentioned my boyfriend's brother's name as a person of interest to get a read on. In a surprise revelation, Jubal brought forth the energy of my boyfriend's father instead. A man who had been abusive to my boyfriend's mother and who was killed by his ex-wife's partner in self defense.

"Yes, he is here. He was very angry when he came, and he slept for a long time. He is aware of you and *he likes you*."

Shaken again, this wasn't working out as I planned.

Let's go deeper, I thought.

"Do we come back again after we die?"

"That is one that your fellow humanity really struggles with. You are spirits, having an earthly experience and you are placed here to learn lessons and to connect with your fellow kind in love. Each life experience will help you become who you are meant to be."

I was quite accustomed to the idea of reincarnation and was already a believer. That notion had stuck once I heard of it.

"Could I come back as a cat?"

A metaphysical chuckle ensued. "No, you won't come back as a cat. A cat will forever be a cat but can take different forms. A house cat can come back as a lion, a cougar, or a panther. A dog can be a pet as well as a wolf. They stay within their general family. Animals can come back into your life in another form if they choose to. Your childhood family dog could seek you later on when you have your own family. The same goes for people. You can be in numerous lifetimes with those you love— multiple or infinite lifetimes."

"Really?"

"Yes. You and your mother in this life were together in another life long ago. You chose her to be your mother in this life."

"Why do I feel like I have no idea what I am doing in this life? Everything seems so hard. Everyone else seems to know what they want to do for a job, but I can never decide. What is wrong with me?"

"You are a relatively new spirit, and in your last three lives you have died rather young. That could be the reason you feel ill-equipped."

"How did I die?"

"Once you died by gunfire, another in a concentration camp, and once by illness, taken as a young child."

Suddenly scared, I asked, *"Will I live very long this time?"*

I readied myself. Tears welled in my eyes- *maybe I did not want to know.*

"Yes, this time you will have a long life."

A breath.

A low gong rang in the room, as our time together was nearing an end. Jubal wished me well. He said how he had enjoyed watching me and my brother as children, running and playing in the room when my mother had come to see him years ago. "How I love to see the little children."

His final note before leaving and having J.P. come back: "You will have a good life this time; it won't always be easy but you will find your way. Just believe."

That hour felt like minutes. I was grateful for a snapshot into the universe and how things worked. I will say that after his comment that I didn't know the man I was supposed to marry, I more readily paid attention to the red flags that came up in my early relationship. I had felt so certain, but if not him, then who?

I wasn't sure how I was going to find that man, but somehow, I knew I would.

~

Didn't grow up Christian, Me 2011

I'd been exposed to many religions since I was a child. Many friends had offered to take me to church, in hopes of recruiting me, or saving me somehow from the grips of hell promised to an infidel. I'd been to a Mormon church Bible study group, where I mostly remember the cookies that were served. A Catholic friend had me go to church with her, and I remember a lot of singing out of an old book, and the shuffle of sitting up and then kneeling onto the upholstered bar in front of us throughout the ceremony. I could never tell when we were supposed to get up, but there seemed to be a special code that only the people that belonged there knew.

I went to Bible camp as a kid because my best friend wanted to go, and she needed someone to go with. At that time in my life I think there were only three types of sleepaway camps you could go to: Bible camp and Girl Scout or Campfire Girls camp. Since I wasn't a scout and hadn't been a Campfire Girl for a while, Bible camp was the way to go.

We bunked up in an old cabin and were given a camp counselor. There were classes we could take for crafts, and some religious things we had to do in the daytime such as saying grace before meals. Mostly it was a time for me to watch people and wish I was like them.

They all were in this belief that Jesus was their savior and everything in their life should revolve around that. God was to be #1. I hadn't grown up with this idea.

In my early days, I craved to be included, to be happy and to have something bigger than myself to believe in. So I listened to them with my little eight-year-old brain and gave my heart to Jesus after archery class one day with the help of my camp counselor Taz.

"You are now covered in the blood of Christ — you are saved."

Well, thank God. Sharing that moment had gotten me out of many a conversation in the years since. People that wanted to bring me into the church as an adult or were worried for my soul, I was able to ease their concern by *sharing that information.*

When I got into the relationship with Mr. In Between, I knew that religion would come up. Initially I wasn't asked to accompany him to church, and my salvation was nary one of his concerns. He had enough going on himself. Sleeping with a woman he was not wed to for starters. It would chew on him, but we felt a lot of feelings and some of them were sexual.

Finally it was becoming too much and he needed to make a decision: marry me and make me an honest woman or break it off. The words that started the ultimate choice really came from his daughter and at the time I saw them as a challenge to overcome.

"Dad, I think you need to marry a Christian woman."

From her tiny mouth to his ears, and then out of his mouth to me. A line was drawn.

When I think back it was probably a loving thing for her to say, and it most likely would have been a good idea, but I was on high alert. I wanted my man, and dammit, I was not going to have some kid take him away from me! He was my personal Colin Firth delivered from the Universe to me. No way honey, not on my watch, I thought.

So I went to church, and I gave my all. I bought into that thick old black book that held stories meant to keep people on the straight and narrow. We'd marry in the church and have a pastor say God's words, "til death do us part."

I'd become the good and dutiful parishioner and help out at the church daycare center (it was in my wheelhouse, and there weren't any tests). I'd stop swearing for the most part and would get baptized right along with his children in front of the entire church. Even my daughters agreed to come watch.

I could do this. I could do anything. I could reinvent myself into a new life, I could become anyone I wanted. I was an expert watcher of people, someone capable of taking on any persona if it was what I thought I needed to do.

Really though, I was just looking for happiness and since I hadn't found it in my old pagan ways, maybe I would finally be happy as a good and wholesome Christian wife?

I committed to God, Jesus and the church, and was accepted into the family, and as often as I would sit amongst the congregation each Sunday, I would wonder to myself, "When will it take?"

When will it feel real to me, and right and easy? Why do I still feel like I am on the outside begging to be let in. I've waited and waited, hoping the Holy Spirit would wash over me any second if I just kept going. Singing along to the songs as the words flew across the big screen, I prayed with my eyes closed and begged for His grace.

$$\sim 3 \sim$$

Professor Cate staggered to the restroom one last time before falling asleep. Climbing back into bed, he set the traveling book on the nightstand and turned out the light. He had read through the little blue book six times already and finished his bottle of wine. It was late.

He found himself thinking long and hard about any similarities he felt from the stories inside and if he might actually be connected to the author. He appreciated her courage and the magnitude of what she was hoping to accomplish with this mission. To be seen in the massive landscape of humanity like this. So bare, so real. Sharing her memories in hopes of others seeing themselves in the words, too. If not in the literal sense, maybe in the subtext. Many of her lessons touched on things others have dealt with. She shared so they might not feel so alone.

Alone, like he felt. Her words had given him company for the first time in a long time.

He turned over and moved to lie on Natalia's side of the bed. He wished he could have shared this book with her. She had been journaling for years, and even talked about writing her memoir someday. Once they had started traveling and seeing places together, that is.

Right before she died, she talked about how each of them had the job of helping others reach for their dreams by way of education. *Their* lessons helped students prepare to enter the world more successfully, more equipped. They were *conduits* to launch students into *their* own dreams in a sense. But he and Natalia had let their own dreams fall to the back of the line. Tears filled his eyes.

Natalia would have loved this woman's big idea. *Their* biggest dream together was to buy a run down winery and build it back up together. Jeremy closed his eyes and thought of his love, Natalia.

He drifted off thinking of possibilities and awoke with an idea. An idea with a name...

Escape.

Suddenly Pre-nuptialled Me, 2011

*W*ith Mr. In Between I had a place to live, new children to care for and a house to make feel like a home. Our wedding was right around the corner, too, so basically I was starting a whole new life from the ashes of my old one.

I went wedding dress shopping with my daughters and they would be my bridesmaids. My new stepdaughter was assigned flower girl duties and my stepson would be the ring bearer.

We'd found an adorable old church to marry in, and invited only a few people, mostly from his side of the world, with maybe two or three from my side other than family. I was stepping into a new life and felt I had left most of my old one behind.

Three days before our nuptials I was handed a document. One drafted by a lawyer.

"If you don't sign it, we won't be getting married."

It was a stab. The idea of a divorce already baked into our wedding plans. One that would become a sore spot in our life together and another way I felt held in place.

The document would be in full force with me receiving no part of anything he currently had with the agreement dying off after twenty years.

"Since you don't have anything and aren't very good with money, I need to have this in place in case we split up. I need to protect myself, my children and my assets. If you don't sign it, we won't be getting married. My lawyer suggested that you have a lawyer look at it to make sure you understand what you are signing and since you are broke, I'll pay for it."

A slam mixed with the expectation that he really didn't believe that we would be forever together. It was a piece of paper handed as coldly as if given to a stranger. To further drive home the idea that he had bailed me out and that I would <u>never</u> be an equal in his eyes.

What could I do? I signed it. We kept separate bank accounts; everything *was divided. It wasn't the kind of marriage or start I wanted, but I had no choice. I was living there, I had moved my family in, I had the dress, the location, everything was decided.*

It's okay that he wanted extra protections around himself and his children in regards to his finances, I just question the delivery and the timing of it. Cold, unfeeling, and harsh is how it felt. Maybe there was no way to soften something like that?

I told myself that he was trying to protect his children if something happened to him, that they would be the beneficiary of any assets, not me. I get it. I understood what it meant as he explained it to me in detail, and why he had chosen to do it. It was at the encouragement of his ex-wife, his kids' mother. I get it. I tried not to care.

But it made me feel really lousy. There was no way around that. When legal restraints are put on love, it becomes more of a business arrangement. That signed and binding prenuptial agreement would be added to a folder of what little I had in our new home together. A file containing our marriage certificate and engagement photo as well as my bankruptcy files.

I had sold or gotten rid of most of my belongings already. His house was already set up and had no room for my stuff. I tried to believe I could make my mark on this house and in this family, but it would be like trying to push a boulder uphill for a while. I hoped it wouldn't be long.

We married in a small ceremony and a friend made our cake while the other guests brought potluck foods, some in the tradition of his old country.

It was a nice gathering, but I noticed when the photos came back that the photographer must have had the hots for my husband. It was so obvious as many or most of the photos of our ceremony were of my new husband, with hardly any of me or of us together. Possibly it was because I had gained weight from the stress and bad diet at the time. Another thing I would suffer on about. Or maybe my absence from the photos was a foretelling of the future.

As we blended our families, we needed to schedule better and have more organization, a real effort. My daughters were with me every other week and were not of an age where they had any interest in another Dad. Mr. In-Between didn't try to bond with them either. And maybe that was a good thing?

I, on the other hand— tried to mother his children. In the only way I knew. To guide, to teach, to let them have consequences for their own choices.

That was not the way they had been raised so far, and the oldest, a daughter, bucked hard against any attempt I had to teach her anything. Not to my face but through her father, as he would tell me under no uncertain terms not to try to act like her mother or expect her to do anything around the house or listen to me at all. She had him wrapped around her adorable little finger; a daddy's girl in every sense of the word.

"You are not her mother," he told me after I had asked her to pick up her backpack or something benign like that.

Um, duh. But hello, she doesn't sleep in her own room, she doesn't pick up after herself and she doesn't know how to even pour herself a bowl of cereal or get herself ready for school. She's ten.

Her brother, aged six, drank mostly out of a toddler sippy cup filled constantly on demand with a sugary chocolate milk mixture, warmed to the perfect temperature for him. He literally held his cup in the air when he was playing video games and we were to fill it up for him. As many times a day as he wanted— he rarely ate actual food.

At home and in public he was handed his Nintendo DS anytime he made so much as a peep. With his games he sat quietly, staying small and out of the way so that his sister could shine. She was the family favorite whether they had proclaimed it or not. He did know, though.

Neither of them knew how to ride a bike, or had taken any classes to learn anything beyond what was taught in their religious private school. No music, no sports, no summer camps. I guess they had told their parents that they didn't want to, or maybe they hadn't been asked? They had slept with their parents since birth, most likely contributing to the ultimate demise of their marriage and had never been left with a babysitter, only their wonderful Oma. Spoiled much?

With a new maternal mission in place for myself, one that would help these kids develop into contributing members of society, I set my teeth in for the long haul, knowing it would be hard, and I would be fought against every step of the way.

I started with their bedrooms, decorating them while paying attention to their interests and favorite colors. If I made their personal spaces fun for them, maybe they would be happy to sleep there, or be in them with their little friends sometimes. It worked.

Next they needed to learn to ride bikes, as I knew if a child doesn't learn to ride a bike, they will struggle with other things later on in life, too, especially if they have any other type of issue at all. A friend of mine had told me that when her son was diagnosed with autism. She researched and got him into all the best programs, and that kid of hers learned to ride a bike, and eventually drive a car. It was important and I made it happen, wondering if my stepson might be dealing with autism.

They did it and it was great, and I continued to try to expand their worlds along with their father. We'd go hiking, and be outside in the fresh air.

Taking more walks and exploring the wilderness around the house. We went camping and made s'mores outside in the firepit.

I made a special effort to teach my stepdaughter how to cook. She had a natural knack for it and also loved art. It was one of the ways we could bond together. We carved pumpkins for Halloween, something they'd never done before. Getting their fingers in the gooey innards of the pumpkin grossed them out. I helped them with costumes and encouraged them to take taekwondo, to see a glimpse of what they could really do.

I wanted them to do activities because I wanted them to be able to relate better to the kids they would be meeting in public school. They had been pretty sheltered in a private Christian school slash daycare center for most of their childhood. I knew how kids could be cruel, especially to children who were different or acted spoiled. I knew this firsthand from my own childhood.

With two foreign-born parents and even though no one asked me to, I took ownership of their assimilation into American society. I wanted them to have a great big American life, and their current view of the world was pretty small.

I will continue to work on that, just try and stop me.

~

~3~

Jeremy Cate walked out of the Dean's Office after his two weeks notice was up. He wouldn't be teaching the summer session this year, and most likely he'd never teach again. He packed up his desk and headed out to the car. His entire tenure had fit into one box. His list sat on the dash. For the first time since Natalia's death, he had a plan. More than a plan, he had something to look forward to.

He pulled into his driveway, grabbed the list, and sat on the front porch to make a few calls. First, his real estate agent.

Krystal Costa came over quickly and was pleased to take on the listing of his house. He signed the paperwork and crossed that off his list.

He had stayed up all night the night before, looking at wineries available for sale that were all over the country, and found one right in his own backyard in the celebrated Yamhill County of Oregon.

Jeremy wandered around the big rooms of his house with a roll of painters tape. Putting tape on everything he wanted to keep, the rest could go. He didn't care.

The things that reminded him of Natalia would stay with him. She was still a big part of this journey after all. The picture of them that his mother took, the vase they picked up in Rome on their honeymoon. The old fashioned cat clock that she thought was hilarious. All of his books on wine, the scrapbooks, a pillow from India that Natalia just had to have. Many things would be going with him.

He called his two favorite students and asked them to come over. Summer was in full swing, and he asked them if they wanted to make some cash.

"Of course."

"You two pack up all the things that have tape on them and put them in storage for me until I tell you where to bring them. You get to keep everything else to sell and can share the money."

"That's a lot of book money!" said one.

"Yes, sir!" said the other.

He handed them a spare house key and one hundred dollars to rent the storage space. He walked them out and said goodbye and good luck.

Upstairs he packed a large suitcase of clothes, Natalia's photo, Book 3, and his toiletries. He was out the door in minutes.

~

To The Best Of My Recollection, Me, 2011
and beyond

As I will go into more detail in the pages that come, I have almost completely stopped my journaling in this section of my life for fear my thoughts would be found and used against me. From 2010 I felt forced by certain circumstances to hold many thoughts about my life inside, to wrangle with and figure out as best I could.

I will call this part of my life "living unauthentically."

~

~3~

J eremy had about a fifty-mile drive to where he was staying. He would arrive just in time for the Turkey Rama Festival. This year, he would be seeing McMinnville, Oregon at its finest.

It was his first visit to the challenged winery he had been eyeing for the last few years. A new life pursuing his passion for wine was about to be realized. He'd be doing it for Natalia as well as for himself..

They had scrimped and saved and made sound financial decisions in anticipation of doing just this. Even though he was alone now, he felt her with him. Every glass he would try would be different on this trip and considered research for the empire he would build. He had things to think about on the way. He would stay in Yamhill for a few days to see if that was the right place for him.

Jeremy had done his research and purchased the place he had seen in *Winery Northwest* magazine. He'd set about rebuilding the vineyard, updating the small cabin on the property to live in, and building a large barn into a tasting room and event space.

Jeremy envisioned making a place for the little traveling book, too. He'd put it on display in the tasting room once he opened for the many visitors to read as they lounged.

Maybe someone would see themselves in the pages and maybe he would help it find its way back to the author.

~

L.T.

You were the gentle giant of our homeowner's association. A white beard without mustache, your head full of ice colored hair- you exuded an air of *All Knowing*. Resembling Santa Claus but more of a European fantasy version interwoven with history, elegance and significance of a being thrust from the ages.

You lived simply, surrounded by art and nature in a one story home along a gully. You had two daughters as I did, and grandchildren that would climb you like a jungle gym.

You could see auras. Once you told me that mine glowed white hot like your mama's. There were times when I was fired up about some kind of injustice or challenge faced by our organization and you'd calm me down enough to look for answers, always teaching me to look at the bigger picture.

Once you said that I should run for president of the United States. The idea was mind-bogglingly absurd.

In your deep and firm voice, you doubled down. "From any government position, you are no more than seven steps away from the biggest office in the land."

While I never sought any office above my little dally into our homeowner's association, I held onto his idea that perhaps I was somebody special enough to have some kind of gift to share.

Although our interaction ended when I left the position, I imagined that someday we might meet again and chuckle at the chaos we started that turned into progress and to celebrate the park we worked to organize and have built for all the little ones who came to play.

I will never forget your kindness, your godly calm in any storm and how you tempered so gently this twentysomething's urge to make her mark on the world.

I pray my aura still shines just like you described.

~

Jeremy's winery label "Escape" is finding fans in the Willamette Valley area. He has found his new love: winemaking. *Find Me Book 3 of 5* sits in a prominent place there in the tasting room and has been read by many. Signatures covered the pages themselves and spilled onto the back cover. Jeremy even added more paper to the back to handle more signatures, but as of yet he hadn't heard of anyone recognizing themselves in the pages of the book.

After everyone had left for the night, he sat in his winery tasting room and looked around. He had built this place from his mind and the collected past dreams of himself and Natalia.

He thought back on his emotionally empty final year as a professor. How he had blindly wandered through his days, walking the halls in a state of shock after Natalia passed. How he had been both physically and mentally absent from class so many times, only skimming the homework that was passed in.

His days of feeling like a ghost. That moment of seeing the book on the old sofa in the commons and then reading it had given him the courage to move on and pursue his next step.

He had kept the book long enough. The whole point of the book was to be moved around so many could read it and share in it.

Even with the many who had seen it, no one took it away to complete its destiny. Out of anyone he knew, his sister was the most well traveled. She might have heard of some of these stories, or might know what to do to advance toward the author. She was about to have some time on her hands, waiting for publication in a journal to accomplish her PhD in Human Development.

Suddenly feeling guilty, he started to wonder if he had actually done harm to the author's request by keeping it for so long. He wrapped it gently in bubble wrap and placed it inside one of his beautifully hand-branded wine boxes. That box went into a cardboard box and he spread peanuts around before closing it and adhering the address label. Christine Cate in

Wyoming, Jeremy's once near-professional globetrotting half-sister, would be getting a special surprise.

He was passing it along. *Finally.*

~

~3~

Christine Sacajawea[1] Cate of Laramie, Wyoming, received a package from her half-brother. Her birthday was a week away, but Jeremy never sent gifts. It was her fortieth: a big one, she figured, so maybe that was why. She cut the tape with a knife and pulled out a lovely wooden box branded with her brother's winery logo. Sliding the door from the box, she was surprised to find a used book instead of an assumed bottle of wine. Was it a self help book?

Jeremy had made some pretty major changes in his own life the last few years, and he had become annoyingly chipper when they spoke on the phone. Here she was studying all the time, trying to acquire her doctorate after leaving the country in her twenties, much to her parent's dismay.

She had worked odd jobs while cobbling together a Bachelor's degree in Anthropology, adding a Master's of Sociology from the National University of Singapore a few years later. Her entire collegiate education was away from the States.

It made classes harder to transfer sometimes, so she took extra just in case. She had learned by age thirty that taking advantage of universal opportunities to help teach English as a second language or tutoring at each of the universities was the best way to get an education, income, and a place to stay all at the same time. It was an atypical path to a degree, but she was a one-of-a-kind person, too.

A wanderer. Curious about people, where they came from, and what made them tick.

Christine had long since run out of money and friends' couches to sleep on, but after her mother Aiyana's death, it felt like time to grow up. She moved home to be with her dad and settled in at University of Wyoming to finish the educational path she sought years ago.

---

1. Sacajawea is the preferred spelling by the Eastern Shoshone Tribe at Wind River. See back for more resources

Her mother's life insurance policy had paid for this last year of college tuition and her dad supported her with living expenses, as she helped around the house. Christine had spent so much time couch surfing and being nomadic over the last fifteen years, it felt strange to actually have a bed to call her own.

Her final dissertation had been all-consuming. Her base theory was that obesity in women, outside of medical causes, stems from a toxic parental figure. It was something she could relate to. Not because of her own parents, as they were together forever and had only been separated since her mom died.

The theory had come from the life and death of her close friend Jessa. Christine met Jessa in elementary school and they became good friends. The two were always giggling in the back of the classroom in Mrs. Mc-Clung's second grade class where they often got into trouble. Jessa was a "*larger-boned*" child, but it hadn't bothered her from what Christine could tell. Not until her father came back into the picture, when she was seven years old. From then on the beratement was constant, and her father would often criticize Jessa in front of Christine.

"Look at your *little* friend; you could eat her for breakfast," he would say, and then slap his hand on his thigh and laugh. Jessa would go from the lighthearted friend Christine knew at school and shrink into someone Christine didn't recognize as she neared the days end when her father picked her up from school.

Jessa had spent years battling her feelings of unworthiness, the demons of not being loved as she was. Never feeling she deserved a good life, all because of the unrealistic expectations of societal beauty standards.

Jessa's father had left the family for the first time when she was five, coming in and out of her family home, and breaking promises to her mother until she was ten. Then he finally moved out and got a place of his own.

Forced into a shared custody situation, any time spent with her father was also in the company of whatever drugged out, *skinny*, "girl-friend-of-the-month" who she was forced to call "*mom*." It had caused more damage to Jessa than anyone knew. As she grew into womanhood, her father became meaner and even more cruel to her, often suggesting she might start taking a little meth as a diet aid.

At times it looked like she had developed some sense of self-worth, but it was usually attached to losing some weight, and those losses were not always achieved in the healthiest way.

The summer of her freshman high school year, she started battling both anorexia and bulimia. She vacillated between the two for two years before finally letting go of her need to control her eating altogether.

When Jessa was sixteen, her father left the area with fake mom #7 or so, but by then Jessa was thoroughly damaged. She believed as her father had told her, that no one would want to be with her. She started drinking to cope. At first, stealing her mother's booze at home, and then once she turned twenty-one, she would stay out late at the bars. After Jessa's mother died, Jessa sought whatever affection she could find. Often touch came in the form of romps in the backseats of a number of college boys' cars. Sexual interactions often came by way of a good-old-boy bet by the man's inebriated friends. Sometimes the men's drunken talk after the deed gave them away, or once Jessa saw an exchange of cash under a table when she went back into the bar.

Two of these hookups had led to her darling children into whom she poured all of her energy. She never sought out the men who were fathers, as she never wanted to see them again. She had her monthly check from her dead mother's social security and worked two jobs to make enough money to support her and her children: one at the courthouse filing case verdicts, and three nights a week cleaning real estate offices.

While Christine was away for ten-plus years traveling, she received the news that Jessa had taken her own life. An overdose. The note she left read that she wasn't happy and believed that she never could be. That she couldn't try anymore, and that she had no more fight in her. She just couldn't bear the idea that she was being judged every day for the way she looked.

While Jessa had freed herself with the act of what must have felt like an unsolvable existence, her decision orphaned her two children in the process. They were adopted away to a relative in another state, thankfully far out of reach of Jessa's terrible father. It was sad, devastating, and Christine couldn't help but wonder if she had been around if she might have been able to help her friend. Jessa had seemed on the upswing the last time they spoke as she was animated and making plans.

Jessa shared that she had met a very kind and amazing man named Adam. They had fallen deeply in love and he could see her and the light inside of her behind the darkness. They were set to marry, and Jessa reached out to her father in one last effort to attain the visual of the happy family she had longed for. With her beautiful heart she told herself that her father must have evolved in the time they had been away from each other, but instead she found him to be his authentically toxic and shaming self. His attacks started up again in earnest via every way he could reach her and

Jessa again fell back into a hopeless state.

Even Adam couldn't break through the muck of her unworthiness. Never feeling worthy of such a love, she pushed him away. Jessa was beautiful and it was such a waste that one prominent and horribly malignant person can do so much damage to another.

Christine's dissertation theory was that detrimental upbringings could only be counteracted if there was some sort of intervention either by counseling or another significant source of emotional support before the age of sixteen.

Christine had reached out for actual stories on the internet to help pad her study. Her website and her Craigslist ads placed all over the country had received over three hundred responses that she could use as samples. Her work was complete. She had sent in all of her paperwork, research, and findings to the faculty and could now relax. She was free for two weeks, until it was time to come before them and present the information and defend her position.

She'd been stuck in the house studying, compiling and organizing her notes for nearly three months. Her skin was stale from lack of air and sunshine, and her brain was intellectually blotto. She couldn't concentrate on the book her brother sent her just yet. She needed to let loose a little. Spending a few days out in nature and going out with some friends at night should help her to unwind a little.

Desperate to get out of her head and escape some of the grief and sadness that she felt for her friend, Christine wished that Jessa had had someone to fight for her, to stand behind her and push her into being her one true self, like she had. Her spirit was pulled to thinking about her mother.

Christine set her newly gifted book on the bed and went to take a shower. She slipped out of her sweatpants, leaving them in a bunch on the bathroom floor. No bra, her sweatshirt soon joined the pants on the mound. She had been up for hours.

She rinsed her two-day dirty hair, feeling the coat of grease lessen. The luxurious shampoo suds left her hair squeaky clean, and she added some conditioner. Her hair, a rich black with faint streaks of gray was long and full. She wore it back mostly, to fit her idea of what a "doctor" would look like. Her deep brown eyes, slightly dull from lack of sleep, still had glints of the gold flecks directly from her mother's Lemhi Shoshone-borne eyes.

When her mom died three years ago, something changed in Christine. She began to really understand her mortality and place in the world. Yes, she had experienced death losing Jessa, but her death had been her choice, on her own timeline; her mother's was not.

Death often happens when it is least expected. A life just stops. Her mother's death had spurred an action inside of her to make her life count. To help others. She hoped she had figured out the right way.

She sat down on the floor of the shower and let the water run down her face. This was where she often prayed.

"Earth Mother, please show me the way to live and provide guidance to others. Allow me to meet new people and inspire. Please send love to my mother. I miss her so much."

Christine sat for a long time, until the water started to chill. She turned off the water and stood, hoping that her prayers had been heard. She tossed her towel onto the bed, accidentally covering the book.

Find Me, 3 of 5, would have to wait to get some attention. Christine strolled into her walk-in closet, nude. Pop had given her the master bedroom when she moved in.

One, because he didn't want to sleep in there without his wife, and two, to make sure Christine had enough space to want to stay awhile. Without his wife, the house had become too big and echoey to rattle around in alone.

She didn't dress up much. No need. Playing pool or darts didn't demand any uniform. Putting on a brown and white gingham cowboy shirt and blue jeans, her long hair wet her shirt so she put it back quickly into a braid. A few tendrils fell from the elastic band and she left them. She tossed her towels over the shower curtain bar and wandered out into the living room to see her dad.

"Pop, I am going out. I've been cooped up too long. It's not the company, I promise. I just need a beer and to get drunk somewhere outside this house and to hang out with some of my friends."

"Oh, sure honey, you go play. You have been working really hard. I'll be fine."

Christine kissed her father on the head and said goodbye. She climbed into her dad's Taurus, and found herself line dancing at the Running Horse Tavern until late into the night.

No more worries, no more deadlines, she was free for the moment.

In her couch surfing days, she felt that freedom. No one was keeping track of her. She let her heart point her to her next destination whenever she started feeling too settled. Many who knew her thought that she was wasting time or wouldn't amount to anything. Christine knew what she was capable of, but she felt like moving around. She wasn't quite sure why.

Quietly, she used her house key in the door and crept down the hallway. She was wiped out all the way around, brain and body. She tumbled face first onto the bed, brushing the book on the way down. Craving slumber, she lightly tossed it away from herself and snuck in under the covers, taking off items of clothing and tossing them out to the best of her ability. She managed to get down to her underwear and bra; that was enough. She fell into a deep sleep still wearing the glass-beaded earrings her mother had made for her.

~

K.C.

You lived across the street from me when we moved to the dream house and neighborhood. You were nice and friendly but kept to yourself a bit as you had quite the houseful. One daughter, the oldest, and three sons. You appeared to be juggling it well.

It was another one of our bunco nights and you were hosting. We all gathered in your comfy great room. Kid's artwork covered the fridge, but everything else was neat as a pin. I wondered how you did it.

I was in the middle of a dilemma. Have more children or just stick to the one I had. See, I loved my first child so much. So much I wondered if I would be a good mother to another. Was there enough to go around? She was smart, easy, and I felt I was doing a decent job at raising her. Could I even love another child as much as I loved her? Would I play favorites?

I said just as much to you that night, probably the most I had ever said to you. You told me about your kids.

"Girls, are easy when they are young, but grow moody with age and hormones. With boys when they are little, you can just look at them and know what you have. They are energetic little monkeys when young but grow easier when they get older."

"But what if I have another kid and I can't love them the same way?" I asked petrified.

"You will, your heart just grows."

And the answer was simple and matter of fact and suddenly my fear subsided.

My heart will grow.

I still make your famous chocolate mint cookies with the swirl of melted Andes mint on top every Christmas.

Both my kid's love them.

~

~3~

Christine stirred while fully inside a vivid dream. She was standing in a golden pasture admiring the vast mountains before her. At first she is alone, then she feels a slight tap on the shoulder. She turns to see her mother holding the reins of a beautiful brown horse with white speckled hindquarters. Her mother doesn't speak but motions for Christine to mount the horse as she holds the animal steady.

From above, Christine holds her mother's gaze, trying to interpret her unspoken message. She looks just as when Christine last saw her. Her mother's grayed black hair is pulled back behind one ear, one of her favorite glass beaded rose earrings hangs colorfully almost to her shoulder. They were a gift from her own mother, then handed down to Christine. Her wrinkled and tanned hands, so beautiful and strong. Her mother hands her the reins.

Taking the straps in close, she felt her mother's strong hands squeeze onto her closed fingers, tight around them, in an almost hand-hug before stepping away and smiling an all-telling smile. With no warning, her mother wallops the animal on the backside causing him to rear up and take off running away in the opposite direction of the mountains, and away from her mother.

Out of control, Christine tries desperately to steer the animal back to where her Mother is. She wants only to be there with her mother again, but the horse won't stop. Finally, after what seemed like many miles, the animal slowed.

She slid off the beast's back and both she and they collapse near one another, surrounded by a field of sage and striking yellow mule's ears.

Christine looks up into the blue of the sky. Brush-footed butterflies dance all around her. The green of the leaves and the mustard yellow of the blooms remind her of the colors of the Pow Wows she attended when she was younger.

She can hear the faint echo of her mother's voice in the wind as the stems sway.

"It's time for another Vision Quest, my love. You must go."

Christine could feel her mother's spirit with her as she awakened from her beautiful dream.

She rubbed her eyes and sat up, fluffing her pillows together into a nest. She leaned back into the cloudlike fabric.

The idea of having a Vision Quest of her own had made her leave the area in her youth in the first place. A tradition told to her as a young girl by her mother. It wasn't common for a girl to go on them though; it was more of a coming of age tradition for boys in her mother's family tribe. She would forever be Aiyana Sacajawea of the Shoshone at Wind River's daughter.

Her mother had taken her side when Christine announced that she was leaving at just nineteen. She remembered her mother's words as if they were tape recorded on her heart.

"Let her go. She is a free spirit. We cannot keep her here. I see my sister in her; she also needed to roam in order to find herself. She has the middle name and the blood of my ancestor, the great Sacajawea. It means a woman who pulls a boat upstream. Her journey might not be easy, but she has her own path; it is her way."

As her father sat with the decision, he knew that his wise wife was right. His Aiyana was always right. Christine was not easily tamed. Her trajectory was already set, and her place wasn't here. Over time he got used to the idea.

A tear fell from her eye. Being away so much had cost her precious time away from her mother. She was sure that she had more to learn from her, but it was too late. She was grateful for the dream that brought her mother back to her. With a message she would never forget.

Maybe I do have another vision quest in me? Maybe I could start with what Jeremy sent?

Grabbing her glasses from the side table, she wiped the lenses with her top sheet and placed them over her nose. There, now she could see. Three of five stared back at her in gold metallic letters. Weird. This book didn't have an inspirational cover that most of the self-help books do: the highly-graphic covers, filled with promises that if you read this book you would be a millionaire, find your one true love or become the person you've always dreamed you could be. Simple title, no promises, no guarantees of any kind.

She turned it over. No publisher, no author bio.

Strange book. Immediately upon opening it she found a request for help.

Dear Reader,

This traveling book is my secret mission to live a more extraordinary life from within the confines of an ordinary one.

Only five copies of this book exist and this has made its way to you; you are now and forever a part of this story.

She read the rest of the excerpt while getting pulled into the idea. This person needed help, she wouldn't be turning away any more people who needed assistance. She didn't want to wonder what more she could do.

The stories inside were raw, and introspective. Easy to relate to, imagine, and be drawn into. She hoped she could relate to them in the way the author needed her to. That she knew who the author was and could take the book back to her. But no.

Maybe she could help by creating a website? Broadcasting this out to the world might amplify the results. She could do that. She had been very successful in compiling data from her sources for her thesis.

She could reach out to different people in other locations, a new goal was bubbling up in her head, but her heart pulled her back to what her mother had said.

"It's time to go."

~

Oh, No, I Might Have Made a Mistake, Me
2012

My revelations didn't come all at once. In the beginning of our marriage I was not in a place of strength. I was in a place of shame, failure and desperation. It wasn't an ideal time to enter into a marriage like that, but now it is done. I had believed we would be together forever. I wanted to make it so.

The further I got from the bankruptcy, the loss of the business, the loss of my home, the more power I grew back. I had decided the only way forward was to give myself grace in a big way. I wasn't the only person who had lost their job, business, or home, I was one of the many over the last five years who were catastrophically savaged by our national economic situation. It wasn't all because of my choices and decisions— those were probably the least of it.

I gave myself some absolution for the affair I had while married to my first husband. Not that I would ever forget it or put myself into that situation again. It happened the way it needed to for a reason I hoped to understand one day.

I gave myself grace for taking a chance on someone else, even though on the face of it, he wasn't a great person for me. I was trusting to give Mr. Fun a chance to be in our lives and to try to better himself and his relationship with his daughters. I had helped him have a second chance with them.

It is only in forgiving oneself that we can unburden ourselves from the lifelong guilt and look rationally at the lessons instead. If I spent my whole life begging for amends, beating myself up or doubting what I was capable of because of these things that happened that I felt I had learned from, it would be a waste of life that I had left.

As I came to understand these things with time spent walking alone outside, learning to dance again when I was by myself or going back to the things that brought me joy, reading "The Secret" and "The Alchemist" again and getting back to my writing, I discovered that I was getting stronger.

Strong on the inside. This is probably when the real problems in my second marriage began. When I dared to share an opinion, or ask for a certain thing, I found that the answer was not always to my liking. We'd argue, or he'd get quiet, which was almost as bad. There was an aspect to our relationship that made me feel insecure and fearful non-stop. He held <u>all</u> the cards, and I wasn't even allowed to sit at the table. I was about as impactful of a decision maker in the house as was the youngest child when he was asleep.

At least he got a new bed for us. That was something. Over our first year I could paint the walls an approved color but little else changed and I was again living in another woman's house. It might never feel like home. His artwork and his kids' pictures were up everywhere; we— my daughters and I were just taking up space. I didn't have a spot for any of my things. I had to negotiate for everything. We kept separate bank accounts; nothing at all was blended. It didn't affect him if I went to the store to buy food for us and had my card rejected because of low funds. It never felt like he had my back.

Any home projects we'd attempt to do together always turned into a fight. He would tell me that whatever I was doing was wrong, or he'd ignore me when I showed him something that might work better. As time went by I stopped asking to do any projects at all. It was such an ordeal to work on anything together. And I <u>loved</u> house projects. I felt at such a loss not being able to represent myself in "our" home.

Most of my friends had fallen away, either because I moved or because we spent so much time with his. We ate the food that he and his kids liked, celebrated Christmas the way they did, and went to his church every Sunday. We never watched football or did any of the things I liked to do like going to art galleries, taking road trips or even just walking around town to see what was up. I missed my old city, my friends, my house and felt plunked into the middle of a soulless place that I would never have chosen to live in unless I had to.

Once active in the bedroom, any romantic encounters fell to a slow drip, and they were always the same pattern: this foreplay, the deed, and then sleep. There was no tease, exploration, or newness— any sex life was dulled into a routine activity once or maybe twice every couple of months, if I was lucky. He was always tired, or needing to get up early, or not in the mood. I waited patiently for something to change.

He blamed my weight gain for our lack of a sex life, him punishing me because of the ten to fifteen pounds that I packed on after discontinuing my thyroid issue protocol diet and just going along with whatever the rest of the house wanted to eat. Often fried this or fatty that.

He wouldn't go walking with me even though it would have been good for him. His smoking kept him stuck in his old limitations.

In an attempt to make it work (although I don't think I was actually aware of it), I started acting in ways I thought he might appreciate, to try to get him to be as in love with me as he was in the beginning. I would style my hair like he liked it, up and off my neck. I wore clothes that showed my bust, although rarely in front of the children, because ew.

I made more of an effort to be friendly with his mother when deep down I had no respect for her for being so toxic and abusive to him growing up. If I was giving myself grace for all that I had done, I guess I could give her grace, too. It wasn't like she had had an easy life. We all do what we know to do.

I wasn't in a place to second guess my decision now; I had to make the best of this. I could be who he wanted me to be- I think I knew what and who he wanted. I had my actress side in my first marriage and was fairly good at it, until I wasn't. I could play a new role, a new character. I'm smart enough to solve this puzzle, to fit myself into his life and this household.

Aren't I?

~

~3~

Christine organized the items on her desk in her bedroom. The stacks of research for her dissertation were piled around her. She had grabbed a box from the garage and started piling them all into it. After sending her paper off to the journal and defending it in front of the panel, she had just found out it was to be published. Finally, everything could be put away for good.

One more thing.

Walking back to her desk, she grabbed the little blue book off of the bedside table. She flipped the page on the spiral book to the prologue and placed it face down onto her copier. She printed out the pages as she went, even the ones with the reader names and locations. Some of this could be useful. She really hadn't come up with a plan yet, but she could do something with it eventually.

Placing the stack inside with her dissertation evidence, she put the top on the box, and placed it into her closet for storage.

She sauntered into the kitchen to show her father what had come in the mail.

She sat across the table from him and placed the medical journal in his hand.

"I made it, Dad. My work is in this journal. Look! I'm a PhD. You can call me 'Doctor'."

She hadn't seen her father cry since her mom had passed. These tears were different. These were tears of pride. He sat and looked at her, and she smiled.

"Dad, say something."

"Your mom and I had many sleepless nights because of you, my dear. Traipsing all over the world, never in one spot for very long, you were pretty hard to keep track of. We always wondered why you left, what it was that you were searching for, and why you couldn't find it here. Now it makes sense. You were on a journey; one I didn't understand. But now I get it. You have always been so smart, smarter than this town, smarter than anyone around here. Smarter than me. I am the proudest dad in the world right now. I was before, and I always have been proud of you and your brother. But this makes me feel like I can stop worrying about you. I'm not sure why. But it gives me peace."

Christine reached for her father's hand and squeezed it.

"I've always been okay, Dad. I'm just on my own path to get there. I want to help people heal what's bothering them on the inside. What keeps them from living their best life. I want to help them conquer the fear that's holding them back."

Christine and her dad's eyes filled with tears.

"Let's go get ice cream."

Ice cream had always been the reward of any celebratory event in their family. When she graduated from high school, when her brother got his Master's of Education, they all had gone for ice cream.

"Sounds perfect, Dad."

They piled into his 2006 Ford Taurus and drove to the nearest Dairy Queen. Christine grabbed a Dilly Bar while her dad ordered a Peanut Buster Parfait. They celebrated her accomplishment together.

She didn't have the heart to tell him she was leaving again for another one of her Vision Quests the day after tomorrow. She'd be spending a week or so in Italy.

~

Craving My Books When Life Feels Empty, Me 2012

I haven't heard a peep about my books. I wonder how long I can hold onto the idea of this dream. How long can I tell myself that what I picture in my head could actually happen?

There have been numerous moves now and a name change. Would the people I wrote about even bother?

I walk the planet feeling that I have no idea what I am doing. Every single day it's a guess. Did I make the right choice there, did I say the right things? Do I appear as clueless as I feel?

Life for me is about the journey, not the destination. I believe that with all of my heart. To rise and try to figure out what's next in this extraordinary/ordinary life that I have been given.

Constantly in thought, I search for answers everywhere I can. It is the never-ending quest of a crusading soul. Many had been inspired by my wish for an extraordinary life, challenged, to ask for more from themselves in their own lives. I bow to the ones who have inspired me either by doing or by sharing their unsettledness, wishing things in their life were different.

It is my desire to feel life fully and pay attention along the path. I ask it not only of myself but of the others who joined on this tour. I have been writing mental postcards for most of my days. Photos on one side, sentiments or wisdom on the other. I collect them in the mailbox of my mind.

Someday when it is time, I will pull the crammed box out of the depths and relive my memories. Maybe when my body is no longer pliable and capable of much more than introspection. When the time comes if one is lucky enough to live past the age of demands, and live into the time of just knowing.

All of these memories, plus the dream of seeing my five little volumes will carry me through.

~

~3~

Christine Cate is lying on a beach chair on the banks of a dark pebbly beach in Atrani, Italy, sipping her first morning espresso. What was supposed to be a week-long vacation to celebrate her PhD, had turned into a two month long sabbatical before the Fall term started.

In all of her travels abroad, she had missed this country altogether. The people were beautiful here, dark complected from generations of working land and sea. She loved the families she saw, their culture, and the amazing food.

The winds smelled of fish and possibilities. Her angst of leaving shone behind her mirror-finish sunglasses. The airplane ticket home, this time, was unchangeably booked.

Her new job back at the college was to start on Tuesday. She had signed on to be an adjunct professor, working part time at first to take up the slack of a slowly retiring Women's Studies Fellow. The rest of her time would be used on building the website to find the author of that mysterious book she had received.

She imagined her perfect setup. She would work and teach during the day, then after hours, tackle one geographical area by area using Craigslist. She'd post the memories from the book into a "Missed Connections" post to see if anyone could relate to them, and keep a record of any responses she got. Reach out to strong possible contenders.

It would be like a big secret science experiment and *she* would be the one to make the discovery. She was already planning to write a book about it. With her copies of the memory pages as well as the names that were signed in the back, she was all ready to start as soon as she could sit at her computer back home. She had brought the book itself with her for the trip just in case she had any eureka moments.

It was ten in the morning when out of the blue, a large, muscle-bound fisherman walked over to her and handed her a hearty fish. The gesture caught her off guard. They hadn't even met. She hadn't done anything to signal that she was in need of a fish. He smiled at her with a great mischievous grin and walked off.

"Um, *thanks*?" she murmured as she pulled her towel over herself to keep the juices from getting on her legs.

Cupping her hand through the gill of the fish she managed to get up from her chair and pack up her things, staring after the mysterious man. She had planned on being here the whole day, but now she had a fish that required refrigeration. It would definitely not keep long with the sun beating down on it. It would make a lovely dinner though. At the café near the parking lot, Christine asked for a bag of ice. It would hopefully be good enough to keep the fish cold for the twenty-minute moped journey back to her small casita.

Placing the fish in the small fridge in the corner of her very basic kitchen, she looked around for other things to go with her fish dinner that evening. No veggies or potatoes or pasta in the house. She'd need to go to the market.

She showered and would let her hair dry in the wind as she rode her rented blue Vespa to Maiori, a few towns over. She parked and settled into the view of the Piazza Mercato. The marketplace was bustling. People were wheeling and dealing for the essentials like fruit fresh off the tree and vegetables that had been harvested that morning. A magical kaleidoscope of colors, smells and sounds.

Out of the corner of her eye she spied the same brawny fisherman who had gifted her the fish. He was selling more fish out of large baskets spilling with ice. Talking in his native tongue, his head flew back in laughter often as he talked to the people around him. He handed out fish after fish and crammed the money into his fallen open shirt. He sweat from the heat and hard work and his skin glistened, *he looked downright yummy.*

Who was this fisherman that had broken through her quietude on the coast today and asked for her attention? Hadn't he seen that she had been keeping to herself? How long had he been there under her nose during all of her days there in Atrani?

True, she had spent most of her days reading under a large sun hat while looking longingly out over the ocean. Hours spent mentally preparing herself for the long boring days ahead of sitting behind a desk in the cold weather and dealing with people on a regular basis.

This position would require standard hours, strict practices and a very traditional lifestyle. Maybe she would be okay, her adventurous life stance would retire into the life she thought she needed. Her talents, her learned information would allow her to help others.

Thinking about it now, her learning and position would allow her to help others, *help others*. She wouldn't have direct access to the ones who might need her the most.

Snapping back into the moment, she inhaled, not realizing she had been holding her breath[1] . She felt faint and sat down on the edge of a large planter.

Her days would be spent in a dark office with the light of a single desk lamp shining its way over masses of papers filled with other people's opinions. She would be working for a colleague whom she didn't like on her best day.

Sudden dread. Ultimate trepidation fell over her as she felt dread at the thought of the office but good gazing at the hunky Italian fisherman. His eyes were sunken happily from the non-stop grin on his face. Wrinkles from years in the sun aged him but not in a bad way. He was tan and content.

Content.

A fisherman is always searching for the next fish, using the knowledge most likely passed down through the generations. Maybe he hadn't seen the world beyond these waters and rocky banks, but it didn't matter if he was born in the perfect spot for his soul to light. The sun shone on his bare arms, his muscles pronounced. He passed out fish after fish until there were no more and started packing up his baskets to go home.

Christine felt embarrassed as he caught her looking at him in the distance. He made his way over to her and sat down. In his best English, he asked if she liked the fish.

"Yes, it is beautiful. I plan on having it for dinner tonight. Would you care to join me?"

His eyes twinkled at her and she blushed.

"I would be honored," he placed his sun kissed hand on his chest and gave a little bow.

They exchanged names and she gave him the address of her tiny temporary abode.

He left her sitting there wondering what in the hell she was thinking.

In three days she would be gone from this place. It was her last adventure before winding down into the societal-expected section in her life. Finally, living life like a responsible adult. She'd focus on throwing money at her Social Security account for her later years. Retirement, being there for Dad.

---

1. haha

Sitting there, watching the market square so full of life, the scene stopped her cold.

She felt oddly at home in the chaos of this place, the busyness of the day, the unknown night ahead. The kind stranger who had touched her with a gift of a meal, randomly seeing him again miles away from where their eyes initially met. She hadn't noticed him, even though most likely he had been there the whole time. She'd been in her head a lot.

She gathered a few items into her basket. Some shallots to add flavor to the fish; some fresh sage to sprinkle over the crispy skin; fresh pasta; a lemon; olive oil; and garlic. She'd add curls of fresh parmesan and parsley. For dessert, a mixed wine-grape tart with homemade crust accented with a reduced balsamic glaze.

Davide promised to bring the wine. His name seemed to fit him. One could easily see him fight a giant and win, yet it was his tranquility that felt like his ultimate strength.

She instantly felt safe at the thought of him. And maybe a bit too homey.

She tied her basket to the back of the Vespa as she started toward home. Or the place she had called home these last two months.

Opening the aged wood door, she laid the food on the counter and took some butter from the fridge to warm. She cooked the tart, and set everything else out to cook when Davide got there. Fresh pasta and fish don't take long.

Christine changed her clothes. Putting on a soft flowy skirt and peasant shirt that bared her cleavage a little, she felt beautiful. She placed her mother's exquisite glass bead rose earrings in her lobes.

The tart smelled divine and she was barefoot and ready to cook when he arrived.

Standing in the doorway with a bottle of wine in each hand and a bouquet of sunflowers tucked under one arm, with a loaf of bread tucked under the other, Christine laughed before taking the wine from him to let him present her sweetly with the rest.

Red was for before the meal and visiting, while the white would go perfectly with their fish dinner. The bread he brought was dipped in fresh olive oil mixed with garlic and puddles of balsamic. He opened the bottle of red and poured some into two wine glasses. He held one out to her.

"Saluti to new friends and beautiful beginnings."

They clinked glasses and he had a seat at the table in the middle of her kitchen.

"Tell me about you, Cristina. What is your story?"

Christine told him about how a dream had enticed her to be there, how she had lost a friend that spurred her into studying and becoming a doctor. How she had lost her mom. Her new work opportunity back home. That her plane ticket was days away.

His face fell at the news of her leaving; she knew she had totally killed the mood.

He had only just gotten her attention even though he had been watching her since she first arrived, her great big hat shielding her face as if the sun would burn her skin off if it was exposed. This woman moved around the kitchen so skillfully with purpose. Heavenly smells overtook his senses, making him salivate.

He had been imagining a nice candlelit dinner with her, sitting together and sharing some wine. He wasn't interested in a tryst; he wanted something more.

As they spoke, sometimes the words would get mixed up and they would laugh but it wasn't awkward. The lulls in the conversation were few and far between. She asked about his fish business and he told her that he had been at sea for many years. No children, no wife. No woman could stand a man who smelled like fish every day, he said with a laugh.

Christine hadn't smelled fish when he entered; he must have found a strong soap. He smelled of a man and that was all. They finished the bottle of red with bread, and were completely relaxed when he opened the white wine. She served the fish and pasta, sprinkling some fresh zest from the famous Amalfi lemon she bought over the whole plate. They devoured the feast.

Gratified, they looked at each other. The day had turned to night and candles lit up the room. He moved to the couch, and she sat next to him. Close. He put his arm around her and found that she fit nicely into his shoulder. She snuggled in.

"Did you like the wine? It is from my brother's winery in Amalfi. He followed the other one of the family businesses. My father was a fisherman and my mother came from a winemaking family. We get together every Sunday, I would love to have you come for dinner and meet the family sometime."

"My brother owns a winery, too, how funny. But I'm leaving on Sunday morning," she said. "That would have been wonderful."

"Must you go?" he whispered, not daring to look into her eyes and let her see the disappointment he felt. The question hung in the air.

Christine sat, her head full of confusing thoughts. She closed her eyes and settled back into him. They could have this moment.

She had made a commitment. All her education had led her to the new job. Back home, she finally had a plan. She was going to be a grown up now. Pay taxes, pay Social Security and live a regular life. Be an orthodox person who goes to their job every day and waits for old age to really do what they want to do.

The other side of her said, "Look at this potential adventure! Look where you are, who you are with and imagine the possibilities of being here and living in this extraordinary moment! Why be typical, and sit in an office grading papers when you can have an adventure in one of the most beautiful places on the planet? Are you crazy!?"

Muddled in her thoughts she snuggled a little closer. This man, unknown to her this very morning, had somehow become someone she really wanted to get to know.

Davide and Christine sat for hours talking. When the light of dawn started to seep into the windows again, he hugged her, kissed her on both cheeks and left her breathless for the day.

"If you must go, please know that I loved my time with you. If you stay, I'd love to see you again," he said. She hadn't slept and he hadn't slept but it didn't matter. They had spent a wonderful night together, two souls searching for something else and finding each other instead.

In a sleepy daydream as she looked out her window, she heard her mother's voice in the rush of the coastal wind.

"Fall into the unknown, my love, and see what lies ahead for you."

~

Adrift Again, But Not of My Own Accord, Me 2012

The company I was working for is folding. Investors have said "enough is enough". Our boss is having health problems and he removed himself for a time and I was put in the management position. That lasted about a week before the boss got bent out of shape and came barreling back. There was no saving this company the way it was, there was too much upkeep and not enough sales.

A few of us decided that we wanted to start our own company doing a similar thing. The shop guys have looked at a space and I will be in sales. It will be uphill as our products are expensive and the contracts that come take eons to get paid for.

After approximately three weeks I have cut myself from the group; there are too many mouths to feed and not enough business. My husband is not one who has the tolerance for entrepreneurship. I am looking for work again. Again, again.

The time off is giving me moments to think, dream, wish.

If only I could be a writer —live this purpose that seems to have a grip on me. If the passion was placed in my heart, why oh why is it something that feels unreachable?

~

~3~

Christine Cate missed her plane. After having rescheduled her trip back to Wyoming three times, she tossed her final plane ticket into the Tyrrhenian Sea. She couldn't go home. She'd found the place where her soul felt tranquil. She *was* home.

She sent her resignation for a position that she never held from the internet café in town. A simple word in the subject line of a reply was all that she received: "Affirmative."

Now to tell her father and her brother.

"Dad, I've met someone. I'm going to stay here for a while." she said, expecting a fight.

"Honey, I've met someone, too. I could never replace your mother, but Pearl is very nice. We met at bingo and she has been coming over and having dinner a bit lately. We have a nice time together. It's okay. Live your life, Crissy, follow your heart. I will be okay."

Could it be this easy? Tears fell from her eyes. She was happy where she was and happy for her dad, too. How was everything so great? She'd had such a different plan for everything. And then she changed gears, and it was still okay. Better than okay. Really, really, great!

Davide met her at the door with a glass of wine and a hug. He was staying more and more at her place although his place was bigger and more homey.

"How did your dad take the news?" he asked.

"Dad was great. He's met someone, too. He told me to live my life, and that he is just fine."

"Let's get you packed up. I want you to stay with me. Let's see where this all goes."

With that, Christine could breathe. She no longer had to worry about other people's expectations of her. Everyone around her would adapt as she had to the situation. It wasn't their life to live anyway, just as she couldn't live theirs for them. Why did she think they had such strong opinions about it?

Yes, she would need more schooling to be seen as a doctor over here, maybe. She hadn't even looked at that yet. Right now she would be content working at a flower shop or even cleaning fish to fully pursue the possibility of this life with Davide.

In one of the most beautiful, welcoming places she had ever been to, Atrani had opened its arms to her. From behind her dark glasses, from underneath her large sun hat, she had seen the light. At last.

Christine walked into her love's family home on the hill to meet them the following week. She was met with smiles, hugs and kisses on both cheeks. She was overwhelmed by their warm welcome. Davide hadn't brought a woman to dinner in a long time. She must be someone special. They drank wine, laughed and at the end of the night, she and he left for his small casita, and falling asleep in each other's arms.

After a session of very passionate lovemaking, of course.

~

Another Job Interview, Me, 2012

I heard about a position selling home materials in a showroom. It was about a forty-five minute drive from my house on one of my least favorite freeways. I guess I have opinions about that sort of thing. It wasn't something I was particularly excited about but it was a job, and I needed a new one. I needed a chance, or something to help me build up my confidence in the world again, so this might have been it.

I arrived on time and was given a tour, introduced to the other people who worked there and shown the warehouse and where I would be sitting if I was hired. Then I was taken into the manager's office for the typical grilling: What have you done? Who are you? What can you do? How much do you think you are worth? Etcetera, and so on.

I handed him my resume as I always print out a copy and bring it with me. Someone told me to do that and I will never forget it. As I sat still looking around the office, he glanced at it and said he was impressed. I had a lot of experience. I had managed to really get around in the industry which I suppose to him wasn't a terrible thing, but to some others it had meant I was a job hopper. A definite bad thing.

Yes, I could do the job. I was comfortable working with all types of people. He made a point to let me know that the preponderance of their clientele were of Asian persuasion with some East Indian customers making up about a quarter on top of that. All fine and dandy, I tried to convey. I was a good listener and would key in on anything that any customer said was important to them.

"Good." he said before going into more of the responsibilities of the day.

"We have a staff meeting at seven thirty each morning even though the job says it starts at eight. I expect you to be here at least fifteen minutes before that."

Okay, I think in my head, there goes seeing my kids before they leave for school. Awesome.

"We will expect you to work one or more days during the weekend and the hours are long since our clients need to come in after their own work day."

Okay, longer than a typical workday. Ten hours at least, and that is before the commute in which I expect shit traffic every single day. Not to mention the miles on my leased car. Love it.

"And we pay commission only, but you will be given 'an advance' each month which will be in the amount you choose. If you do not make sales up to your advance, you will need to pay that money back. You have three months to get there, or we will have to lower your monthly allotment."

Okay, so if you have no customers coming in here, I can expect to spend the majority of my life here for no pay, and then get dinged if I don't pick the magic number I might sell to. Got it.

I knew from my previous business that forecasting was not my thing. It's like guessing with no evidence whatsoever, or maybe it is just hoping for the best. It was always so interesting that people could say, "We forecast making 100K in profits this year."

How? Are you fortune tellers?

Then came the question that I either misinterpreted or didn't handle in the best way.

"How do you handle stress?"

I thought for maybe a second about all of the things that this job was going to be: the dashing in at the crack of dawn for a daily boring meeting to talk about boring stuff, with terrible hours, a rough commute and movable or non-existent pay. And even after all that, he was going to stress me out and expect me to handle it?

"Well, in the last two years I have lost my company and my house and had to sell most of my belongings. I declared bankruptcy and moved to another state. Since I am here and still up walking around, I guess I handle stress pretty well."

His eyes grew wide.

"Um, sorry, I meant do you run or do yoga or something like that?"

Those answers had never occurred to me. My answer was my answer. I was surviving. As best I could. Bragging about yourself in a job interview when your view of yourself is in the toilet is hard. But I guess I was able to do that too—enough that he offered me the job.

I didn't end up taking it. For my husband it was about the mileage that I would have to put on the leased car, and we didn't want to get fined at the end of the contract. Mr. In-Between had signed on with me as my credit rating was garbage and I had nothing to drive after selling my car to pay off the loan prior to the bankruptcy.

Life was shit, but I was still moving forward. Getting out of bed and trying to find my way with the scraps of self I had left.

Lord knows I didn't need that boss stressing me out, more, on top of it all.

~

K.K.

We met at an interior design class in our rural small town. We were both young moms and trying to figure out a way to be creative and make extra cash while still being there full time for our kids.

At our first class we immediately bonded, both taking in all of the information that was given by the teacher- a seemingly well established designer in her sixties. She had a certain flair that felt a bit outdated, but we were there to be sponges.

Outside of class we would gab on the phone and eventually we invited each other over to our respective houses. Yours had a more homey farm-style look while mine was oddly eclectic, filled with funky antiques that activated my imagination.

For several classes, we took field trips to each of our classmates' homes to see what types of style we had. When it was my turn, the teacher seemed a little awe struck. In her effort to get more on top of the reactions I was getting from my fellow students, she asked me, " If your house was engulfed in flames, what in this room would you grab first?"

It was a question no one else had been asked. In my youthful view I picked up a little metal gnome bank that my mother had purchased for me in England on a recent trip.

I would soon be admonished in front of all. "I think it would be best to prioritize your family photos instead of any little knick-knack."

I had been spanked by her verbally. Put in my place. I felt set up. Of course I would be saving those things first, I told myself. She took me as a vapid, materialistic kid who didn't understand what really counted.

You, K.K., were understanding of my embarrassment. We laughed it off, and eventually schemed of going into business together helping others make their homes more beautiful. *Giving that hoity-toity designer a run for her money in our small town.*

We planned our business launch date and came up with a name that incorporated both of our names into a cool logo.

Something happened so it wouldn't be so. Maybe you told your husband of our intent, or mentioned it in your circles, because pretty soon after, you said that you couldn't be my business partner because I didn't belong to your church.

"Have you even given your life over to Jesus?" you asked incredulously.

I told you about my moment at sleep-away camp and about the conversation I had with my camp counselor, Taz, when I took Jesus into my heart and you seemed appeased. In your next breath, you spoke as coldly as words could ever be—*that if I didn't join your church, we couldn't be friends anymore.*

After some thought and soul searching, I wasn't willing to change my entire worldview to go into business with someone who was so set in their own way of seeing the world that they had no room for any other thoughts.

And we went our separate ways. It was kind of a shame because I think we might have worked well together.

~

*G*od has been teasing me for a while. What exactly is He trying to tell me?

Having different experiences within the walls of a church was not out of the ordinary to me, as I had a few much earlier in my life while going to a new church with my mother. One story is as follows.

I went to church with my mom after a full year of her bugging me to go. She said she had found this great, new, non-denominational church with leaders she just loved. She was absolutely sure I would love it, too.

So after months and months of her badgering me, I finally said, "Okay, but if I choose not to go back, you can't bug me about it, and I DO NOT want to touch anybody." I knew my mom would 100 percent be interested in a touchy-feely church, and I braced myself for the experience.

We arrived and walked in together, finding a place to sit in the middle so I had a good view of the stage, and many of the other people as well.

The music started. Boisterous, happy, energetic.

The pastoral pair, a husband and wife team, started down the aisle to raucous applause and cheers from the audience. People on the inside edges of the pews stood lifting their arms into the aisle as if to build an arch for them to pass under. It was as much of a Jimmy and Tammy Faye Bakker moment if I ever saw one.

Okay. I sat and waited for what would come next.

The husband sat in a chair off to the side of the stage and the woman took to the podium.

"Hello, everyone! Welcome!"

Cheers erupted from the crowd.

"We are going to do a little something different today, I want you to reach around you and shake hands with the other people."

I do a death stare at my mom before behaving myself and shaking hands with the people around me, all the while smiling and nodding like a good girl. Touching already. Ugh.

"You know, I think we can do a little bit better than that. Give those people

around you a hug." bellowed the pastor to all of us.

Wow. I thought. What a day to pick to come here.

And I hugged the people around me.

She spoke up again. "I think we can do an even better job at relating to each other this morning. I want you to reach in front of you in the pews, and give that person a little shoulder rub."

I looked in front of myself and was shocked to find myself sitting directly behind a man with a hunchback deformity. I didn't even know people had that condition anymore.

Well, what could I do? I reached in front of me and gave that man a nice shoulder rub before looking up to the ceiling and saying in my head to the Guy upstairs, "Very funny, God. You got me– hardee har."

From then on, I kind of expected God to play little tricks on me, or maybe he was just proving to me that I didn't belong in any of those buildings.

Another church visit, another experience. It was Easter time, and my good friend M.K. is religious. Another friend and I had flown in for M.K.'s birthday as a surprise and we agreed to go to Easter Sunday service with her family.

I felt a little out of my element because I hadn't had very many experiences in houses of the Lord throughout my adult years. It was a newly remodeled church, and M.K. was so excited to show it to us. Everyone was nice and there was a good message, typical of what I imagined for the occasion.

While I sat listening, I got a whiff of something, and looked around to see if anyone else was smelling it, too. Oddly everyone was fully in tune with the pastor and no one seemed preoccupied with anything else at all.

But I was totally distracted. Why was I smelling farm animals? So strong it was like I was sitting on a bail of hay in a well used barn.

After the sermon, we moved out of the lobby, and we started to walk back to the car.

Her husband and kids were up ahead, as I asked her as quietly as I could. "Hey, I smelled something weird back there; did you smell it, too?"

"Hmm, no, I didn't smell anything. What did you smell?"

"Not sure why, but it smelled like farm animals." I said hoping I wasn't being obnoxious.

She looked at me with a strange face, "That's so weird, because the building used to be a barn, but not a lot of people know that. I've never smelled anything like that in there."

I took that moment to refresh over the other two experiences I had had in churches as an adult. The time with my mother had activated my sense of touch- this time, my sense of smell was affected.

Another time with M.K., before she moved across the country, I had gone to her previous church, too. As we sat, the Pastor asked for God to enter the building. People had their hands raised in invitation and their eyes closed. As a watcher of people, I kept mine open. As the choir sang, a beam of sunlight shot in through the back windows. It had been pouring rain outside only moments before. So that time was a sense of sight.

I'm still waiting for my sense of taste and hearing to be triggered in some way, in some church. You just never know, so I guess I will try and enter the buildings that house the beliefs when I am invited. Maybe I am supposed to experience all of the senses, or maybe God is just playing with me— for a jolly good laugh.

~

~3~

Jeremy made the trip somewhat reluctantly, as he was working on his first batch of a new wine. The vintner he hired assured him that everything was to plan and he would let him know when the harvest was complete and the pressing had begun. Everything was well in hand.

"It isn't often that your professionally-single sister gets married. I had to be here. I needed the evidence. Plus it doesn't hurt to drink some great wines."

Even though they were adults, Jeremy knew how to get a rise out of his little sister. But this hardly felt like the time. Even though they had different mothers, he had grown to love his father's new wife Aiyanna who raised him after his mother died early in his toddlerhood. Christine would always be his little sister. He was so happy for her he could burst.

This trip would be memorable in more ways than one. Getting to see his sister walk down the aisle and meeting the new part of the family, with roots in the Amalfi coast wine families. Jeremy was in pure heaven. He had already strolled through their vineyards a few times, and was promised some cuttings to take back home with him. Another grape variety to play with to either add to his already planned wine or to make into a new blend.

Christine, Jeremy and their father looked out over the back deck of the big main house, facing the ocean. In the distance she pointed out her soon-to-be husband's boat and the beach where they had met.

It had been months since Davide had presented her with the fish and she had been writing a self-help book for others struggling for purpose and adventure at the same time. Living responsibly while being a free spirit. Chapters about how to see your faults and how to forgive yourself. How to be your own best friend.

Right now though, she was drinking in all that was in store for her. The joy she felt in her heart and the smiles of her family filled her with a contentment she had never felt before, but had craved so desperately.

Jeremy asked to be excused. All this love stuff was compounding in his head how alone he felt without Natalia. Lonely inside, he was happy to have the draw of the production facilities to hone in on.

He *was* fascinated, as well as overwhelmed, walking through the old stone buildings with their hand-chiseled cellars holding the old wine production mechanics as well as the newer halls with the state-of-the-art technology.

Davide's brother Mattia met him as he walked. Mattia wished to practice his English. His soon-to-be new brother-in-law spliced off tendrils as they walked the vineyards, handing them to Jeremy to put into small pots to start new plants back home. They continued to walk the grounds.

Jeremy liked that they still used the old equipment for their special *Old World Reds*. Using the old practices of stomping and screening and the giant oak barrels gave him a feeling of peace and belonging. Mattia left him to attend to one of his helpers.

Almost four years ago Jeremy had left his position as a professor at that small community college when that strange book changed his course. Who knew such a small item would launch him into pursuing the dream he and his beloved wife Natalia had shared.

Maybe the little blue book affected his sister as well, reaching for what could possibly be.

Now, as he stood in front of these ages-old casks of systematically fermented juices just waiting for their time to shine, he confirmed to himself that he was on the right path.

Over the peaceful hum of the machines, he heard the passionate inflections of a conversation in Italian approaching. He couldn't let on how impressed he was so he averted his eyes as they walked passed.

The fact that he had been accepted as family from the moment his sister decided to marry Davide made him feel comfortable and welcome. With his father and Pearl planning on marrying on Davide's boat on this trip as well, everyone was happy.

He had only produced enough wine to give out for Christmas presents in his first year of actual production. Now that he had a few years under him and his vines— he would work towards managed growth. The timing of this trip was perfect, to learn and to dream a bit more.

His vineyards were about to go to sleep. Most of the wineries around him were shutting down when he left and since his outfit was still so small, he could take off. He had asked his new hire Paul to stay in his house and look after his dog while tucking in the vines for the winter. Paul heartily agreed to be in charge. Paul loved plants more than he did people so Jeremy didn't worry at all about the leaf babies he had left in his care.

Jeremy imagined his vines starting to show their bright orange and red colors before the leaves fell. He had decided to extend his stay in Italy through the winter and, given that this part of Italy and Oregon State shared the same seasons, he could be learning while everything was sleeping back home.

Jeremy concentrated on learning their processes and inked out on paper how he would scale and improve things back home. Over dinner one night the idea came up that the Italian part of the family could offer exclusive U.S. distribution to Jeremy's winery as an additional source of income for both of them.

Tastings of *their* wine could happen at his tasting room and bottles and cases could be sold from there. His cut of the profits would allow him to buy better equipment. *They* would benefit from a larger audience and new excited customers. He was honored to be included with some of the big players in the world of wine.

His sister passed by his bedroom door, "Hey, I think you should take this back with you when you go. Pretty sure the author lives in the states, and with the language barrier, it might not go as far here." Christine handed her brother the traveling book. "Maybe put it back where it was; at least there, it was getting some action."

Jeremy hugged his sister tighter than either of them expected. So many things were lining up perfectly for all of them. So many wonderful things to look forward to. So much to tell Paul back home, so much to set up and so much to put into place.

It had all started with that strange little book and an *Escape*.

~

~3~

The sun rose that day with promise. It was Christine and Davide's big day. Two families from different continents would merge to celebrate the fated couple.

Christine Cate wrapped a white silk robe around herself and walked out onto a private terrazza on the back side of a stone and stucco house built hundreds of years before. She sipped a strong espresso from a hundred year-old cup that had kissed the lips of hundreds, maybe thousands of persone. Looking out over the beautiful Amalfi coastline, everything here had history. Hand-carved stone terraces planted with ancient grape vines were showy in their reds and golds of the season.

She couldn't wait to get into her dress. She looked back smiling over her shoulder at it, as it hung there waiting for her. Its sheer creamy undersheath covered with a full length handmade overlay was woven in the different designs of Italian bobbin lace techniques. With its deep V-neckline and sheer bishop sleeves, the dress was sexy but classically elegant.

She'd felt so lucky to have found it in an old vintage shop while in Milan with Davide a few months before. As he wandered off to look at the old fishing rods strewn about, she had gently pulled the dress from the rack and handed it to the salesperson behind the counter. At the time, she prayed it would fit.

Paying for it quietly, she smuggled it out of the store with little notice to him, other than she was carrying a bag when she wasn't before.

Once home she had gone straight into the bedroom and locked the door, which he found odd at the time, but he did not press. She pulled the antique dress on, gently over her figure, pairing it with some satin kitten heels she had purchased at the open market for a party the week before. The dress fit dreamily, to her relief and glee, and she teared up at the thought of wearing it to marry her love someday. He hadn't even asked her yet, but she knew he would.

That day was here. She slipped on the gown right before her father knocked on the door.

"Can I come in, Chrissy?"

"Yep," she called out, not taking her eyes off the reflection in the mirror.

Rutger Cate, all gussied up in a suit and tie, walked in and his eyes welled with tears. His daughter was a radiant beauty. She looked *so* happy too.

"Aw, Dad." Christine reached for her father and hugged him as she started to tear up as well. In the hug, her hands brushed a package which he held behind his back. As they parted, he placed the parcel in her waiting hands.

"Something from your mother. How she wished she would have been able to see you on your wedding day." The present was light, and billowy and wrapped in a pastel salmon-colored tissue paper.

Christine unfolded the paper and lifted free a gossamer, ivory-tinted veil.

"It was your mother's. She wore it for our wedding after adding her special touch to it. The original veil was a gift from my mother to her— her *"something new."* Well, your mother took that once simple design and added her own flair with her incredible, traditional beading. Glass beads with freshwater pearls and white dentalium shells which held significant meaning in her heritage. Looks to have aged to the perfect ivory to match your gown, meant to be."

Christine felt a rush of wind from the window and her mother's presence swirled as her father placed the veil on her head.

"It's perfect. You are beautiful, just like her. Your mother was such a loving, kind, amazing woman. When she came into my and Jeremy's lives after his mother passed suddenly, I never thought I could love anyone again. Her spirit and air showed me that life was still full of possibilities, one only had to look into the sky and ask. She is with us today, *I know*."

Christine and her father dabbed their tears again as he stuffed at least a dozen tissues into his coat pocket for the day.

Jeremy knocked on the door and entered. Seeing his sister through new eyes, they glistened. She deserved all the good and wonderment that she exuded. His powerful and once wandering sister had lived her life as she wished, never caving to what others thought she should do; her decision to stay here now was no different.

Christine linked an arm in each of theirs as she held a single white rose. They floated down the stairs into her future.

The older generation guests scurried into the small runabout trucks from the winery with the bride, while the younger guests and the groom hopped on Vespas decorated with white ribbons and flowers to get down to the town hall for the ceremony.

Christine was led through the back door at the local registry office, and when she walked into the main hall, Davide stood captivated and in tears at the sight of his bride. The ceremony was short but meaningful. It was wordy with big gaps with one person speaking part of the program and an interpreter speaking what was said right after in English. For the English parts, the interpreter spoke in Italian to the relief and joy of Davide's family. Both families were appreciative of the translators.

Christine's father read a Shoshone love poem aloud before the couple was pronounced husband and wife. Some of its touching intent was jarred with the interpretation but Christine and Davide focused on the meaning.

"Fair is the white star of twilight, and the sky clearer at the day's end;
But she is fairer, and she is dearer, She, my heart's friend.
Fair is the white star of twilight, and the moon roving to the sky's end;
But she is fairer, better worth loving, She, my heart's friend."

There was not a dry eye in the room. As the couple kissed, great cheers and whoops came from both sides of the family. All the way back to the villa they received honks and well-wishes from strangers on the street. Christine happily hung on to her husband, riding side saddle on the Vespa all the way back to their reception.

Friends of the family had been busy while they were away. As they all rounded the corner together, Christine could see the garlands of Italian Cypress and a garden with Star of Bethlehem flowers tied with flowing ivory ribbon swagged across a rustic wood tunnel pergola, showcasing the most beautiful view.

Crisp white tablecloths sat underneath gold chargers and clean white plates had a single grape twig with dried grapes and a bevy of Star of Bethlehem flowers were placed in its center. Silverware, unmatched as if it had been borrowed from friends and family from miles around sat alongside each plate ready to help with the enjoyment of each morsel. Two wine glasses were placed at the corners.

Food made with love waited in hand painted tureens across countless tables waiting for guests to enjoy family style. The feast of rabbit stew had been cooking for hours already, started by Davide's mother and his sisters in the old earthen kitchen outside. Together the day before, all the women, Christine and her father's new love, Pearl, had prepared Ndunderi di Minori for the day: cheesy little pasta pillows made with ricotta and farro flour to be doused in a rich traditional meat ragu.

There would be a toast to the bride and groom with bottles and bottles of Franciacorta smuggled back from that same trip to Milan while passing through Sarnico on Lake Iseo. Christine hadn't thought a thing about

Davide stopping by a fellow winery to pick up some "supplies." They knew how to surprise each other.

Instead of a wedding cake, the guests were treated to their own personal-sized lemon delight cakes from the *Pasticceria Sal De Riso* with a side of limoncello poured tall in cordial glasses for dessert.

Their wedding day could not have been more romantic.

Christine Cate, now Christine Sacajawea Accardi, sat at a large table on the veranda of the familial house with her now husband Davide.

As her father sat to the right of her with his new love Pearl, and her brother to the left visiting with his in-laws, she felt forever home.

~

K.B.

Another loving mother figure. You were my first serious boyfriend's mom. I sure lucked out when it came to you. Always nice, welcoming and very loving towards me and your other son's girlfriend. You had had a hard road in your relationship with your husband, my boyfriend's father.

I remember having a conversation with you after we had been in each other's lives for a few years. I said how I couldn't understand how you would have been with someone like that. The idea of a strong and together woman falling prey to a man so heinous. You shared one of his sick moments, so twisted I dare not share here and give someone ideas. My heart ached for what you had been through, and would forever for how you escaped him.

Strength and character have nothing to do with finding oneself a victim. You were one of two extremely vibrant women I knew that had succumbed to an abusive partner. Thankfully you both escaped.

I remember how you would cook for us and sit with us. We had dinner as a family most nights I was there. You even let me stay over with your son once we were committed to each other and you knew we were sexually active anyway. I think you liked the company.

There were a few times you actually crawled in bed with the two of us, me on one side of your son, you on the other and honestly it wasn't as weird as it sounds. You were crazy for your boys, and your sons liked these girls and so you loved us like we were your extra kids.

I remember your crack-like cornflake cookies, and how you always nailed our Christmas gifts. Traveling with you to New York and to your family's generational home in Connecticut was amazing.

I remember when we told you that we were engaged and you burst into tears. It wasn't that tearful happiness type of crying, it was something much different. Like an "Oh no!"

I felt so hurt. What had felt like an acceptance of all of our years together suddenly felt yanked away. Like I wasn't good enough for your son.

As an adult I think it was just that we were still so young. You didn't want us to possibly make a mistake or make such a big decision at our ages.

I willed to myself that it wasn't because of me that you broke down like that. Maybe that moment was in the back of my head when I decided to end it.

I will always have a daughterly love for you, even though it's been years since we've spoken. As a bonus mom placed in my life, you were a great role model for me to aspire to, in your strength, in your love of your children and your survivor attitude.

~

Letting Go of Another Part of Myself, Me, 2013

There were many ways I twisted myself to fit in for the ease and the peace of the household. The pretzeling was entirely unintentional on my part, and I am sure his part as well. When I first came to the house, I was a novelty for the kids. I was funny and playful and I felt I had something to offer this family. I had a hope of making a difference.

I had done some stand-up comedy and people often told me I was funny. Mr. In Between was heavily invested in being the funny one, so I got quiet and became the straight man to his funny self.

I found myself encouraging him or letting him take the lead when it came to any conversation in a group or at a party or such. I hid in the background and even listened to his favorite kind of music while we were in the car- to his old style rock and roll instead of my preferred contemporary and hip choices.

My artwork was too boisterous with its sweeps of red that to me spoke of passion but to him spoke of the blood he had been exposed to in the wars back home. I didn't fight to have it displayed anymore once he told me that, as I didn't want my art to be painful to anyone.

We watched TV shows he enjoyed and watched an obnoxious amount of action movies during our time together when the kids were away. Talk about blood. Anyway—

Long gone were my documentaries and foreign films with subtitles and even my earth-friendly living habits. When I got here, I was just grateful for anything. Anything was better than the nothing left for me. Over time, I grew to miss all of those creative outlets I used to pursue.

The time I had to write. Sitting and talking with my mom and my daughters. Making art. Walking to work because I lived so close. Participating in the social events in my old city. Seeing my friends- that new group of people I had found while in my greatest growth period of my life. All of it was missing now, and as much as I would try to pull some of that into my current life, it was just too hard and too far away for me to keep it.

Setting aside my writing. It was also a "frivolous" way to spend my time when there was actual work to do, or chores to catch up on. I made it my purpose to be someone who was useful, helpful, and in service to others.

I let his dreams become my dreams: A cabin on a lake, owning an airplane, continuing to live in this quiet suburban neighborhood. Settling in again after loving and thriving in my up-and-coming funky urban neighborhood when I was single.

I went along with everything, and rarely thought back to anything that I loved, longed for or wished for myself. I was tired when I got there, a beaten pulp of a human being, punched down by life itself. Was it any wonder I didn't have the ability to fight for what was best for me, if I didn't truly know what that was?

In my head, if everything I did and knew was wrong, it made sense to let someone else run my life for a while. So that is exactly what happened. I didn't consciously mean to have things go that way; they just did because I wasn't aware or strong enough to challenge it.

The differences between us stacked up, one on top of the next. I was being buried in a berm of invisibility in my life, with no shovel or even a spoon to dig my way out.

It was for the good of the family. The best for everyone else.

Or so I thought.

~

~3~

Finally back home in Dundee, Oregon, Jeremy dropped his suitcases and walked into the old barn that was shaping up to be the new showpiece of his winery. One of his beautiful photos of the Amalfi coast would be blown up and centered over the tasting bar. The used casks from Italy would be delivered in about two weeks. The burgundy countertop made from recycled paper he had commissioned for the bar and the reclaimed wood for the fronts had been made in his absence and he was starting to see the whole thing come together. His own wine wouldn't be ready until next year but he could start the frenzy for the Accardi wines now.

Natalia would have loved this. Seeing the pieces blend like the notes played by an orchestra for a perfect symphony.

So much had happened since losing her. The long lonely days after she had died. Wasting away at the college waiting to be with his Natalia. And then, the book that changed everything. Not just for him but for his sister, too, moving them both out of their comfort zones.

A belief that there was more. That life continues and it is up to the person to seek out what comes next. His short fling with the real estate agent when he arrived here didn't last since she headed back to Arizona in the off season then decided to move there permanently.

The travel and the working on the wine formulas and growing a business had kept his mind busy for a while now. The lack of female companionship was okay. He had been alone for years.

Maybe it was time to hire someone to help with the business and marketing side. Maybe he'd take on a business partner? If he could find someone who knew how to entertain and run big functions, that would be the most help. He knew how to *attend* a party, but not really how to *throw* one. He could even rent out the whole campus if he needed to for larger functions.

Jeremy placed an ad on Craigslist > Portland.

Wanted:
Someone who knows how to run events, from weddings to corporate parties to smaller get-togethers. Sales and marketing to help build the business.
Very important: Love and understanding of wine.
Escape Winery - Jeremy 555-2589

Jeremy received seventeen phone calls by evening. He was totally overwhelmed. He had no idea there would be such a response. He called back and asked everyone to email him a resume to look over.

Ten actually did. One gentleman with zero experience seemed to have pulled random facts about wine from the internet. Two others were underage and wouldn't be able to legally pour wine for any event, so they were out, too. A few were marginal but nothing to get excited over.

A woman named Sky, looked fantastic on paper, pulled to the front of the line. She had started as a line cook in a small café, then had purchased the café five years later. After selling that business, she started a small catering business in the Portland Metro area for ten years specializing in corporate events. There was a two-year gap in her employment that made him wonder, and would ask her about when they met, and then a job as a sales rep for a local wine operation that recently went under.

A traveling wine woman with experience in events, corporate parties, cooking and wine. Too good to be true. Jeremy put a star on her resume and laid it on top of the others. Changing his voicemail to tell others to send their resume if they were interested, he placed his phone in the kitchen on silent and headed off to bed.

He'd look further tomorrow, but for now, he was tired. Too tired. Tired of thinking, tired of doing and completely done juggling it all alone. He showered, put on some pajama pants and slid into the nice clean sheets the housekeeper had put on his bed.

It was good to be home.

~

Letting Go of Myself Even More, Me, 2013

Writing. Maybe it was for the better; not writing meant there was no more evidence to go back and read. It was painful. In this house I let things happen around me and to me, my role is to support those around me. Giving everything of myself and having little left over was a pattern I just couldn't seem to kick.

This relationship has been pure drama from the start. Intense and hungry in the beginning, very typical of how I roll.

After a big fight, I had thrown my engagement ring on the ground and stormed off.

I wonder what would have happened if I hadn't picked it up again.

I believed I could live with our very different levels of religious beliefs, but the longer we were together, the more differences surfaced. Without my writing and being able to vent and let go, the thoughts swirled non-stop. A cyclone of unhappiness had me in its grip.

~

Stepparenting is Tough, Me 2013

I never wanted to be the bad guy. But I knew that sometimes kids need to have some parameters around them. Goals, something to work towards. I spent a lot of time watching and paying attention to what my stepkids liked so I could better relate to them. In the beginning, when I was just a girlfriend, I was the fun one.

Then I moved in and started playing my normal motherly role and I was no longer fun. I didn't mean to become un-fun. I don't quite know how it happened. Pre-me, his time with his kids was a lot less. He had them every day after school, but then they would go back to their mother after dinner and they spent every weeknight over with her. He had them every other weekend; that was the only time he had them for overnights.

Getting kids off to school wasn't possible with him working the early shift. Because I was there, his kid's visitation schedule could finally change. We made it so that we had his kids when I had my kids so we would have ample alone time together. Things went along nicely for a while, and I thought it was okay, that we'd found this new way together.

I hoped that our kids would just blend together, become chummy and care about each other. His children were still small when I came on board but my daughters were older, pretty much set in who they were. And as much as they were nice to the little kids, they didn't actively go out of their way to become brothers and sisters together.

I must say here that I am so appreciative of my daughters and the lengths to which they supported me in this relationship. They believed it was what I wanted and indeed it was for a long time. They sacrificed and made pretty serious adjustments to be there for their old mom and I will forever be grateful.

I wish they would have shared their concerns earlier on, but as children, I think they didn't really feel like they had a voice, or, as I hoped, that they were just living their own lives and not worrying so much about mine.

Things were messy. When we all moved in together it was an opportunity for me to have my dog back with me, my best buddy, C. My ex-husband had taken him after my house went away. I was happy to have him around but the other people in the house were annoyed that his nails were long and clicked on the downstairs laminate floors. He was old and his breath smelled and I didn't have a lot of money to get him fixed up.

At one point, my stepdaughter said she wished he would just die. Definitely the dramatic child in the house, she ended up writing me an apology for her outburst and all was forgiven, but I knew C did not have as many fans in this house as he could have. He was an old dog, and he snored and slobbered, all of which was completely adorable to me, but he was not the type of dog this new family of mine really liked.

I tried to bring different points of view into the house. With me, we would carve pumpkins, get our hands all gooey in the guts and eat the seeds after we cooked them. Halloween costumes were elevated. One year, my stepson hadn't wanted to dress up, then suddenly he changed his mind and wanted to go to a Halloween party he had been invited to. Quickly, I grabbed a bunch of bubble wrap and wrapped it around him and he went as a "bubble boy." All the kids at the party were popping him all night long.

I brought vegetables into the house, expecting them to at least try some new ones. They had never had 'salad' for dinner. I tried but it didn't last long. As a bunch they were all pretty set in their food ways.

Every attempt I made to add something new to their lives, their diet, a change in their rooms was met with a negative reaction at first. "No way." "We don't want to."

My kids were just way easier at this point. I literally had to give them a look and they stopped doing what I did not want them to do and straightened up their behavior, whatever it was. His kids were not wired that way.

I wanted my extra kids to feel loved, cared for, and that I was on their team. This commitment was more than I had with Mr. Fun's kids. With that break, I cut off seeing them for my own protection, to remain away from Mr. Fun, although I kept up with them on social media, and cared about them and they knew it. I have wished them happy birthdays for years and often think of them.

For these extra kids, I had vowed to be around. Even when it was hard. Even though their mom lived less than a mile away. I wasn't trying to be their mother, I only wanted to mother them when they were under my care.

We had all promised to co-parent these kids and make sure they felt loved, supported and were given every chance to live the biggest life they could. Or maybe it was just me who was pushing for that?

If they were living here in America, I wanted them to know how to protect themselves out in the world, online, and to know what to look for and how to do stuff.

Sometimes I'd wonder if the grief or pushback I got from them was because their father was not all in with me when it came to our life together.

I hated when everyone else in both houses would run around like crazy trying to fix whatever issue his kids had found themselves in, instead of having them learn from their own mistakes. I wanted them to get that they were responsible to keep track of their own things. I had let my daughters learn that, and they usually took care of themselves in regards to remembering their schoolwork or responsibilities after that. I knew it would help them in the long run.

I felt like I was constantly shrugging my shoulders in this life. Trying really hard not to let things get to me. This was my life now, and these were my extra kids; it was time to make the best of things.

I grew to love them, each in their own way, and I hope that I made a difference in their lives. Maybe someday, if this doesn't last—they will know that I did my best.

~

~3~

Sky had been working a temporary position in a high school cafeteria. The kitchen had been a disaster in her view, so she stayed late, off the clock to clean. It was nice to be back in a commissary, even though she was mostly serving up processed and already prepared items.

"Just warming things up," she said to herself. She longed to start—*really* cooking again.

Entertaining. Sharing her love of all things food and maybe with a little wine.

Sky sold her restaurant *The Saucy Tango* and spent the proceeds taking care of Grannie G. who had fallen in her late-nineties and wasn't able to move around without help. Fortunately, her mind was sharp and she had no trouble communicating. The two of them were the only family each other had. Grannie G. had died peacefully in her sleep six months ago.

She felt as though she was starting all over again, but her time spent with her grandmother gave her peace. Sky had learned to cook from her, and how to host a party.

One party they had hosted was named after a foreign movie *Babette's Feast*, a story about a refugee French housekeeper who wins the lottery from her native country. She then uses the winnings to provide a once-in-a-lifetime feast for her newly-found family in her new country. The whole town is ripe with speculation as to *when* she will leave their little hamlet to become the rich aristocrat that her lottery winnings would now be able to provide. Sky remembered it as a rather lovely tale.

Picking up her voicemail with her secret code, Jeremy's voice came on loud and clear.

"Hi, Sky. My name is Jeremy Cate and I am the owner of Escape Winery. I am looking for someone who can run the tasting room while I am working other angles of the business and help out with parties and events. I would like to talk to you about your impressive qualifications. Please call me back. 555-2589. Thank you."

Sky was thrilled to get the call. It had been her last ditch effort for a regular job on Craigslist the night before that led her to send her resume. She had been tuckered out but told herself she would not go to sleep until she had sent at least five resumes out, no matter what they were for.

It wasn't a kitchen job, but might be really great. She was excited to return the call the next morning, on Saturday.

It was answered on the second ring.

"Hello, Escape Winery. Jeremy speaking."

"Hello, Mr. Cate. It's Sky Meadows, I'm responding to your message that you left me yesterday. I am very excited to hear about your winery and what a potential job would entail."

"Wonderful. So happy you called me back. When do you have some time to stop by and have a chat?"

Sky was wiggly with excitement and danced around her kitchen as she thought. She tried to hold herself together and to be professional.

"I have some time today, if that works for you. Where would I be going?"

It is in the hills of Dundee. I am still building up my vineyards and waiting for the grapes to be perfect for the first release. In the meantime I am acting as a distributor for my sister's husband's family winery out of Italy. We are trying to build their brand here in the States, and it will help me keep my enterprise going and build a nice reputation. Today would be great, if you can!"

Wow, Sky thought. This is the coolest job ever, and Jeremy sounded beyond nice. It could be an amazing opportunity. She wanted in. Perhaps the high school kitchen deep clean could be a parting gift?

Sky took the lead, "How about two o'clock? I could use a ride in the country. I'm excited to see what's happening out there."

"Two o'clock is perfect. I will text you the address. Is this a cell phone?"

"Yes, great! See you then."

Sky hung up. A text quickly buzzed on the screen with the address.

Sky twirled around the room, she had such a good feeling about this job. With tons of experience in wine, entertaining, running events, and sales of wine, she was a shoo-in.

She just had to convince him. She slipped out of her pajamas and into the shower. Her long red hair wetted under the showerhead and the water ran down her face. She positioned herself to take full advantage of the jets on the small of her back.

Lugging around the big pots at the school cafeteria this week had been taking a toll on her forty-eight-year-old body. She wasn't as young as she used to be. But hell, she was a lot better than she used to be in a lot of other respects. She shampooed her locks and turned her attention to shave her parts. Legs first, then pits.

She had let her womanly area go for a bit, as she didn't have anyone special in her life, so it remained natural. She stepped from the shower onto the mat and dried her body first, then her hair. She wrapped the towel around her hair and walked buck-naked across her bedroom floor to the closet. She needed to pick the perfect outfit. Something professional yet casual enough for a first meeting outside on a property.

The Pacific Northwest was pretty casual anyway and she didn't want him to think she was going to be high maintenance. In truth, she would probably do the job for free if not for those pesky rent payments and bills.

Grabbing a mid-length skirt and a button-up denim blouse, she placed them on the bed to see how they would look. She liked the bleached out denim shirt but not the skirt. Too fancy.

Instead she grabbed a pair of nice medium wash jeans and buttoned up the top, leaving the top two buttons undone. She added a leather belt she'd picked up at Goodwill, with a silver belt buckle placard with a big S insignia on it, no doubt for Superman, but she'd claimed it for herself—*Sky*.

Grannie G. had left her some Indian jewelry with turquoise and Red Jasper. That would go well with the outfit. A beautiful chunky bracelet and necklace.

Her hair was naturally curly and it had started to dry in wavy long curls that circled her face like a wreath. She had long ago made peace with her hair. Having once fought it, pulling it back so tightly it looked like her face was stretched, not anymore.

Working in kitchens, it needed to be up, but when she was home, she would let it fall free and loose. Today was no different. She grabbed a barrette in case it got too unruly on the drive. She dusted her cheeks with some bronzer to make it look like she had been outside lately. A quick flick of mascara and she was done.

Swiss cheese on toast, open-faced, with a thick slice of an heirloom tomato and salt and pepper was a perfect late breakfast. Allowing herself to recuperate from a long hard week at the cafeteria, she had zonked till ten and goofed off until twelve-thirty. She had to go. It was a good hour to get out there and she didn't want to be late. This was too big of an opportunity to mess up.

She poured some day-old coffee into a travel mug and started the engine of her Ford Escape. No, it had not escaped her attention that she drove a car with the same name as the winery. Maybe Jeremy would think it was a sign.

She certainly hoped so.

Maybe it was.

~

Maybe it was.

~

Isolation and Seeing It In Others, Me 2013

I *have felt alone where I am for a while. This place is familiar but is missing the soul energy that I felt in my last place. It's like I went back in time to the cul-de-sac years of my life, only I wasn't the young stay-at-home mom surrounded by others who were all in the same boat. This time was different. There wasn't any of the same camaraderie I felt back then.*

I remember when I moved to this place, technically in a different state but separated by a bridge and a max of eight miles or so from the majority of my friends. It certainly wasn't as far as it felt.

As we planned an engagement party to celebrate our impending union, I invited everyone I knew, wanting people to meet my soon-to-be husband. I was excited and wanted to share my happiness with them.

And people didn't come. It was either too far or the party didn't fit into their schedule or maybe it just wasn't something they could get behind, despite us being friends. Maybe they weren't my friends anymore and I had no idea.

The people who did come felt like the ones who lived on the outskirts of my life. The acquaintances who popped in and out and hadn't been the big movers and shakers of my life thus far. It was lovely to see them in a different way and I appreciated them making a trip over the bridge to come see us.

While it was lovely or as lovely as it could be, I wondered what I had done to repel the majority of the people in my life. Maybe I had become too much?

Too much drama, too much chaos, too little stability. Maybe my instability would rub off on them if they hung out with me—who even knows anymore. I felt the gap and stayed in my head about it, believing it must have been me.

Mr. In Between hadn't invited many people; it was more of an event for me to try to hold onto some semblance of my old life as I entered a new one. This move felt like my first divorce all over again. Starting over, trying to find my place in this new situation that already had all the pieces and parts set before I even got here.

What would I contribute? Could I make new friends? Would I find a new tribe? Would I ever come close to the community and involvement that I had and felt at my old place. Or was it all gone?

I dove into the church-things hoping to find new friends, but none of them took. I worked at the daycare on Sunday mornings watching the littles, the younger the better as I didn't have the church-speak to actually be a good steward of anyone's religious journey. In the baby room, I could just sit with them on the floor and play and I wasn't expected to download any of the biblical knowledge that needed to be taught.

My best new friend during this time was actually my husband's ex-wife.

For whatever reason, I had never been hung up on being jealous to the point of avoiding anyone's ex and with our common interest in my new step kids, it gave us enough to talk about which was nice. We have the same birth week and are similar in a lot of ways, so that made it easy to talk to her for the most part, even though we didn't always agree on the parenting "styles" that we each thought would be helpful for whatever challenge we were both dealing. She became a friend- someone who knew my husband and how he was and I would confide in her sometimes if things got bad.

Mostly I was alone. When my daughters were with their dad or I was in and out of employment, I spent an awful lot of time alone. When I did leave the house, I'd take walks alone for hours, playfully scrambling up and down dry riverbed rockways hoping to ease some of the hopelessness I felt.

As they left for college, I had to sit with my choices. Most of which was punctuated by the fact that I had no friends that called or invited me anywhere or even thought of me in any way or with regularity. I was an island of self, adrift in a sea of sadness and isolation— with very little hope of it changing.

When an invite did come, I didn't want to bring my husband who was always trying to make some joke or be anti-politically correct, spouting his ultraconservative views all over my liberally-minded friends. I couldn't take him anywhere without risking embarrassment so we only went places where his friends already knew him and accepted him as he was. His friends became my pseudo-friends, placeholders for ones I used to have.

In an effort to have a place to write that felt safe, I started an online blog I kept to myself. I didn't use my real name, and it would have been hard for him to find. If I couldn't write at home, I could on the interwebs.

While out in the world I felt the isolation of others as much as for myself. Here is an excerpt from one of those moments:

The Age of Invisibility:

Today I noticed something enough to write about it. I was at the store and I saw many older people in their senior years, walking with their heads lowered as if apologizing for being in the way at the store. They are slower in the *checkout. Sometimes they can't reach the items that are put high on the shelves. And they are just old. Like it's a bad thing.*

We (the younger set) walk the store with our heads up, vibrant, hell-bent on accomplishing our mission. Us with our smooth skin meander through the makeup aisle wondering about the next eyeshadow blend, the newest lip gloss to press onto our taut lips. As if that is important. We have full use of our bodies, we walk fast and our minds are sharp. We can handle the self-scan checkout systems, no problem. We use our ATM cards and remember our pin number. We get annoyed when they write a check. Or have a coupon.

I want to point out right here that their little exchange at the checkout** (while we are in a hurry, and they purposely got in the line of their favorite checker who is friendliest to them) **could possibly be the only human interaction that they have that day, or WEEK.

Imagine.

They got up early and primped their aged skin as best they could. A little rouge to cover up the lack of sunshine. They had their hair done the day before and put a cap on last night so it would keep for their weekly trip out to the store. They ate a light breakfast and drank only one small cup of coffee so they wouldn't have to use the restroom with its fancy-schmancy turn-on -by-itself faucets and self-dispensing towel holders that are so complicated, or worse yet those weird air dryer machines that are called a "knife." This trip is again a multi-hour planned ordeal. They caught a bus, or maybe drove (which is probably pretty scary with so many of us crazy youngsters on the roads, zipping around each other and ALWAYS in such a hurry).

They arrive to find that the contents of the store have been rearranged again, and everything is so high-priced they may have to make decisions about what to buy or if they need their medicine this time. They keep their head down, trying not to bother anyone or be in the way. They hurry through the line with the hard stares of the younger people with their screaming kids in the cart, trying to get home for naptime. They are rushed and it is over-they have had their outing for the day/week/month.

A few weeks ago, I saw a woman trying to help her husband out of a car and into his wheelchair. She was a smaller woman, her husband much larger although now frail. I asked if I could help her. She politely said no, as if this was her duty- what she had signed up for and she would handle it, come hell or high water. They were finally out of the house and going to enjoy a McDonald's coffee together. Duty. Mixed with love, perhaps- hopefully, or just duty.

With duty comes the idea of burden. Again, I sit with the societal rein- forcement that the oldsters are not needed, or troublesome in our world. It's beyond sad. Her proud moment of saying that she could do it herself had cost me, too, as I wanted to help and might have felt good about being there for a stranger. We feel good helping others. Being there for others. I left our interaction feeling sad.

Another thing people are hung up on is pride. The oldsters are proud that they can take care of themselves. They have outlived, outseen and outplayed this whole world- who are we to help them?

We live on a double-edged sword of wanting to help each other but not wanting to impose. Not wanting to bring attention to the fact that some things just aren't as easy as they used to be. Acknowledging that is serious business.

On the job, I met a woman named Margaret. Margaret was also my maternal grandmother's name, whom I loved dearly.

I automatically had compassion and an interest in the well-being of Margaret. I was selling carpet in a flooring store when she came in with her daughter. Her daughter was a little older than me and her Mom Margaret must have been in her late eighties. Such a sweet little old lady. She was visibly nervous.

It was her first real purchase of anything substantial since her husband died and she was wondering how it would all work. Her furniture would need to be moved, her family photos in frames, everything. I remember her ruminating aloud about how she was going to pay, finally settling in to using some of her savings for the project.

As she waited for her project to start, she came into the store a few times while I was there, her eyes watery with nerves. Finally she asked me point blank if it would be okay.

I don't know who reached for whose hand, but suddenly we were bound. I held her hand and gave it a tiny little squeeze to let her know things would be okay and then we just stood there, and I didn't want to let go, and she didn't want to let go. Her little hand reminiscent of my grandmother's- nestled into mine took me back to that last time I saw her. Her skin soft with wrinkles. Such a comfort for us both.

We need to realize that we as a society have— right now an unending supply of adoptive grandparents waiting to be taken in.

We live in a world where we ignore each other. Partly because we feel useless to change another person's circumstance. There isn't a way—yet to fix "old".

Loving people, in acknowledging them and seeing them, requires giving, and perhaps a commitment from each of us to make a difference.

And we're busy. So busy with our stuff. Busy with our kids' stuff and work and everything that it takes to keep a house going or to stay above water and off the streets ourselves.

I wonder what would happen if we started connecting? Asked our oldsters about their life? Think of the riches that lie inside them– the wisdom.

What have they seen, heard, lived through? What could they teach us? The cultures where they honor and seek out the wisdom of the elders really have something.

And I can't unsee them, and you can't unread this. It's out there.

The least we can do is smile and be kind.

It Feels Good to Be Writing Again.

~

~3~

The trees on the roadside blew slanted in the wind and Sky left her car windows open to dry her hair.

Jeremy was somehow standing there on the drive as the welcome wagon when she pulled up. He was also wearing jeans, much to her appreciation. A handsome stranger. Wavy brown hair that curved around his face and jut into his eyes just slightly. He brushed it away his eyes as he walked towards her car.

"Nice car," he said. "I have one, too." He chuckled as he pointed up the drive to another Ford Escape that was blue. "I had to buy it, because *you know.*" He seemed warm and authentic.

A smile crept across her face. A bond had been made. He shook her hand and asked her if she'd like a tour.

"Yes, I would love that."

Jeremy was in his element. Sharing his winery geekiness, showing the latest technology he was implementing to his organization and running on about all of the different types of grapes that he was growing, or hoped to someday grow with someone who knew what he was talking about.

They walked the rows of the vineyard, sometimes in silence with the sunshine strong on the sprouting leaves. There was an ease between them, as if they had known each other much longer than just the last few minutes.

"I'm really excited about this next space; it's probably much different than others you may have been in. Jeremy led Sky past the house and over a small hill. On the other side they scrambled down a steeper grade where a door was tucked into the hillside. A graveled path nestled in front of the door and a makeshift road led up to the pathway. "This is our aging chamber. I usually come at if from the other side, but we were closer from where we were to go over the top and now you can see what it really is. We made ourselves a little man-made cave here. The hillside looks like it's a part of the landscape. Can you believe how natural it all looks?"

A craggly old door teased of age but Sky couldn't tell if it was just part of the optics. Jeremy opened the door and the hinges creaked with authenticity. It was dark and cool inside, rocks of all sizes and shapes slathered in with mortar. Large bell lights hung sporadically down the center of the shaft adding to the visual of an old hidden place. There was a smell that was neither good nor bad- was it one of possibility?

Sky wished she would have brought a jacket or sweater. Next time.

"You have really got something here; this place is downright cool," Sky shivered as she spoke.

Jeremy sensed her chill, "Yeah, I keep meaning to leave some jackets in here in case people need them. Something with the winery logo on it, ya know." He winked and it surprised her, and maybe him too as he abruptly motioned for them to leave. They warmed on their walk back to the main area of the property.

The last stop was the tasting room. Jeremy flung open two great metal clad doors on the front façade of an old barn. A newly poured and polished concrete floor shone with the utmost attention. A large map of the world was embedded into the design prior to the sealing with a star on their exact spot. Newer black-encased windows had been placed into the ancient wood walls punctuating of old and new coming together. Large ancient timbers braced the ceiling for strength. It was massive and dramatic yet had a homey feel.

Small bistro tables, just waiting for people to sit and admire each other over a glass of vino, the bases were wine barrels with glass beveled edge tops. Very thematic.

A monstrous half-circle bar had a counter made of a material that looked like a solid pour of fine wine. Her eyes questioned, as she slowly caressed the top. "This is beautiful."

"It's paper, mixed with a resin. Recycled paper actually; it's green."

Being green and sustainable was very important in this region and to Jeremy, and this was a stunning accent. "Plus, this material is perfect for wine tasting, as you'll never see a stain. Any mishap will only add to the beauty."

Sky studied the front of the bar that was faced with reclaimed wood. Each chunk looked to have a tinge of wine color on it as well. "How is this possible?" she asked as she ran her fingers over the craggy pieces.

"Those are from the massive old French wine casks, each piece cut, and placed into this beautiful pattern to allow some of the interior wine staining to stay visible. It may lessen over time, but for now it's stunning."

"Wow, you have put a lot of thought into this. *This place is gorgeous.*"

Sky spun around to take in the whole space. Another view showed a few taller tables with stools and an Eames couch in the corner hung out with some easy chairs. Not the ugly Archie Bunker kind of chairs, more like a traditional Mission style.

This guy had class. A large Southwestern rug sat underneath a seating area and a coffee table held a single book on a pitched frame in the center.

Sky could not resist. She walked closer to the enticing seating area. "What is this, a little reading material? About the winery?"

"Not exactly, but sorta. That book has kind of a special place here with me. It is a book capable of changing lives. I know because it changed mine and my sister's as well."

"Find Me. 3 of 5," said Sky.

Jeremy looked at her and spoke, "Hey, yeah, take it home. Read it over the rest of the weekend and bring it back with you on Monday at nine. If you want the job, it's yours, I have a feeling we might make a good pairing."

Sky grabbed Jeremy's hand and they shook with vigor.

"Great! I really want to be a part of this. You are building something amazing here, the potential is enormous. I have been dying to be a part of something again. I was just waiting for the right thing to come along. Thank you, Jeremy, thank you so very much."

"Terrific!" Jeremy's calm smile and how he grasped her hand with his other hand as they shook, made her feel very at peace about them working together.

"I will be here. Nine a.m. sharp." Sky placed the book into her bag and started out the double doors towards her car.

"I mean, you already had the company car, what choice did I really have?" he laughed.

Sky laughed. "No choice at all," she called back.

"We can work out all the details on Monday."

"Perfect! Enjoy your weekend."

"You, too. Enjoy the book."

Sky got into her car and started the engine. An overwhelming feeling of relief came over her as she realized that she had found her new-something. A new role with a new company and with a very nice man with whom to build whatever this could be.

Jeremy walked into the old cabin and Sky heard the screen door slam. A call buzzed and she answered, it was the temp agency offering up another weeklong job starting Monday.

"Click one to accept this position, click two to deny."

Sky was delighted to click the number two. Maybe forever.

No more temporary work, temporary life or living arrangements. She had something to hold onto and work on. She turned out of the drive toward the big city. That bright sunny afternoon kept her company all the way home.

~

Finally, a Position, Me 2013

*A*n outside sales job peddling some green building materials. Working with someone I liked and got along pretty well with. We had similar brains, but he was a bit more hyper than me, always on the move or trying something different. Even when in business mode, his attention scattered to an invention he had thought of or wanted to bring to market.

The position was basically unpaid, but I had somewhere to go most days and there was the promise of big paychecks if I could get architects to spec our products. I had an entire state to sell to; surely I would be able to make some money.

I knew what I sold and I liked the product which is often half the battle in sales. There was always something to learn though. I remember going to a business and I got a little spicy with the owner, in a playful way as we bantered back and forth.

"I'm going to sell you something," I teased.

"Only if I decide that I want to buy from you."

Yikes, he never did buy anything from me, and hardly ever anyone else from what I heard.

I tried at this job, going and running presentations, often making food as lunch was a requirement by the companies willing to let their employees listen in. Outgo, outgo, outgo.

We will see how long this lasts. But at least I can say I have a job.

~

~3~

Sky read the book Jeremy gave her from the winery at home over a glass of red wine. It was such a fascinating concept. She closed her eyes and thought back to her own moments with the wide range of people she had run across in her days. Had she made any impressions on them as they had on her?

As enticing as it was to think about, the book didn't inspire her to reach back into her past and call anyone. Any old relationships were dead and gone in her eyes and heart. She was quite content to be on the path she was on. Settled and proud of how she cared for her grandmother in her last months, this life of hers had given her tons of experience and a whole lot of memories to reminisce about when she got right down to it.

And what about this next chapter? A new job, a new boss and the exciting uphill that came with building up a business. She was giddy as she rose on Monday, early to get to the Escape Winery. If things looked like they were working out, she might need to move. This hour-long drive would get old for sure.

With no experience in workday traffic out of town, she left early, arriving well before nine.

Jeremy waved her into the tasting room. The furniture had been slightly rearranged since her visit. A new but vintage-looking podium took prominence under the great big window near the group seating area.

"I thought I could put the book on here. I found the piece over the weekend at a local antique shop. It looked like an old church podium. There was room for something special to sit up on top and storage shelves below. What did you think of the read?"

"Super interesting. I liked how it was filled with snapshots of time, snipped from a moment between two people. Such a range of memories; you can see how a whole person can develop out of snippets like that. And the idea that a single moment can mean so much to someone, *you just never know.*"

"*Exactly.*" Jeremy looked up into the rafters while nodding in understanding before turning back to Sky, "I anticipate we will have a good amount of people through this coming season with the launch of the *Old Country Reds*. Maybe someone who visits here will see themselves in the stories and help the author get her book back. I have been hoping to help that happen to honor what the little book did for me. That book inspired me to take a second look at my life, after my wife Natalia passed away. It pushed me to think of what I wanted and where I wanted to be."

"I'm very sorry to hear you lost your wife. If you ever want to talk about her with me, I'm open to that. I just lost my Grannie G." Sky pulled the book from her oversized macramé bag, and placed the book cover side up onto the podium. "It's a perfect fit."

Jeremy smiled and looked at Sky. "It sure is."

"What do you say— we *escape* into the office and brainstorm a bit. I have some ideas, but I would love to hear what you think, too.

"Love it," Sky smiled. She knew things were going to get interesting.

~

Technology is Such a Tease, Me 2014

A little gift that would have changed everything. A Christmas gift from my daughters to attach to my keys so I wouldn't lose them, as I did sometimes. A tiny GPS locator practically the size of a quarter! If only that technology would have been around when I sent out my traveling books, then I could have kept track of them. I'd know exactly where they were and who might have seen them.

Maybe I could have gotten one back by now? Called it to me with a blip or a whir or driven whatever roads to get to it. But alas, that type of sorcery was not available when I sent my books out.

When I am alone and thoughtful of the piles of shit in my life, I crave knowing where my books are. Are they having a better, more exciting life than I am? I certainly hope so. I see them gallivanting all over the world, touching and inspiring gobs of people.

I wish I could.

Perhaps one is just around the corner from me. This secret adventure of mine I've kept locked away in my heart. I still believe that this crazy idea is possible. That this little life of mine could count for something. Even in this chapter of limitations and often hopelessness, somehow my story might rally others to make their lives bigger.

In the quiet, I still believe.

Sigh.

~

~3~

E scape Winery was hosting its first big event since the opening: a wedding. This was not a typical wedding either. It was a traditional Hindu wedding or *Vivaha*. Sky had spent the last month scouring the area for inspiration to learn more about the traditions of the guests and couple. Sky spoke to anyone with an East Indian background that she bumped into. She wanted the event to be *perfect* for the couple.

She needed it to be, not just for the bride and groom but for the winery. It was their first big chance to put their venue on the map for other people wanting to reserve a space. If the family felt honored, celebrated and cared for on their big day, Sky and Jeremy would feel accomplished in their six months of working together.

Before contracting with the venue, the family had visited to see the space and hear more about their accommodations. They were served a beautiful light buffet of vegetarian cuisine cooked by Sky herself in a nearby shared commissary.

Luscious bowls of cool soup were made with the freshest peas and mint Sky had picked from the garden that day. A single pea sprout sat atop a swirl of coconut cream. The newly added winery vegetable garden wouldn't be able to produce enough to serve the entire guest list on the wedding day, but the hand care and hospitality made enough of an impact to show that Escape Winery cared about the freshness of the food. Served chilled and in traditional hammered copper bowls, it was a delight of the first generation Indian parents of the bride and groom. Beautifully fried triangular shaped samosas with potatoes, peas and onions in a decadent spicy sauce were served, along with aloo tikki potato skewers, with a fiery hari chutney.

The tables were decked in an underpinning of white tablecloths with richly colored satin remnants criss-crossed in reds, oranges, yellows and teals. The family was quite impressed when they saw the efforts that Sky and Jeremy went to in order to make their family feel special.

The bride and the groom and the parents excused themselves to walk the grounds after the meal, and when they came back, it was a resounding yes from all.

"We will need it next month. We will send you a list for all of our needs. We will need the main house, and we saw that the house next door is also available to rent so we will need to call the owner of that property. We have multiple ceremonies that take place over the three day period."

Sky spoke up, "I have anticipated your need for the next door property and have arranged for it to be available for the groom's family for as long as required. I have also inquired with another neighbor about *their white horse.*"

The family's eyes lit up and they happily nodded to each other before walking over to shake hands with Sky. *This woman had done her homework.* This was the perfect place for Adesh and Avantika to get married.

"Thank you so much for the opportunity. We are honored to be able to entertain your party for this beautiful event," said Sky as she walked them all back to their limousine.

Strutting back into the office she plopped a butt cheek onto the edge of Jeremy's desk. He looked up expectantly.

"Well...?"

"We got it!" She raised her hand to get a high-five. He came around for a hug instead.

"Way to go! It's all because of you. Yes!"

"We have some work to do to get it perfect, but it will be dynamite. I am so excited!"

"No doubt in my mind that you will make it just what they dream. Let me know what I can do, okay?"

"Well, you'll have to move out of your house for the week, and I called to rent the neighbor's house next door, and um, *we're gonna need a white horse.*"

~

S.S.

You were the one who challenged my status quo. After nearly a lifetime of avoiding women who looked like you, here you were, and you were not going anywhere. You were my imagined nemesis in your being tall, blonde, and thin.

As you stood with your husband with his Tom Selleck mustache and your two little kids holding a pie for us the day we moved in, I saw that avoiding you was not going to be in the cards. We were next door neighbors, you had kids, and your daughter was nearly the same age as mine. It wouldn't be fair to my little one to keep the two of them from playing together, so I was going to have to challenge this long-set idea that you were better than me somehow simply because of how you looked.

I don't think I shared with you all of the rumblings that went on in my head each time we were together. My inadequacies festered under the surface of my skin each time I saw your neat and clean house, your perfectly coiffed hair and seemingly idyllic life.

As the years went by, you became a best friend, someone to share my doubts and concerns with in my mothering. Our families grew together like a comfortable knitted sweater. Your daughter and my oldest became best friends, practically inseparable. Shared garage sales, parties and watching each other's kids in a pinch.

When your daughter was suddenly afraid of dogs, you decided to usurp a possible lifetime of fear for her by adding one to your family. Your dog and my dog became best friends and there was suddenly another set of play dates to plan.

One day, your golden and my pug were wrestling as they did on the front lawn between our houses. Playing, frollicking, being silly puppies together. In their tussle, your dog's mouth got stuck on my dog's collar and in her frantic, she started thrashing to get it free. This caused my much smaller dog to be tossed to and fro, the collar actually folding into itself, choking him. You were there and saved him. I will forever tear-up just thinking about that. You saved my dog's life.

A trip to the vet and weeks of watching his swollen bloodshot eyes slowly go back to normal, we agreed no collars were allowed when they played. Breakaway collars will always be my personal pet policy because of that day.

Years spent next door to each other, my daughters would have the perfect childhood memories that I never had, with a band of other caring mothers to help carry the burden.

When your son was being shunned by the other children for his behavior, I softly suggested that maybe he should be evaluated, to see if there may be something else going on. I remember the concern on your face at the thought of it or that something in your life might not be as you'd once hoped. Something out of your control and with unknown ramifications.

I tried to buffer the point. "It's not you. Nothing that is going on is a result of how you have mothered. You are an amazing mother, sometimes you get a kid and there may just be something extra that the parents have to work around."

I don't know if my words were comforting and I don't remember being kept in the loop as things progressed, but I know that you were and forever are an extraordinary mother and friend and I am mighty glad I got over myself enough to be friends with you.

~

Mothering is Who I Am, Me 1994-Forever After

*I*n total at any given time we had four offspring in the house, two of his, two of mine. My oldest moved back home to attend a local university rather than the one she started at, and took a bedroom at the end of the house for the most privacy. Her boyfriend from Seattle would come to visit, but was never allowed to sleep in her room with her, even though they had been intimate for years. "We" had moral standards to uphold; after all, this was a religious house.

My youngest, here mostly on school vacations and weekends while finishing up her last year of high school, was busy with school and cheerleading and had a boyfriend who lived out of town. They would talk often on the phone while planning her train trips to visit him about once every couple of months or so, once we approved of him, that is.

My husband's children were behind mine in age; his oldest, a daughter. She loved experimenting with makeup, fancy nails and hair styles, she craved views and likes on her social media pages. Her inborn style, beauty and natural elegance made me feel like something of an ugly, old, chambermaid in my own home. But it was fun to watch her grow into a young woman. Even though things had been hard in the beginning, my interest and concern reached her heart and we grew a special relationship despite our challenges.

Her brother was a bit harder to crack. He was a bit of a loner, often in his room playing video games for hours, only coming out to seek something to nibble on while deep in gaming. He didn't have any chores assigned to him so his summers were his own. When school was in session, he would get home from school, have a snack then head straight up to his room. Dinner would come and he would stick around for the meal and then back to his room to either play his games or watch other people online, playing the games he liked, in order to learn new tactics.

One day, there was an interaction that I will never forget. He was sitting *at the kitchen peninsula at the home computer, while my daughter and I sat at the dining table.*

"You know, I think if both of you were gone right now, I'm not sure I would even notice."

He didn't even look over at us when he said it. It was said as matter of fact as if he had stated, "I just ate a sandwich."

She and I just looked at each other. We hadn't been speaking to him, and there was no segue into his statement at all. He was just sitting there thinking to himself that he either had no connection to us, or that he was surprised to realize that he had little connection to anything at all.

It made me start looking at him closely. I had been following a young man and his organization in his efforts to bring more awareness and acceptance of self to people on the autism spectrum.

The organization, Autism[1] Experts (AE) out of Seattle, Washington, teaches seminars to parents and children on the spectrum offering tools and an understanding of how to live easier in a predominantly neurotypical world. I watched the group's online videos and posts and wondered if my stepson might have some of this going on. The more I listened, the more convinced I became that something in what they described and what I was experiencing was similar. I was determined to help my stepson somehow.

As many times as I had asked him to clean up his room, the task was never completed, it wasn't until I tried one of the AE's suggestions of writing down the steps of cleaning a room that he had more success. He seemed to wander off in his head a lot, or fixate on certain movements or sayings he thought were funny for months at a time, gleefully laughing beyond what the action or joke seemed to warrant.

There was a time when he was six years old that he was sitting on his legs watching a movie, and he suddenly started screaming as if he was being murdered. I ran to him, trying to see what was going on, how I could help, only to realize that his legs had fallen asleep and his tiny movement had made his legs go into the pins and needles phase. The sensation was something so foreign and terrifying and he wasn't aware that something like that could happen. As it lessened I talked him through it, telling him the why and what caused it so he could avoid it in the future.

---

1. This organization was originally called Asperger's Experts at the time of this scene, however I have changed it here in unison with the organization circa 2025. The founder has thousands of references with the former term. See back of book for resources and websites.

He was always on some sort of a device, so sometimes I would just sit and watch the screen with him, asking questions about what he was doing or what the goal of the moment was. Pointed, direct questions with an easy answer; not open-ended questions that pulled him out of whatever he was doing. I paid extra attention to his likes and what got him excited and eventually painted one of the video game characters on his bedroom wall.

His sister, forever praised and celebrated, didn't need any extra attention.

I committed to fight for the younger one to take up more space in the house, to be noticed. It would become one of my goals. Making sure this kid had everything he needed to become whatever he could be, despite anything that might make it harder for him.

I stuck up for him when his father yelled at him for taking a different way home on his bike than the rest of us. I praised him for his independence. I would bake and play board games with him or whisk him away to go geocaching. That was one of my favorite ways of bonding with him, as we had a task to work on together, and it got us both outside, solving a little mystery. It was something the older kids weren't really interested in doing.

His insistence in that statement–that he wouldn't miss us- wasn't a reflection of how bonded or not bonded he was to us; I felt it was simply a disconnect that he couldn't explain. I appreciated him thinking enough of it to say something.

When he was starting high school he went through a patch of depression, anxiety and felt overwhelmed to the point of missing many days of school. He started counseling and we parents (his naturals and steps) went to one session together with his counselor—just to compare notes amongst ourselves and to help the therapist know more about his home lives.

It was there that I brought it up- that maybe he had a little Autism going on.

"No, he's just an introvert like me; there is nothing wrong with my son," said his mother sternly.

She drew a line, right then and there. There would be no discussing it further. Even the counselor dropped it.

I was told at home never to speak of it again. The protection that his mother had provided might make his options smaller, but she didn't know.

She only knew to protect. Protect him from names, labels or judgments.

"There is nothing wrong with my child."

I didn't say that there was. I only said he may have some additional challenges and don't you think it would be good to know now?

She threatened to remove him from our house if I questioned it again, and I had to relent since he wasn't my son. I would help where I could and support him if he did need some extra conversations around what was expected from him or how to navigate things.

I never felt so hopeless as to watch him struggle through everything when he might have been handed some more tools to make his life easier. And a whole community to belong to.

Still wanting to help, I thought maybe we could get him a dog. I was actually pretty depressed myself by this time, and I had raised a puppy before: my one-of-a-kind pug, and companion and love for over thirteen years. We had to put him to sleep about two years prior and I'd battled the idea of getting another one, mostly because I didn't think I could love another dog like I loved him- a similar view and worry I had about having a second child. But it was probably time, and I could use someone in the house to go on walks with.

So what kind of dog? My pug had not been appreciated by the more traditionally minded people in the house, the ones who only saw cute and fluffy as the best pet. So I found one that met the ideals of my husband with the adorable factor more in line with my stepdaughter's wishes.

I wanted the dog to be my stepson's, something that was his own to have and take care of; not his sister's, or his father's either. I pushed to have only him go to pick up the puppy, but in usual fashion, the sister came, too, and the dog turned into everyone's. I thought we decided that brother could name the pup though; it felt like my one and only win in this battle.

But by the end of the week, my stepson's chosen name had fallen away and was replaced by the one his father picked. That little man was on the bottom of the heap again.

We all grew in love with the little pup and I took up most of the care and training as per usual. She wasn't my preferred breed, a little bit stuffy and foo-foo for me, as I preferred a dog with some sort of imperfection about them. I did fall in love with her though. Somehow, maybe in the back of my mind, I picked her because I knew I wasn't long for this house anymore, and maybe her presence could take up some of the gap after I left.

Ignoring my spidey senses about my stepson was difficult, but I had no other option. My insistence had made it so that he was rarely able to come over anymore. I wondered if his mother worried I might have a conversation about what I thought. Which I eventually did, subtly, posed from an innocent angle.

One day, he and I were home alone, sitting on the couch. He sat petting the new puppy as she basked in the sunshine streaming in through the window.

"Hey, you know how _____ just got diagnosed with ADHD?"

"Yeah,"

"What do you think of that, do you think that it's bad, do you think any less of him?"

"No, not at all."

"Do you think that if you had something going on like that- you would want to know?"

"Yeah, I would want to know."

I left it there, knowing that his wish was going to sit like a broken promise of what could have been.

I knew that if he knew, he would be okay with it. And I also knew that if a child received a diagnosis before they turned eighteen they might have more resources available to them through state programs that could continue with them through life. I felt an urgency to get to the bottom of how he was but I held my tongue and kept quiet, silently begging for something to help him from another direction.

I kept seeing AE with their classes, seminars, world traveling adventures, and workshops, not to mention their dedicated game servers where other kids with similar brain styles could gather and play, socializing together from a safe and pleasant distance at first, oh how I wished he would have been able to be a part of it.

I did my best to learn more about autism and ADHD, and prioritized time to honor the things he liked to do. I kept more of an interest in him, sometimes instead of his sister. Just to even things out with the adoration of her by the rest of the family.

To be asked to step aside like I was, as if he were none of my concern was a blow. But I know I tried.

I sometimes think about how he will react when he finds out his mother purposely kept us from investigating these sources because she didn't want him to be labeled. She didn't want him to be seen as different from the other kids. But he was. Is.

His epiphany moment will come someday and the questions will be asked to his parents. "Why didn't you get me more help? Why didn't you ask my teachers? Why didn't you do more when you saw me go into myself and not build friendships or take steps that were necessary for me to move into adulthood?

I didn't think that my partner in life would be my saboteur. It wasn't necessarily on purpose, he just never stood with me, even when he knew I was right. I didn't want to be right and I didn't want there to be a thing; but if there was a thing, the best way to handle it is to acknowledge it and get the tool box chock-full of good ways to accommodate and help, not to shut off the conversation. It felt like just another way he and I weren't compatible.

I can't answer those questions for him, if my stepson asks. It just wasn't my call.

One of the hardest parts they don't really talk about in parenting a stepchild, is you more often than not have zero say in the health and well-being of that child.

For me though, I didn't have a say in this household in many of the different categories; this was just one. But it was probably the most important one to me.

I would have given up my chance at the rest of them just to know I did everything in my power to help him have more answers growing up, or to not have to wonder so much of the time. If only I could have spared him that feeling or of being alone in his head most of the time.

Being "just a stepmom," I had to step back and hope for the best. Believing he would find his way even without me as a part-time tour guide. I can't fix everything. I can't save everybody. I wasn't sure I could save myself.

When I entered the picture I naturally assumed that all of the kids would be mine to mother. That having an <u>extra</u> mom would be a good thing, and not a bad thing. An enemy of the state. I know I have done a lot to teach him some of the things that will come up for him. I taught him how to make scrambled eggs, we picked berries together and I taught him how to start the washing machine. Since I felt pretty decent about how I had mothered and grown my two, adding a couple more shouldn't have been a big deal. Right?

No matter where I would be, I love them both very much and am grateful I got to see their personalities appear, and watch a lot of their successes in life.

I hope I will leave a happy memory in their hearts when I am gone.

~

~3~

After misreading the invitation, Sarla Beti arrived at the Escape Winery at twelve instead of two. She hadn't been out this way before and was surprised at the colorful landscape of grape vines and outbuildings. It reminded her of Italy and going there with her family as a child.

The parking lot was empty. With no one around, she wandered the grounds looking for a secret spot where her friends might be waiting. Cracking open the door to the main tasting room, it was vacant, but welcoming just the same. She pulled out her invitation from her purse and looked closely at it.

"Oh. That's why I am here alone. Nice one, Sarla." she said out loud to herself.

Going back to town would mean she would pretty much have to turn right back around and come back to still be on time. Better to just sit and wait it out.

She noticed a seating area in the corner by the expansive windows, and a book set up on a stand. She wandered over as it looked like a cozy spot. She wouldn't bother anyone there. She could wait and maybe read that book until her friends arrived. Then she would either tell them how foolish she'd been or perhaps she wouldn't share that after all.

Sarla picked up the book off of the stand and lowered herself into one of the wide leather chairs. It enveloped her. She was small in stature with not much else on her five-feet-two frame other than spirit, drive and luxurious locks of long black hair.

She had worn one of her favorite sleeveless sundresses in bright green and draped a light yellow dupatta over both of her shoulders to the back. That way if she was given the option to have her own henna designs done, it would be easy to have it out of the way.

She crossed her legs and tried to sit up as straight as she could, but the cushion of the chair made her sink deeper, her feet shooting over the cushion in front of her. Rearranging herself again, she tucked her legs underneath herself and rested one arm on the side of the chair to be able to hold herself and the book in a comfortable way.

The book was tattered from viewing. The title "Find Me, 3 of 5" was barely legible. Mere hints of gold print adorned the blue cover. Sarla opened it to the first page and read the inviting plea from a secret author.

This would definitely kill some time. Usually one to follow the rules, Sarla felt a little sneaky, as if she had stumbled into and read a stranger's diary, but it was exactly what the author asked for.

She read an excerpt about the author's grandmother and how she chose to marry the man she loved rather than the one who might have been better suited to her.

Marriage. She had been mulling it over for a while. Pulled back into reality, she glanced out over the tasting room and imagined it full of people all dressed in bright colors, with the music floating over everyone enraptured in dance.

Avantika and Adesh had found each other in their heritage's old-fashioned way. An arranged marriage through a family contact. Each had written a dossier of their likes and dislikes and what they were looking for in a spouse. It told of their religion and regional heritage. The document was *the* introduction to each of the potential partners.

Often, ads were placed in the local Indian newspapers of who was looking for a spouse for their child, niece or nephew or close relation. It was the way it had been done for thousands of years already in their culture. Not the newspaper and newly online part, but through word of mouth, messages, or traveling often great distances all with the goal of putting two suitable people together. Sarla was very aware of the process as her mother had been talking with her about it for most of her life.

Her mother had been after her lately to make up a biodata profile. Mother offered to do it for her if she were too busy with her work, all so they could start the process of getting her married. After graduating from law school and having passed the bar two years ago, Sarla landed a great job at a firm in Portland. She had a nicely-sized contemporary apartment and a small dog to keep her company when she was home. Some of her spare time was spent with a wonderful group of Punjabi friends, the same ones that were coming together for her almost married friend, Avantika. She had only been to two Hindu weddings as an adult, and attended a few as a child where she sat mesmerized by the scene, a dream of color, love and culture— *everything felt so magical.*

She'd been to a number of western weddings of her work or school friends recently, and as beautiful as they were in their own way, they didn't have the jewel tone flourish and richness of spirit that she herself craved.

The idea of her own wedding seemed far, far away. Often troubled with the process, she knew that she had a choice to make. She'd been torn about dating. Should she dedicate her time to look for a *love-marriage*, or enlist and trust her friends and family to help her find someone? She didn't know which way to go.

Dating, specifically online dating, seemed odd as no one knew these people she would go out with ahead of time. She would have no connection or affirmations as to what type of family they came from. That crop would also include people not from her heritage or even her country, and how would she reconcile that? Would they convert to Hinduism, or would she leave her own family's values behind. Maybe a hybrid of both?

She closed her eyes and imagined herself in a traditional western bridal gown, white with intricate lace and some beading. She tried the dress on in her mind, spinning in front of a mirror before changing out of it into a red satin and chiffon dress embroidered with florals and vines reminiscent of mehndi with exquisite gold beading. Bangles on both arms and theatrical earrings and neckwear all in yellow gold. That felt better. As she sat she confirmed that yes, indeed she would want a Punjabi wedding. She opened her eyes. Yes, that felt like home. Now how to acquire the groom? *That was still undetermined.*

After checking her watch, she read more in the little book. Reading about the author and dating a boy outside her religion...hmm. This book had a lot of useful things to consider. Would she, could she marry outside her religion? What of any children they had together; how would they handle that?

Yes, she wanted her spouse to share the same values and background. Okay, now she was getting someplace. Who knew she just needed a little time sitting alone and some real life examples to put some answers into place for herself. Her mother would be thrilled.

Would she ask for help in finding the man in an arranged marriage situation or would she go looking for herself in the massive village online? Western men most likely wouldn't understand all of the traditions and the big one of keeping sex for marriage. Often she would hear all about her friends staying over at their boyfriends, and how it was almost expected to share a bed without even a plan on marrying. That seemed odd to Sarla. It was a huge commitment, and enjoying each other in that way should only come after they had decided to share their lives together.

Sarla squirmed to keep her legs from falling asleep. As she adjusted, the book fell to the floor, falling open to a new entry. She picked it up and righted it on her lap.

B.E.

B.E.

You were cute, blonde, tall and lean when I met you. The new roommate of an old friend I was trying to reconnect with. I was just out of a longstanding relationship for most of my late teen years and into my twenties, you became my second lover. Using your time building a business refinishing fences and decks for people, you were begrudgingly independent as college was not for you.

The more time I spent at the house, the more I felt a pull towards you. When we finally decided to spend some time- just the two of us- my friend didn't mind, as she had seen the electricity sizzling between us.

We'd take walks, have picnics and shack up in your room enjoying each other's company. One time after a nice bout of lovemaking, I lay on my side, nude, looking at you. Your eyes ran over me and you told me that I was so beautiful. I am sure I thanked you in the moment before hiding myself in the covers. I was uncomfortable with an admiring eye. It was the first of a near-lifetime boomerang effect that would happen whenever I felt the danger of being really desired. Even by those who I claimed to love.

Suddenly I was back to that scared, out-of-control feeling of my molestation as a child, and I started gaining my *safety* weight. You didn't seem to mind, though you didn't look at me in the *same way* either.

As you were dressing one day, I noticed some whitish bumps on your *self* and asked you about it. You said you didn't know what it was, that it had been that way for awhile, but that you were sure it was fine. *Stupidly, I believed you.*

Soon after, I noticed some bumps on me. There wasn't any pain or itching but since you and I had unprotected sex, I went to my doctor and was told that I had contracted genital warts. I let you know what was going on, and you *said* you went to the doctor to get it handled. For other reasons that didn't matter anyway, we broke up.

Thus began my lengthy painful campaign of weekly trips to my gynecologist. Long cotton swabs were dipped in some sort of "acid" and then pressed into my lesions. Over and over he applied the potion and I could hear the sizzle of my skin and feel it, as no numbing meds were ever offered. I lay there each day, trapped in the stirrups and in my head regretting evermore that I had left my stable long-term relationship thinking there were more fish in the sea out there. I'd caught something on my second try!

Money out. Pain, not to mention a huge amount of shame to carry around with me tossed in as well.

The operation lasted over three months, before I was finally *cleared* of the problem. But something inside me had changed. Not in my down-there, but in my head.

My mindset. Sex wasn't the fun sport it had once been; any pleasure I'd found had been replaced with something else. Sex became a risk that could bring me pain, shame or potentially fatal implications. This ailment also put me at an increased risk for cancer someday.

Instead of doing the mental healing and forgiving myself for being naive to the potential issues, I turned inward and punished myself instead.

There would be no more enjoying the act, or allowing myself to be so vulnerable as to have an orgasm with any partner hereafter. *I was done.*

I didn't deserve that pleasurable feeling after being so stupid.

Life went on.

I thought I was free from the issue until the virus sprang up again, right before I was about to give birth to my first child. I cried for days. This terrible circumstance still had a hold of me. Stealing more from me-that of the joy of the arrival of my first child. Instead of that jubilation, the doctor had talked me through the risks of my passing it on to the baby as it moved through the birth canal.

My doctor and I did our best to eliminate the possibility, but my shame and self- blaming were activated again, and any joy I'd gained back for sex was gone again.

B.E. - I sincerely hope you kept better track of your dick after that.

~

Always the Weight, Me, 2014

The origin of the life jacket poundage happened pretty logically when it comes down to it. The powerlessness I felt with the molestation at nine, reaching for anything to help gain control again. I'd lost any semblance of safety and I found most of my solace in food.

When you are a kid, you don't register as to why happen and how to manage a trauma, things just are. I went from a scrawny kid in fourth grade to a rounded kid in fifth, but things didn't really change that much in the other ways.

As puberty came on I started being noticed by boys more. Some thought I was cute and they teased me. With my little extra, I attracted only the ones who liked my personality versus the ones who were only interested in my looks, so there was some safety there, and I didn't have to add any more than the original fifteen.

I had relationships and physical ones and I didn't feel the shame that I could have felt with my naked self being exposed- somehow I had already connected with them on a deeper level and anyone I "loved"- loved me the way I was.

Over time I have noticed an oddity that I wonder if others experience as well. Sometimes when I wasn't paying attention, the safety-fifteen fell off.

When I married my first husband, I had a little extra but he didn't care. The fear didn't rise up as he wasn't particularly complimentary about my appearance, or anything else for that matter about me and we went about making babies, an automatic weight contributor. I ignored a lot of my own self-care in giving to the family as often happens with new moms.

As my thirties moved into my forties, I noticed that when I was not in a relationship, I would often slim down some but not all the way. I'd attract the next one, then once he and I were an item, I would pudge up again to avoid any attention from anyone else, nothing drastic, just my little safety-jacket of excess.

It happened again with Mr. Fun. I was slim after the divorce because I could hardly eat with the stress and was walking miles and miles each day with my job.

We were lying together, naked, as people do and he looked at me just so.

"God, you are beautiful," he said. The exact same words that had sent a shiver in me the last time and I did the same thing the second time. I hadn't worked through any of it, hadn't been paying attention to the why and what happened next. I felt unsafe. Weeoo-Weeoo!

Pudge back up. Stop taking care of myself. My regular reaction of being uncomfortable in hearing a compliment, while yearning to be admired by the ones I gave my heart to. It doesn't make sense, or does it?

When I met husband number two, I was much thinner. In my life with him, I again set aside every health-based priority for myself and fell into the really unhealthy routine of our recently joined household. On came the fifteen plus more.

*He did marry me despite my extra-extra weight even though **he was not okay with it**.*

By then we were rarely physical. It was months in between our lovemaking sessions. When things got harder and we needed to work on things, he would always bring it up.

"I told you that keeping a healthy weight was a requirement for us being together, you need to work on that." Never mind that me prioritizing him and the kids was a big part of the reason I wasn't healthy. To make life a little bit easier.

I would go through spurts of hitting the gym and running, and some would come off but not all. At this time in my life I also was dealing with a chronic, hidden illness, extreme unhappiness and the overwhelming feeling that I didn't even matter in my own life. So there's that.

We didn't even screw on our honeymoon in Paris, with the Eiffel tower in full view of our hotel room. So lame.

There would be no unconditional love with this one. No understanding. Only his judgment and his preferences that kept me unsatisfied and hopeless in our life. Maybe it was a little bit of a test to see if he would love me as I was.

Whatever the reason, this weight thing has complicated my life in so many ways. Keeping me safe from attention, protected but often rejected.

When will I feel okay as I am?

~

~3~

S arla read the last line of the B.E. excerpt from the traveling book and slammed it shut out of shock. Her face reddened as she looked around before exhaling a breath of sheer epiphany.

Placing the book back gently on the coffee table, she walked out the doors to see if any of her friends had arrived yet. She hadn't bothered to write her name in the back of the book and she was glad. *No need to pin her name to that story.*

Cars were starting to pull into the parking lot and she waved and walked over to them. She wished she hadn't read about what the author had been through, but at the same time, reading it had helped solidify her decision to either go with a matchmaker or lean on her parents to seek out a husband for her on her behalf.

She didn't want the extra risk of falling in love with the wrong person, or having to muddle through men who might not share her values. Yes, it may be old-fashioned, but the practice continues on in modern times for a reason. She knew many arranged-marriage couples live out their lives very happily, her own parents included, because they start out with the same goal in their hearts. Learning together as they make their way through the years as a team.

She would set some minimums with her parents though, as she had heard of some women having to give up their careers once they married. She loved her career, and couldn't imagine doing anything else.

When her friends arrived, they all sat and laughed and talked while watching the henna artist decorate the bride's hands, feet, and up her arms, before the guests were also given some designs to cherish and remember and celebrate the occasion. They laughed and enjoyed the choreographed dances prepared by friends and family of the bride and groom, eating up the yummy traditional food and music of the mehndi ceremony.

It was exactly the sort of day Sarla wanted for herself, someday.

All of it. The big traditional wedding, her one perfectly-picked man just for her.

She believed her family also wanted what was best *for her*. She knew that the man they chose would be well-suited, someone who was also committed to a shared vision of family, tradition, and a long and happy life together.

~

If Wishing on Teardrops was Enough, Me 2014

A lonely wife sits on the floor of her bedroom, wondering how she got here. Again.

She waits to hear a kind word about their lovemaking the night before, yet nothing comes.

Maybe it wasn't real. Maybe it doesn't matter anymore.

Maybe it's time to give up.

She asked him yesterday what he even liked about her that day they met and his answer was just that he saw her.

Did he like her smile, her eyes, anything about her?

What, if anything, does he like about her now?

She feels invisible.

Asking- no, begging- to be touched; he never does on his own. They don't even hold hands anymore.

A kiss in the morning to sustain her and one at night to tuck her in. But what is she to do with the passion and love that sits inside her, wanting.

In the same room they sit, he on his mobile device. She watches him play games and avoid her so long— she picks up her own so they have something in common.

She imagined herself somewhere else and the gap he would feel would be nothing.

She feels like nothing to him, and she cries.

She is a good woman, one who tries hard to make him happy, support him and his children. Make a difference in their lives. Everything she tries falls short. She herself falls short of some large expectation of what he really wanted—someone with an accent, someone who makes more money. She tries really hard to be enough, then realizes she is enough just maybe not for him.

And she doesn't want to leave, start over and be away from him, yet she feels alone most of the time anyway with his kids and his hobbies getting the best of him while she gets the leftovers and the scraps.

They never dream together anymore- practicality is the winner in this house. Zero romance, no imagination, no fun.

We can't do this, we can't do that. We can't afford this but yet we can't take our money with us when we die.

The kids are getting older and soon it will be the two of them. Strangers living in the same house.

Or perhaps one of them will break for freedom.

Or they will both get sick from the lack of love and die of broken hearts.

I can't do this anymore. If you want to stay together, we need to work at this and I need you to SEE me.

Celebrate with me all that we could have. We need to have more fun with each other and celebrate the differences.

I am trying to make you happier and more relaxed by making more money so you can breathe, buy fancy watches and fly.

Touch me, see me and hold me is all I want in return.

I am a good woman.

Love me

Please— before it's too late

~

M.I.L.

In the beginning you saw me as a way of getting more grandchildren. I was young, seemingly fertile and was crazy about your son.

After your son and I married, I did indeed provide you with your first granddaughter pretty quickly. You'd come stay with us to see her but when you visited, it was mostly the two of us during the day as my husband went to work. It didn't take long for the nitpicking to start.

I remember that day when you told me that your *"golden boy"* shouldn't have to lift a finger around the house since I was at home with our daughter. He shouldn't even have to take out the trash.

Throughout the years, you'd find other ways to make me not feel good enough for your son. With your scritching at specks of burnt food splattered on the stove from one of the meals I had made, to refolding the laundry once I had done it already.

"His shirts should be pressed before he goes to work; I can't believe you let him out of the house with a wrinkly shirt." *It never seemed to end.*

Once in an effort to show I did care what you thought, I asked you to show me how to iron a shirt as no one ever had. I really thought it would change things if I tried harder and showed you I was willing to learn.

Years more of trying went by. I'd make sure to have a few large print romance books in your room for every visit. A gift of a candle and your favorite candy or something to wear for Christmas.

I remember the exact moment when I stopped caring what you thought of me, or my housekeeping. How I was raising your granddaughters, really anything anymore.

You were staying with us, and my local sister-in-law came to have dinner. My two daughters bounced in and out of the living room as we all sat together watching the Winter Olympics.

Women's figure skating. Suddenly out of nowhere, words barreled out of your mouth. "Oh, son, I wish you would have married an Asian girl, they're so beautiful."

My sister-in-law yelled immediately, *"Mom, God!"*

I waited for the fallout, or any response from my husband. Nil. Our daughters who were quite small, were sitting on the floor playing, and may have also heard the wish. I wasn't sure. I got up and went into the kitchen to process.

A gauntlet had been thrown.

I was not Asian, not even close. As white as white bread could be. I wasn't slender, graceful, or born with flawless ivory skin that glowed. I would never get there.

I had a decision to make, right then and there to go in, make a stink, fight you, defend myself in front of my daughters and blow up the house. Figuratively, of course.

Instead, I sat. I sat and thought about your life and how things might not have turned out the way you thought they would. You didn't have much. Few friends. A little money, enough to get by and to donate a few dollars each holiday to the girls' savings accounts that you set up. You were a good and loving grandmother to our daughters. Any gripe you had about me, might not be about me at all?

Maybe you weren't happy with yourself? Or maybe you just weren't smart enough to know that your statement in my house, in front of my family, *especially my daughters*, was inappropriate? That answer gave me the most peace, whether it was true or not. I could've taken it as a personal attack and wrecked our time together, or I could decide that you didn't know any better, and give you grace instead?

I took the high road that day, and every day after that as well. I wasn't going to argue, justify or try to prove myself worthy of your son anymore. That wasn't my job. My job was to raise my daughters along with their dad to be kind, caring, self-reliant people.

As long as you were around, I'd have some new large-print books to read by your bedside, a soft towel, regular photos of the kiddos and a comfy Christmas sweater you could count on.

Maybe just a little bit to help keep you out of my hair.

~

Snippets from Heaven, Me 2014

I *just watched some of* The Five People You Meet In Heaven. *I have to say I don't spend much time thinking about dying. I mostly think about living.*

People rarely, if ever, die on terms that satisfy everyone. Somewhere, someone is wishing somebody could stay longer. It's sad, really, to hold so tightly onto ones who go before us, for it is they who get the ultimate freedom from any suffering and uncertainty they carry. Somehow we believe that it is **here**, *on the earthly plane, that* **we are in our most needed place**, *while there are many who believe that* **the afterlife is where it's at**.

I can neither agree nor disagree with either angle. I think and hope that the place where one is at should be the very best place for us to be at any given moment. With that understanding, aren't we all always— in heaven?

Sometimes people hold on so tightly to their deceased members of their family and friends when they are gone, the dead spend much of their time looking back at us guiltily as if they shouldn't have left. They can't fully enjoy where they are because they are caught in the shackles of who they used to be to someone else. Caught in the grips of another's expectations.

People mourn differently.

I mourn sometimes for my grandmother, the regal, M.H. She taught me so much, and I loved her so much, but I knew she was ready to go.

The movie was beautiful. Confirmation that we are connected to the people around us, more intentional than we know. It is a reminder to look closely at those around you. They may have much to teach, and you may also share what you've learned.

If The Five People You Meet In Heaven *is true, we will get the answers to the questions that we have, right when we need them most.*

When our loved ones go, we need to let them go, peacefully, with well-wishes and love. It may just change everything for everyone.

~

Another Blow to My Health, 2015

I had been home, in between jobs and spending my days writing my stories. It felt like a gift. Usually, when I had the chance, words came easily and I could get into a flow. But this time, something was different. Words I had written thousands of times seemed wrong, or I couldn't spell them at all. I was wracking my brain endlessly and I wondered if maybe I was having early-onset dementia or something else was going on.

When I wrote the word "brang" as in "brought" and looked at it— **I knew something was terribly wrong.**

I stepped away from the computer and got quiet. "What is wrong with you?" I said out loud, finding a spot on the couch and plopping myself down in frustration. I had time to write but I couldn't. My brain wasn't working.

My mind raced with the possibilities. Maybe my thyroid meds were off- no they had just been checked, my dosage is fine. I'm not on my period, so I can't blame that either. What could be wrong with me? What is this?

I walked back to the computer and typed in Symptoms of Lyme disease, as something in my head told me to.

"short-term memory loss, difficulty with focus and concentration, brain fog."

I called the doctor's office and made an appointment. I had been in just the week before with a mysterious sore that wasn't healing and didn't pop like a regular zit on the side of my upper left leg. He had given me some cream for it, and it seemed to be helping but it hadn't totally gone away.

Sitting in his office he asked me what I was in for.

"I can't spell like I used to. I'm having trouble finding words when I write and when I talk."

The default answer to any woman after the age of thirty spouted from his mouth. "Well, you are getting to that age where you will have some cognitive decline, plus changes in your hormones play a part."

"No, it's not that. My meds are right, I feel good- it's my brain. It isn't *working right. Then I remembered back, about two weeks ago. I'd gone out to get the mail, and when I placed it on the counter, I saw that there was a bug on it. I glanced at it, then took the envelope outside and shook it off onto the front porch, not thinking anything really other than, it kind of looked like a tick. Over the next few days it was sunny out, so I spent some time reading on the front porch. Then I noticed that bump on my leg, which is still there, and now I can't spell words. Maybe I got bit by that tick. I'm telling you something is wrong with me. Will you please test me for Lyme disease?"*

"That is the most ridiculous thing I have ever heard. We don't really have Lyme disease here in this area, and you don't have that bullseye rash common for Lyme around your bump, so the only thing you really have is that you might have seen a tick on an envelope one day in the last couple of weeks? It's crazy. I'm totally sure you don't have it."

Not an amateur at this point of my life, for advocating for my own health, I challenged back, "Well, then test me. I hope I'm wrong."

"Fine, but we can't draw blood for that here. You will have to go over to the hospital for that test. I'll send over a request. I know you don't have it. It's a waste of time and money."

"I'll go right now." I said, determined.

I drove over to the hospital and gave the blood needed for the test. It would be two days before I had an answer.

Two days went by, and I heard nothing. After dinner I get a call. Oddly, it was my doctor, so I took the phone upstairs.

"You have it. I'm sorry I didn't believe you. There was a delay because the lab got the test wrong. They actually first tested your blood for Bordetella instead of Borrelia-the first one was the test for whooping cough. After I caught their mistake, they said they had enough of the sample to run the correct test and it was positive. We need to get you on antibiotics right now."

In the meantime I had done some homework myself. I wanted to be aggressive with this treatment so I wouldn't develop some of the chronic symptoms of Lyme. I did not have time or energy in my life for that kind of shit.

"I'm recommending two weeks on doxycycline, I can call in your prescription right away."

"I want to be on it for a month, I need to kick this."

"Okay, a month. I'm sorry I didn't listen to you. Your story was just so far-fetched."

"I know, super weird. I am so glad I remembered and put it together. Now I can get better."

A month on antibiotics and the next test showed I was clear. But I know it can hide in the body, and resurface when you least expect it, so I am always on alert. Mostly when I am not able to find the right words, or I have trouble spelling. I am happy I was paying attention enough for my intuition to prod me.

Again, I have learned to listen to what my body is telling me, to question myself and my providers when I have a hunch. Do my own research, not to my own detriment but to help me stay well. Doctors just don't have enough time to learn everything, listen for hours to their patients to put the pieces together. I didn't fault him for being cautious, or even somewhat judgmental— my story was unlikely.

But it is what I do- hold in my mind bits of most likely useless information until it is needed. Then it comes. Taking care of me.

Doctors care, but they can't know us in-and-out like we do. We have to help them learn to listen and fight for ourselves.

~

~3~

The Find Me book sat on a wine barrel end table in the corner window of the tasting room of the Escape Winery. The podium it once sat on had been moved to the conference room about a year ago, as it got better use there. The book, seemingly rarely picked up, sat with its pages tattered, the front cover bleached evermore in the sunlit windows.

Jeremy sat on the oversized leather sofa and picked up the book. He flipped through the pages and to the back to see the many signatures. Perhaps thousands now, his own towards the very front of the list. Somehow he thought it would have been taken from the winery by now, someone seeing themselves inside, written about by the still-anonymous author.

This book had resided at the Escape Winery for more than three years in his first visit before being sent to Jeremy's sister. She had kept it for about a year before giving it back to him when he was there for the wedding. For years it had been stuck with him. Yes, there was a good amount of traffic at the winery, *but was this the best place for it really*? What if the author wasn't in this part of the United States? Jeremy questioned, but something inside told him it wasn't time to let go. It was a feeling he just couldn't shake.

He and his manager Sky had built up the winery into one of the Willamette Valley's most sought after places to visit. A wonderful hybrid business of vintner of their own wines plus the international wine distributorship with his in-law's family in Italy. Hosting upwards of six weddings per year, each one had become an extravaganza.

Their biggest and his favorite—still was the enchanting Indian wedding complete with multiple home rentals, three days packed with ceremonies, massive amounts of food, and music and dancing. Sky had even coordinated for the groom to ride into the wedding ceremony on a beautiful white horse.

She had pulled it off as if it were nothing and ever since she kept dazzling him with her ability to help all of their clients feel special. They often said they felt honored in every way.

He placed the book in his lap, and looked proudly around the tasting room. Sky's touches were everywhere. The space, once a vacant, near util-itarian vessel of possibility, was alive with color and fragrance, not only of the great wines they had developed but the sweet smell of flowers and food always in season.

The wine glasses chosen by Sky were all engraved and stamped with the year. People loved the way the flutes felt in their hands so much, they often sold out of them. Wine clubs often held their meetings here, and their Signature Surprise wine baskets had a monthly subscribers list in the hundreds.

Jeremy had found the perfect person to work this business with, but he might have also found more. He had kept his feelings for Sky secret. At least he tried to. They hadn't ever been out on an actual "date," but spent time after-hours after closing to catch up and talk shop. They naturally spent a lot of time together, working side-by-side every day. Being with her was easy, and he loved having her around. He couldn't imagine ever letting her go, or worse yet, seeing her with someone else.

His life back at the community college felt far, far away. Memories of Natalia would sneak in now and then, but he found it was no longer a daily occurrence. It wasn't that he stopped loving her- he always would. He was just feeling in a space that there was room for someone else. *He wanted Sky*.

How would he tell her that he was in love with her? They hadn't talked about it; he was technically her boss after all. He was pretty sure he would be breaking all kinds of HR. regulations if he asked her out- not that his tiny company had set that all up yet.

He didn't know how she felt. She hadn't brought anyone around as her boyfriend, or talked about anyone in a special way. He couldn't believe that she wouldn't if there was someone. He and she were at the least very—good friends.

Finding himself playing with the spiral on the little book, he placed it back on the end table and got up to go outside. He'd have to tell her soon, before he lost his nerve, or before it was too late and she'd link up with someone else.

Jeremy grabbed his panama hat that hung waiting on the hook to the left of the door and walked out among his vineyards in the bright summer end sun. The leaves were just about to turn into their best colors. Grapes, all ready to be picked. These vines were strong, alive. He felt strong and alive, too. Yes, he would tell her.

As he walked, he imagined circumstances where he might bring the topic up. Sighing and heading back to the office, he turned to see Sky get into her car to go home that night. They each waved at the other per their usual

goodbye.
Someday, he hoped she would stay.

~

C.W.

Another mother figure in my journey. You made a huge impression on me in my early years. The mother of one of my best friends, I was always a little afraid of you with your great big personality, strong opinions and take-no-shit attitude.

My friend was the most capable and independent person I had known and I think I know how she got that way. Taking the bus downtown to get her allergy shots in the sixth grade seemed terrifying to me but my friend did it weekly, no questions asked. Sometimes I would go along but mostly I was scared to go into the big city like that.

Everything in your house was big: events, sheep dogs, Christmas trees. You were always doing big things. You had a California inspired clothing store for a while, a wildly successful restaurant with what is still one of my favorite recipes, and had the entire U.S. Ski Team over before all heading off to Sarajevo.

You gave me what I consider one of my biggest lessons. Your daughter had a birthday party up at the mountain. A day away skiing and a sleepover in a cabin. I don't know if you paid for all of our ski rentals and if you did, thank you, but the lesson came when we were grabbing our equipment to take to the slopes.

I was small and overwhelmed with the task. I hadn't done anything like this before and I didn't have a parent nearby to help me, so I asked you.

"Will you carry my skis for me?"

Your answer was succinct and there would be no negotiating.

"Carry your own gear."

It felt like a bigger message than you just wouldn't be helping me with my skis. This was a life lesson. To carry our own gear, our own stuff. No one was coming to save you.

I told you later what that had meant to me and you hardly remembered it, but you were touched. I remember I have told it to my

daughters in their lives as well.
   Carry your own gear.
   Will do. Thanks.

~

Escaping Yet Again, Me 2015

*A*t the sea again. There is so much more sky the closer you get to the ocean. It teases you slowly until the two perfect horizons meet.

Every two years or so, I leave to be by myself or to visit one of a few good friends who knew me before this marriage. They've known me for a long time, and have seen me through my worst times. They know I am unhappy, they feel it, but there is more to it this time.

Again, I find myself here. My place to exhale. I sit on my blanket with my toes in the cool sand. The grasses sway softly in the wind. The sun plays hide-and-seek with the clouds but I don't care. I have come to hear the ocean. Feel the soft sand hug my toes. Coming here makes me feel small, with my problems being even smaller. Today, I am taking care of myself for a change.

A lady walks past me and smiles. I smile back at her quickly then duck my eyes to remain private as she looks towards me again. I am not here to make friends. She walks with purpose towards the water, only swaying a bit to avoid the crashing waves hell-bent on wetting her pant cuffs. I imagine her, in dire straits walking right out into the ocean— like in the movies.

"Enough is enough," she thinks.

In reality, she has planned this day properly and brought a beanie to hold her hair, while mine ricochets from the sides of my face, smacking me in the eyes. With her further down the beach, I am finally hidden in my spot as the clouds part once again and the sun beams onto my face.

"Is that light for me, God?" I ask.

I snap a photo of myself then point the lens towards the sea. My face is tired from the day. From my life. I am tired of crying about it. I am so very tired of trying.

Challenges have been many in this marriage. Mr. In Between and I are in real trouble. Our differences seem to be stacking up like an impenetrable wall between us. We've tried counseling, but we haven't been able to come together in any way.

We are at odds with our global views, spiritual beliefs, physical needs and wants, our life goals, as well as the little stuff like what to have for dinner.

Mostly I just cave his way to keep the peace.

He often makes household decisions without me, as he feels he can, unilaterally being head of the household. His conservative political views override mine in the bigger sense, while at first we just joked about canceling each other out.

I see some liberal views percolating within his children with their care and inclusion of the people around them. They see all people as valuable. I hope they stay that way.

When I left for this weekend away, I asked him to write a list of what he felt he had to offer and what he wanted for our marriage, and said I would do the same.

I run my fingers through the sand and reach for my journal.

Last time I left a marriage it was because I couldn't grow with my partner anymore. He was fine and stable and even happy in his stuckness.

When Mr. Stability and I parted, there was a divorce settlement and child support to help me make it until I could get on my feet. Not this time. With the prenuptial agreement that I signed I would leave with almost nothing. It was as if I never existed in his life- no harm, no foul to him. But I would have nothing to show for my time and life energy spent there.

Nothing for my efforts and work in improving his home, for the money I had contributed. No safety net at all, and probably bigger than that, I would be walking away from my stepkids, too. I feel like they need me. Could I- should I- give up the rest of my life and any happiness I might find elsewhere to give those kids another lens to see the world through?

Mostly I am sad for what might have been. I thought I was marrying a great adventurer, one who wanted to see every corner of the world together, someone whom I would share my life and myself with. A partner in every way.

What should I do? While I am grateful to have this dilemma as a living, breathing person, I also didn't want to be contemplating divorce again. But here I am.

The clouds cover up the sun again as I start my list. In and out the rays beam. I am cold then warm- it feels a lot like my life: uncertain, mostly, with little control over it. Nothing I can truly count on. I only react and flex to what each day brings. Back to the list.

-What I have to offer:
1. I am loving

2. I am strong

3. *I am wicked smart*

4. *I am giving*

5. *I am a very good gift-giver*

6. *I am a good cook*

7. *People generally like me*

8. *I am funny*

9. *I like to learn*

10. *I like to try new things*

11. *I am a good friend*

12. *I am a hard worker (sometimes)*

13. *I have good ideas*

14. *I have great daughters*

15. *I am a good mom*

16. *I am kind*

17. *I know color and design*

18. *I am beautiful*

19. *I have pretty eyes*

20. *I get things done.*

21. ~~*I am cold.*~~ *(The clouds part and the sun floods over me again.) Now I'm not.*

-What I want in a relationship:
  1. *A soft place to fall*

  2. *Understanding*

3. *Affection*

4. *Sex*

5. *A friend*

6. *Someone to play with*

7. *To try new things with*

8. *Someone to adventure with*

9. *Someone who has my back, as I have his*

10. *A partner in crime in life*

11. *Someone to dream with*

12. *Who trusts me to parent*

13. *Someone who believes in me*

14. *Someone who sees me as a priority*

15. *Someone that knows me*

16. *Intimacy*

17. *To be honored*

18. *Someone who wants me to be wholly who I am*

19. *Love*

The rain comes and I walk back to my car. I crack the window so I can still hear the rolling waves. I kill time watching people before I must head back.
I don't want to go home.
A woman, nicely dressed, appears standing behind the hood of a medium sized SUV. I can only see the top of her. White scarf, tailored brown denim jacket. She walks out into the open to reveal crazy cheetah-patterned hammer-time pants.
I smile.

To be that free. Confident, spirited, so unapologetically herself.
Epic.
I am out of cell phone range. No one can get to me— even if they tried.
I drive home, realizing that I have spent years editing myself down to be the woman I thought he wanted. In this relationship—I have lost myself.

The notion takes me back to a class I took about men and women. The man who shared on stage something he experienced in regards to women.

"I've seen it so often. After getting into a relationship, the woman will just kind of fold herself in behind the man, rather than being her authentic self anymore. The previous 'she' was the person that made us fall in love with them in the first place. It makes me so sad when that happens. Be yourself. Don't let 'you' go."

And I remember that man saying it as clearly as if he were sitting in the car with me now. Yet I have allowed it to happen to myself anyway. My needs haven't been met possibly because I haven't felt important or valuable enough to share them or to fight for them. So much of me is missing in my own home. My hand-painted art is not hung up in our house because I have allowed it to be that way. I go to a church every week for him and because I am "supposed to." I cook what he and the kids like because I do not want to rock the boat.

It is all exhausting and I want off this roller coaster.

I arrived home to the lists I asked him to write and to go over mine with him. I had no anger left from our fight days before. This exercise was about being honest with each other. Getting to his truth and sharing mine.

We talked for a little while, then I showered and we went to our usual restaurant where he ordered the same thing, and chatted up the waiter. The two of them had their usual back- and- forth and I just smiled, like nothing was amiss. My usual M.O.

When we got home, he climbed the stairs for bed. I came up a few minutes later to find him on his phone with the cat on his lap. We started talking about sex.

"You changed," he said. Going further into detail about how my weight gain had made him turn away from me since we were married, and how "visual" he was. My body just wasn't working for him, but maybe he'd try.

He tried to get frisky with me, and I relented, begging what was left of myself to feel a closeness rather than the separation I felt more often than not. It was fast, unfeeling and he collapsed next to me, snoring just a few moments later.

And here I am, still.
An idiot who keeps wishing for more in life, but settles for the crumbs.

~

Do You Want It Right, or Right Now?, Me 2015

A *young couple came into my latest job. They had just bought a house and were seeking carpet that could be installed quickly before they moved in. Selections were limited in that category and the wife wandered off, looking for something better.*

The husband kept trying to wrangle her back over to the immediate selection and they quarreled.

Uncomfortable, I said "I'll give you some time to discuss."

She wandered off again, and he came up to me, lost.

"What should I do? We were supposed to have this done and now it will be weeks if she picks something else."

I don't know where it came from but the words flowed almost instantly, "Do you want it right, or do you want it right now? This decision is one of the first ones you are making in your home together. It might be best to have a space she's excited about and wait a little bit for it, rather than have her be sad every time she goes in that room."

My comment hit the mark. I didn't go into work that day to save someone's marriage. But maybe I did by happenstance.

I wish I could figure out how to save my own.

~

Remembering My Extraordinary Life Wish, Me 2015

*W*ondering if my books had touched people's lives at all, or if they ended up in the recycle bin with the waste paper as my first husband Mr. Stability had said.

That divorce. The idea of a bigger, more extraordinary life had pulled me out of that marriage. At the time I wrote the books, I wasn't ready to blow up my life yet. Things weren't bad enough to leave. So I gave the books the wings to fly that I wished I had.

Now, wishing for an extraordinary life seems to have dropped to pretty low on my priority list. The goal of survival and just getting by has raised its ugly head again in my life.

I spend my days working hard to try and get a job, to find my next money maker. I need to have a way to contribute to this household, or maybe even leave this place and start a new life on my own. I would be fully alone this time. My youngest has been living mostly with her dad over the last year. It is her senior year in high school. It's good, I mean, for her. I wouldn't want to be here either, if I had anywhere else to go. It really is a drag. Hubby doesn't even ask me about my days, figuring I would tell him that I found employment if it happened.

"You could work at (fill in the blank here, with random retail jobs that will make me want to kill myself for the lack of creative outlet), he says, as if to help. Maybe it made sense, but taking a job just above minimum wage wouldn't help me. I needed an income to pay for a full life- rent, food, insurance, clothing, everything.

Since the bankruptcy, my credit is also shit, so I have one credit card with an interest rate that should be illegal, and a bank that might let me have another card if I give them the money up front. Gee, thanks.

He hated his job, and he said "everyone else in the world does too," so I might as well join the masses of miserable people in the world who have their jobs suck the life out of them until they die, often right before they are set to retire.

I've had jobs. Lots of them. I can do many things, but the college degree box that all of the employment algorithms are using makes it so I can't even get past the front gate. I wish companies would look at the whole person, not the readout of where you were, when and for how long. It's tiring, frustrating, and makes me want to climb into a cave.

In order to have anything stick this time, I was going to have to be at least slightly interested in what the job was. Design, construction, marketing, invention. Some kind of creative bent to it, or it would be just another speed bump on my already lengthy stop and go resume.

When I wasn't sending resumes or having job interviews, I would go for a stroll, making sure to go by the rocky swale areas, in between the houses in the neighborhood. I'd veer off the sidewalk and pick a different pathway trekking down the rocks each time I went. Balancing on the stones of different sizes without falling, I'd imagine I was on a backcountry hike in the woods somewhere very far away from here. This exercise became the one and only self-mandated task of my day. Even though this rambling over the boulder-filled expanses got me no closer to employment, I needed it. Something for me.

I didn't care who saw me and it didn't matter. I needed that time to feel adventurous. It allowed the child in me to play, and feel untethered again if only for a little while.

Sometimes when you are unhappy, time passes more slowly. You feel that if you can just get to tomorrow, something might change for the better. But often, when you are living in misery, feeling misunderstood and hiding your truth, each day can feel like a year, too. Then it does become years. That is what happened to me.

I woke up and suddenly I've been married for nearly six years. My yearly attempts to leave hadn't moved me off this spot. Every single time I had suppressed the screaming banshee within me by convincing myself that this is what I deserved, or was where I needed to be. When you feel so low, that you can't do anything, and the world gives you more of that, you have no choice but to believe it, too.

That is where I am. I can't decipher up from down, right from left. I sit so stuck in my own choices in this catastrophe of a marriage. How will I ever feel confident about making a single decision ever again?

*I isolated myself, too. Or maybe I just feel alone as no one seems to call anymore. Maybe they are tired of listening to the complaining I've done for so long with no action to change it? They **know** I won't move off the position. Maybe— if they would check in, I would just lie, and say everything is fine because who really wants to hear about anyone else's bullshit dumb life choices* *anyway? They have their own problems.*

When you have found yourself so far away from who you are, beyond any distance you have covered before, the path back to yourself seems impossible.

If I was depressed I didn't have the usual symptoms. Not getting out of bed in the morning, crying for hours on end. I got up every day, at five in the morning and made his lunch for work, I handled the household. I did everything, because that is what I could do. It was the only way I could contribute, but often these tasks hold no value in the relationship. Only actual money would get me in the good graces with my husband, and maybe I just didn't want to be there anymore? In his good graces, or in this fucking house.

Mostly I felt lost and angry. Anger I would often point at him even though it should have been directed at myself for getting here. I have no one to blame except me.

This was my sentence for leaving my first husband, a kind and responsible man who was actually pretty good-natured with my hijinks, even though he wasn't willing to grow along with me.

In response I had picked the super unstable guy, the one I had to ditch completely in order to try to have any peace again.

Then I had picked this guy- my husband now, a pretty decent replica of the English man I'd seen in the movies. Dreaming of the man I saw on the screen, and the romantic characters that he played, neither of which were real. My imagination has clouded my judgment to the truth of our compatibility; that and my desperate financial and living situation at the time.

None of any of it matters anyway. It is what it is.

The extraordinary life I want is still out there, somewhere. I know it.

~

~3~

Jeremy sat at one of the front tables at the biggest wine event of the year. The Oregon Wine association's *Best of the Year* awards. His category was next. Pinot. His palms grew sweaty as the category was announced and the entrants were introduced. He waved as his winery was called. This was it. The realization of being acknowledged in something he never thought he would be able to do.

Escape Winery had become a great success. Partly due to his passion and perseverance, and partly because of the pairing he had made with Sky Meadows. She brought more hospitality experience, and the feeling of community that his winery needed. She looked at him and put her hand on his. She meant a lot to him. *The feeling was mutual.*

The winner was being announced.

"Pinot of the Year 2015 goes to Escape Winery with Vintner Jeremy Cate."

The audience exploded and as Jeremy rose to accept the award, he grabbed Sky's hand to go up on stage with him.

Together they climbed the stairs and stood side-by-side as he held up the award in thanks. A hand-blown wine glass cut in half was sunken artistically into a metallic glazed plaque. The winery's logo and name was frosted into the glass and the whole piece sparkled in the spotlight.

"I'd like to thank everyone so very much for this award. I dedicate this in gratitude to the three women who have made their most impactful mark on my life, helping me realize this dream: my late wife Natalia who introduced me to the love of wine; a mysterious woman who wrote a book that emboldened me to leave my golden handcuffs job as a college professor to chase this dream; and finally this amazing woman next to me- Sky, who with her genius, hard work and support made this win possible. I love you all. Thank you."

Sky stood there looking out over the audience with the lights almost blinding her. She smiled, blushing at the very idea that Jeremy loved her. She loved him, too, but it hadn't been said. *Maybe he loved her like a sister?*

She really hoped not as she was very much in love with him. They walked back to the table together hand in hand. She noticed that he hadn't let go.

After sitting and accepting congratulations from all their tablemates, Jeremy leaned over and whispered it again.

"I do love you."

"I love you, too." she said immediately, her cheeks warming a little.

"I mean, I *love* you, love you." He squeezed her hand as they sat there together, looking into her eyes without breaking the gaze. It was as if all the rest of the people had disappeared from the room.

This was the beginning of something else. They had worked side-by-side with each other for the last three years. Working to get here. The professional acknowledgement. The regional reputation. Their success. Now this.

The winery's calendar of events was always full. Sky had built up a huge list of businesses that would have their company meetings at the winery, as well as team building exercises, weddings and even a bar mitzvah.

The wine distribution side of the business had exploded with the addition of the "*Mother Country*" wines. Their own introductions of mixed reds blended with grapes from the Mother Country and some that Jeremy had chosen from his own hybridized grapes had been well received.

The business was running smoothly. Jeremy and Sky looked forward to what would come next.

~

You Can Heal Your Life, Me, 2015

As a way to get out and not spend a lot of money, as I wasn't making any, I would wander over to the neighborhood library. Often I would take the younger kids, letting them load up on videos for the weekends that they were with us, and getting some movies to watch myself.

It was a particularly rough time, with me looking for work and having spent the last year trying to build up my accounts in a commission-only sales rep capacity. I felt like a loser in every way one can when looking at their life in comparison to others.

*A title **You can Heal your Life** caught my attention. A video by Louise Hay, a well known self-help-plus advocate and author. I snuck it into my bag after checking it out to watch when I was alone. I was desperate for some soulful nourishment and begged it would somehow fix me.*

Finally alone, I watched the tape narrated by Louise and many of the gang from "The Secret" speaking directly to me in my living room. Pseudo friends long since left behind during the last few years of junk that I had been through.

An exercise she shared hit hard: one of the necessary first steps to healing one's life, she said, was to walk to a mirror and look into it.

Standing in front of the mirror, I winced. My face was puffy, my eyes were red from crying as I felt powerless to help myself. I'd do anything. Even this.

*"Look into your eyes and tell yourself, **'I love you.'** "*

I said it, then again. I didn't break eye contact, I didn't look away. Tears came hard. I hadn't loved myself in a long time. If I had I wouldn't be where I was. I wouldn't have allowed myself to get so far down on the list.

I said it again, I looked closer into my eyes. This wonderful body that made me a mother to my amazing daughters. This wonderful heart that I had that kept beating and loved others. This body that had taken such good care of me despite me abusing it for years with a bad diet, lack of exercise and not enough sleep.

"I love you." The more I said it the more it went in. I did love myself, I had just forgotten or hadn't put it together until now.

Loving myself was key to asking the world for what I wanted, to take up space again and to pursue my passions. To be true to myself. To get back to the "me" that my daughters knew and needed. I had to love myself first.

As people populated the house and the day went on, I held close— my little secret. A mission to remind myself that I was worth love, that I was somebody and I mattered. It would be how I would get stronger to leave. To be true to me.

I am in here, I thought, I just need to get to know myself again, learn what I am good at, and how to take care of myself.

~

Thinking about My Mom, Me 2015

With Mom living far away, I felt like I had lost my best friend. The one who knew me best. If I analyzed things more I would have noticed the similarities of her life with my own. She had asked my dad to leave after wanting a bigger life than the one they had together. She wasn't content with always staying home and watching TV as a lifestyle like he was, and she couldn't convince him to live any other way. He was a watcher, and she, well, she was a doer. My first marriage ended for a similar reason.

Our lives were different in that I had married a second time much earlier than she did. My husband had many of the same qualities as the man she had been in a long term relationship with that cost her seven long years of her life. That was the main difference- my man had married me, most likely because of his religious aspect. He had seemed fine with us shacking up and knocking boots together before his young daughter said something. I am sure my mother would have married that boyfriend if he would have asked.

Mom had also found religion in her late thirties or early forties as I have now tried. She found that part of herself thanks to a friend's recommendation and to help her feel a sense of community after we kids had left.

We each built a business, in similar ways, trying to make it work, sometimes at extreme financial costs to the family. She had declared bankruptcy not once but twice. Moving into very small quarters, even staying in a small cottage in someone's backyard to make ends meet for a few years. Each time she moved, she found her space getting smaller and smaller, until she became too comfortable in tight places- never asking for or feeling she deserved more.

Kind of how I am now. Making myself small to fit here, no matter the cost.

I wish I would have listened to her more, watched and actually learned the lessons that came to her, instead of continuing to make the same mistakes that she had myself.

I had spent so much time trying **not** to be my mother, or thinking I wasn't because I was a stay-at-home mom, or I had money for a while, and married *again, that I didn't realize the gift of who she actually was. I'd be incredibly lucky to be like her.*

Read this book, and this book, she'd say and each time I would reject her suggestion because I didn't have time or perhaps I felt I knew better. Where would I be if I had read all the books? If I'd read 'some' of the books that she had read, or been to 'half' of the places she had been, would I have felt the need to attempt my greatest adventure in secret?

I had cowardly sent my books out into the world, unaccompanied by my name or an easy way to find me again.

Why? Was I ashamed of my life? Or the people that I had met or learned from?

Was there value in having them know what they meant to me? Did I affect them too?

I may never know.

Maybe her life is as mixed up as mine, and the two of us are just spinning around each other, hoping that one of us will be flung out of the lack-filled vortex, finding success and maybe even happiness —at last?

Maybe I am here to break the pattern? So my own daughters do not fall into the same soul storm as I have, as my mother before me?

If that is my role to play in our family production, my becoming small in my own life will not get me beyond it. I cannot break the cycle from here. Something has to change.

Maybe, just maybe, if I can find my way to the truth, I will end up changing things for all of us?

And wouldn't that be extraordinary?

~

I Really, Really Tried, Me 2016

*S**peed train from my original thoughts back in my teens to now. Words in a diary.*

"Religion is a system that some people need —to tell them that there is a meaning to life without actually looking for it themselves."

I imagine having these words read by many will bring out the pitchforks with some people. Especially in this house I am living in.

I'm not trying to say that anyone who lives by and holds tight to the "word of God" is not okay. They obviously need something massive like that to tether themselves to to walk the world. If they get that feeling of security from it, then good.

Maybe for some, religion is more of a placeholder for purpose. Or becomes the main mission of one's life. As in Mother Theresa being put here to inspire and care for others. Maybe their current incarnation is to play a supportive role and bolster the lives of others rather than having some internal and urgent mission to achieve for themself?

It would be an interesting experiment. If one could remove all the metaphors, symbolism and guilt from the Bible, while updating the words into twenty-first century vocabulary, what would be the outcome? A two to three hundred page document on how to be a better person? Might it be one of the very first self-help books?

I just can't get behind the idea that EVERYONE must believe in that specific doctrine in order to be relevant, okay and a good person. That kind of thinking needs to go.

I have tried with this whole "Jesus is the way" thing. I really have. I have gone to many churches with friends, my mother, others and no single "house" seemed right to me.

At this point, I think I know what it is that keeps me from this way of thinking.

It boils down to— I believe in all of it. I believe that there is value for people who need that structure or support **and I believe that every single prophet was placed where they were placed at the exact time and place to profess and enlighten those around them using communication at the precise level of understanding that was possible for those people to understand.** *Perhaps we can advance as education, knowledge and understanding do as well.*

The people don't know much about how the world really works? Fill them with fanciful explanations that help them make good decisions until they do. Check.

A talking bush; a sea that parts; turning those who misbehave into pillars of salt. Let fear guide their moral systems so they behave if they lack the internal compasses themselves.

I believe that the teachings were supposed to inch us closer to loving and caring for one another and this beautiful planet we've been gifted to inhabit.

However, if we can compartmentalize these teachings and place them in relation to history and what scientifically was known at the time and we move forward into the progression of knowledge that we have achieved now, would religion even exist anymore? Maybe that is why we see the division, the controlling ones who shun and shame those different from themselves.

The other religions I have glanced at have similar messages like do unto others as you would have done unto you. Compassion and service to humanity; developing oneself to be a good person in unity with others and nature; and that we all come from one Source- a loving energy who is named all sorts of names but the message is still clear.

We are here to love each other. *It is that simple.*

In every text, in every year and dimension, **that is our sole purpose in life***.*

I wonder sometimes when I lie on the green, green grass and watch the white puffy clouds moving across the perfectly tinted blue sky while the immaculately spaced sun shines warmth onto my face: what if instead of fighting over which god is the best and most important one, we just allow for them all and appreciate whichever we choose?

It feels like there's enough room **for us all to believe and be who we truly are***...*

~

Soon to be Empty Nest, Me, 2016

My youngest and I drove together to pick up my oldest daughter for the big trip north to drop youngest off at school. The same college her sister had left two years ago, it felt a familiar drive.

Youngest and I had spent the last few months gathering up everything we could think of to make her new dorm room feel like home. Bargain hunting, picking up things as we saw them. Going to the garage sales in the area.

Everything that was chosen was a soft pink, baby blue or white. Shabby chic décor was her freshman style. Simple and sweet. Just like her. She was ready to go away. More ready than I wanted her to be. We picked up Sis and were off.

We almost missed the check-in time, hearing that they may give my youngest's room away if we didn't arrive on time. I'm not sure it was an actual possibility, given that it had already been paid for.

I let my two daughters out to run ahead and get checked in while I battled for a place to park. We met in the middle and started pulling items out of the car to take to her new dorm room.

Years previous, I had made the trip with the two of them again to take my older daughter to the same college. She was there for two years, then had a change of heart and came home to a college closer.

I secretly hoped the same would happen with my youngest daughter. Let her go off to college, be away enough to feel independent, then come back near mama, at least for a little while longer.

We set up her room, then her roommate came rushing in saying there was a dorm meeting in two minutes that they had to attend.

*Suddenly, we were rushed to say goodbye. I held her and the tears started welling up in my eyes. I wasn't ready. This couldn't be the way we say goodbye. I wanted to joke around some more, have both my daughters to myself for a little while longer. This couldn't be **"it"**.*

We started packing up our stuff, the tools we brought to hang her pictures, the items to set up her desk. Oldest and I stayed behind with the promise to shut the door when we left. We kept tinkering in the room, making tissue paper flowers and leaving other little surprises that my youngest would find in the days to come.

As quickly as she'd left, our new college student was back, and we were gifted a proper goodbye. She and her roommate were ready for nine months of unsupervised sleepovers. I hugged her tight, and Oldest and I left for home. I'd drop her off in the big city where she lived now before making the long trip home to an empty house.

It is such a strange feeling to leave your child somewhere. We are taught early on as mothers, not to leave your children anywhere. To keep them safe and under our wings. Then we teach them, the best that we can, how to walk this planet and care for themselves. How to make good decisions and stay safe. You hope that they allow the right people into their lives, and avoid the ones that are trouble. Although I have not lost a limb, I often think it might be a similar feeling to when you leave your child somewhere, and walk away.

After dropping my oldest off at her boyfriend's house, I headed back home. Four hours on the road, a big empty van, cavernous and echoey with no one to talk to.

Sitting in my thoughts, I ask myself, did I teach my kids everything I should have? Was my youngest equipped to be on her own? Will she succeed? Will she miss me at all?

The radio stations go in and out and I end up using the seek button all the way home. Traffic. All I want is to get home. Stop. Process, be in the familiar quiet again. I feel like I will just collapse into a pile of nothingness. As much as I want to get home, when I get there I will feel even more alone. In the quiet emptiness, stuck in a life I have not loved for a long time.

I pull into the garage, grab my bag, and put it down in the hallway near the washer and dryer. I sit on the couch and melt into it.

To be devastatingly sad at our time of goodbye would have taken away the excitement that my daughter felt to be there. To cry and weep and lose my shit would have come across that I wasn't happy for her. To act that way would have turned it around to be all about me.

My husband is away for a once-in-a-lifetime trip he has been planning for over a year. I couldn't break down and ask him to come home to comfort me. I need to suck it up. I am happy that my youngest is brave enough and ready to launch and make decisions that will affect her life and her future. I know where she is and I know that she is safe.

My oldest daughter is spending the summer with her boyfriend. In a city hours away, she has started turning what is a bachelor pad into a real-life home for the two of them. Money is tight for her so I bought her groceries and some sunflowers to brighten up the kitchen.

Sometimes I wish I could just wrap my kids in bubble wrap. Keep them safe and secure. Make all the decisions for them like I used to. But wait, maybe that's not a good idea based on current circumstances.

My husband called me from his trip and I broke down. I know this is the way it is supposed to go. Your kids should want to leave and seek their own fortunes and lives. It actually means I did a good enough job that they feel prepared to get out there and make their own way.

But honestly, right now I am just plain sad. Sad that time seemed to go so fast. Sad because this is just the start of them not being with me all the time. Sad that I didn't take more pictures, or keep better journals of how brilliant and funny and amazing they are. Sad in worrying that I might have missed something. But beyond proud of them just the same.

Happy for them both, off living their lives. I let the tears flow. And decide that now is a good time to start working on me and what I love again.

A whole weekend to myself, no pressures, and no expectations for the first time in a while. I have time on my hands, and complete privacy. It had been absolute years since I had this kind of time to myself. I wasn't sure if I knew what to do. Would I leave the house at all? Would I shower, feed myself, or do anything?

The absolute quiet I felt in my first divorce apartment juts back into my memory. Solo with big hairy thoughts. It can be a dangerous place for me. Quiet makes demands of the self. It asks questions, and pleads for answers towards living one's best life.

Even in my aloneness, I am never alone. Part of me is out in the world in the shape of my daughters, and their five secret traveling book sisters cross my mind, too.

Where are my little books? Are they close to me? Can I see them if I squint with these forty-five year old eyes of mine? The thing is, I have met so many more people that have touched or changed my life since I wrote them, since I sent them out, so many years ago.

It feels like I should start documenting an additional set of initials for a set of new set of books to capture my since-discovered people and <u>our</u> moments.

Ooh, maybe a new project. Five more books, filled with my latest initials, the people who have helped sculpt me after the first ones were sent. Send those out as well? Give myself a slightly better chance of seeing one of my traveling books again?

The idea rumbles through my head and maybe I will start drafting some thoughts while I am alone. But not today. Today, I need something to soothe me, a hug of something I could imagine in my future.

Brain droning time. A mellowing. I put on the TV and start numbly poking through the channels to quiet the words and worries zig-zagging through my head.

*The movie **Wild**, based on the book by Cheryl Strayed, appeared on the screen as an option. I had been wanting to watch it so badly. I had wanted to watch it with my daughters as I knew it was a lot about her relationship with her mother. My daughters were not around at the moment, and who knew when the next time would be.*

I grabbed a snack and put on my coziest pajamas and readied to watch it myself. It wasn't the type of movie my husband would watch, so this was the perfect chance.

A woman, a writer,- starts off on a journey to unravel the troublesome bits of herself after losing her mother, by walking the Pacific Crest trail on the west side of the United States. She's never done anything like this before, and she is determined to confront her demons and heal her life.

I sat mesmerized with the images on the screen, struck with her bravery. The vulnerable story, laden with some toxic traits she worked through, compartmentalizing her moments into something she can move beyond. I held onto every bit of that feeling, taking it all in as if I was there walking silently alongside her on the trail. I didn't dare cry as I didn't want to miss one second, one word, having my tears blur my vision of this heart-wrenching and freeing film and its arrival into my life at the most perfect moment.

I had kept my cool until one of the last scenes of the movie. Reece Witherspoon, playing Cheryl Strayed, is walking on the trail and she comes upon a lone llama up ahead of her. It is a foreign view and she is surprised. For me, it meant even more. Here on screen, my spirit animal.

I bawled then, my emotions falling out around me. The sadness of my daughters leaving maybe for the last time.

My daughters, who know I love llamas, had arranged to take me to a llama farm for my birthday last year. Their thoughtfulness, the way they made me feel special that day. They knew me. They knew that I was hopelessly depressed and unhappy in this marriage, and they felt unable to help me, but they could help me feel special on my birthday— that they could do.

I remembered back to a particularly gray soul-day. I had escaped my life for a few hours to return to my beloved old town to watch a friend host an old-fashioned variety show. Upon arrival I found out that two of her guests were locally famous therapy llamas, and I could get my picture taken with them. It was another pull back to the city I loved living in, even in what I had thought were my shittiest of circumstances. Partaking in a group hug with those two marvelous and fluffy creatures will be a moment I never forget.

This llama on the screen was to drive all of those messages home to me.

~Do not waste time.

~Do not delay in telling your loved ones that you love them.

~Do not waste your life by not living it.

~Be your best self.

~Take care of you.

~You can reimagine yourself anytime along the journey

I watched more movies like that over that weekend of Me. I ate what I wanted, cooking up many of my favorite meals including a special one I hadn't made in ages, as my husband is allergic to one of the ingredients. It is one of my grandmother's recipes. Her presence joined me as I feasted on her scrumptious chicken olé.

I call my mother and tell her I love her. I tell her that I'm sorry I haven't read all the books she always tells me to read, and I promise to read some, but she might have to condense the list down a bit. Down to a manageable size taking into account my current age and attention span. Something I can conquer with the low energy that I feel currently.

*I put on **Under the Tuscan Sun**, one of my favorite divorce movies and begin to prepare myself for the inevitable chasm I see coming towards me. After that, my other favorite divorce movie, a foreign flick- **Bread and Tulips**, about another wife who is so done with her lackluster life. It is curious that I bought actual copies of these movies— perhaps it is a sign.*

Something has got to change.

Soon. God Dammit.

~

P.F.

I often wondered why a single woman like you would want to live in a massive house at the end of a cul-de-sac in what was mostly a neighborhood full of young families. Nary a pet around, I was flummoxed how you picked this place. You must have made good money although I don't think I ever asked you what you did, nor did you offer it up in conversation.

For a few years you hinted at a boyfriend you had who lived far away but we never saw him, and then suddenly you didn't talk about him anymore.

My curious side pondered what you did rattling around in that big house all by yourself. Over the years I had kept you at arms length, even though I really wanted to befriend you as so many other people in the neighborhood had. You were well loved.

I remember our chats, with me not quite being able to place what it was about you that kept me at bay. I was stumped until one conversation I had about you with another neighbor. I was saying in frustration that I felt like you never listened and that you always had something more impressive to say once I was done talking.

"Yes, I know. She's a one upper. It gets to me too sometimes, but I think it's just her way of relating to us. She's not really doing it to be annoying, I'm sure. I don't think she even knows she does it. You can tell she is doing it when you hear a '*Well I- then yada yada,* she says whatever it is she wanted to share. "

Fascinating, I thought. I hadn't put it together until she said that, but then there it was, as clear as the nose on my face.

"Exactly! Wow, I am so glad you told me."

Knowing that about her helped me to better relate to her, or at least how to avoid topics and instances that might irritate me. She was in a place of- *trying her best to relate to us*, using any child-related story she had heard or by sharing a job-related anecdote because-she wanted to be included. She was trying to fit in. I get it!

Maybe she had wished that she would have had a family and it hadn't worked out, or whatever, but knowing that she wanted to connect gave me a new way of seeing her.

I wonder if she would have been made aware of her habit, if she could have tried to change somewhat and listen more? If she might have been able to learn and have more impactful relationships in the process?

I share this here because since hearing about this quirk, I sometimes catch myself doing the same thing. One upping someone inadvertently because I can wholly identify with their story, by telling a similar story directly after theirs.

I now know more often than not to stop myself and let whoever is sharing a story to have their moment in the sun. Learning to listen to those around you is a wildly important skill in showing love to others.

We are all just trying to figure it out.

~

Losing My Newly-found Creative Space, Me 2016

*I*t wasn't a real shocker when Mom decided to leave her husband. The rest of us saw it coming and wondered what had taken so long. That guy was a real piece of work.

I met him first as he threw questions at me left and right about sustainable wood options and construction at a small green-building seminar back when I had clout in the subject. He challenged me but I had an answer for each of his jabs and he grew some respect for me. 'Twas the following week that he stopped by the store for another volley of green-life conversation that he missed me and met Mom.

While I worked at my day job and juggled what was left of the business, he swooped in and fancied my mother, leaning in with a keen ear when she declared that she wanted to get married within the next year. Mom treated her proclamation as a challenge and I was in my own type of back- and-forth with my beau at the time, so she had time to go off and get to know him.

Yes, they had a lot of things in common, their passion for the planet being the mainstay. They were of comparable age. He had been married and divorced before but that is nothing even close to scandalous when you are in your mid-seventies in our society.

After I moved out, and the business was closed, Mom found some more projects on her own and they planned a trip together. She was whisked away to Tobago for a two week vacation through his timeshare property membership, and they both started to dream of what they could do together. My determined mom got her wish and my brother and I literally got a phone call after the fact.

"We got married. I hope you will be happy for us. I'm sorry you two weren't here, but we just did it. We will have a reception sometime soon."

It didn't surprise us that Mom did what she said she would do; we just wish it would have been someone else. But there wasn't anyone else in the running. It was a while before I figured out what we didn't like about her new husband, but as I was talking to another friend about my exchanges with *him, she pulled a Saturday Night Live video up on her phone and handed it to me.*

The character Penelope was always one-upping people in every way. She couldn't stand for anyone else to do anything. She had done it before, way better, way more, or she was the first to do it.

That's it! He was a total know it all, and a one-upper- always sharing something that he had done on top of whatever was said. It was super annoying and a total turn off.

My brother felt the same "ick" when he was around and, over time, it just meant less time with Mom. She felt the distance building between us all, but wasn't sure what to do about it. She had wanted this. Remarried for the first time since she was with my dad (they had split up when I was nine), she had to try.

They continued together, him finally becoming a supervisor on some of her construction projects. One time he and I got into a tussle. I was the expert at a flooring company brought in to see what could be done on a jobsite. They'd wanted the new floor to match the floor that had been installed two years prior.

I stated simply that there was no way to have them all match unless they started with all new flooring. He blew his top, saying that I was just working to make a sale, that I didn't care about the needs of the customer, etcetera and so on.

It was then that I declared him (in my head) a total asshole and moved further away from any time spent with him. Holidays were a drag as he would come over and pick stupid fights with my dad and poke needles of annoyance at the rest of us. He always seemed to come and blow up our powder room toilet, so much so that it had to be snaked to get it working again.

I am sure he must have had good qualities, too, but my brother and I couldn't find them. Even his kids were estranged from him. When Mom started telling us about his temper, that was when I got even more concerned, although she was convinced she could take care of herself. He would often pick a fight with her in the car about random stuff, and get himself so steamed when Mom defended herself verbally, he'd get out of the car and take the bus or walk home.

Okay — he proclaimed himself to be a Buddhist...

One evening over a birthday dinner for one of us, my mom and he announced that they had sold their house, bought a sailboat and would be leaving in a couple of months to sail around the world together. Shock.

What business did a seventy-four year old woman have in taking off into the wild-blue holy-shit for months on end, with potentially no communica-

tion most of the time? We were frankly terrified at the prospect.

*Her husband wanted to start by going south to make sure to go around the horn of Africa. That is literally the most pirated area in all the world. I tried to convince him to skip that part, but he shot back, and of course he knew much better than I, **as he always did**. I would try to convince Mom to be reasonable– they did not need to play with actual pirates.*

My brother and I made a side-wager of who would push the other one in first, letting them bob away forever in the crashing blue abyss. My bet was on Mom pushing him since she was a survivor, and way more coordinated.

They bought a boat down in California and packed up a U-Haul truck full of what they thought they could fit on the boat. They liquidated her much-loved furniture and emptied the house as much as they could. We supported her decision over our concerns. A lot fell to me and my brother, as they hadn't found homes for everything and didn't plan on coming back.

I was the good daughter and went to help with the last day of moving, telling her I was excited for her, and for them, and hoped it was all that they wanted it to be. I took the rest of their furniture and crammed it in my garage, selling it off piece by piece until it was gone.

When they were about to pull away from my house, I hugged her as if it might be the last time. This amazing woman who taught me all about life was moving away, not only out of the state for the first time in my life, but she could potentially be gone forever if things didn't turn out as planned.

I was scared but I also knew the importance and urgency of chasing a dream before it's too late.

One had to try.

If it wasn't now, it would be never. Another giant "what if" to wonder about forever and that is just a shitty thing to look back on. If anyone could at her age, she could. I just didn't know about the combination. Were they a good team? Or was this going to be the nightmare version of Gilligan's Island? Only time would tell.

They made it to the boat, but there were unforeseen repairs to make. He said he could do it because he believed he could and, again, knew everything. In the meantime, they filled the boat to the brim, boxes and books spilled over into their car and they started paying boat dock fees while things got fixed.

The engine didn't work, so the boat wasn't safe to be seaworthy. The engine was old and the manufacturer was in Norway so getting parts was a problem. It was over a year trying to get it fixed, much longer and more expensive than either of them thought.

Maybe it was our worry that kept them stuck in that marina. Maybe the Universe knew the open ocean wasn't the safest, best place to be in an often volatile relationship. Whatever the reason, the close quarters amplified the not so nice parts of her relationship and something had to change.

She wanted to continue the dream, but she wasn't happy sitting and waiting on the boat either. After about a year, she came and stayed with us for a couple of weeks. She needed a breather, to visit with friends and family and give him uninterrupted time to try to get the boat fixed as he said he would. She shared the hard stuff they were going through and the doubts she had about the whole thing with me.

She'd sold everything. There was very little left. She'd put everything into the dream and the relationship. Leaving would mean starting all over again. She went back, hoping the boat would be adventure-ready, but it was more waiting, and the money was gone so they had to anchor out in the middle of the bay to stay afloat.

Dinghy trips into the marina for groceries, no internet, only a small amount of electricity daily to run the needed lights and appliances, mixed with the non-stop togetherness with a man she didn't think she loved anymore was too damn much.

When she said she wanted to move back home to the area where my brother and I were, I was glad. I understood her wanting to leave the marriage. I was in the same boat, although I hadn't said it aloud to Mom.

A friend was down in the area and she drove Mom back home to us. Hubby and I were happy to have her come and stay, and I was happy to see her much more. I just didn't know that having her here would complicate my already tumultuous life even more.

How long could I keep up the charade? She'd see through every argument, excuse, explanation. I couldn't lie to her, or at least I couldn't get away with it. She knew me too well for that.

Mom moved in and decided to go back to school to learn website design. Her studies took over my office, the one place I had in the house to hang my artwork and work on my goals and dreams. I set it all aside once again and let her study in that space.

Months later, it was there that we had probably the biggest conversation of my life. The one that changed everything.

~

$$\sim 3 \sim$$

J eremy walked Sky out to her car after the awards event.

"I just don't want tonight to end," he said.

"Yeah, I know what you mean."

He reached for her then and she folded into his arms. They'd hugged before in excitement after getting a contract or a big sale on their wines, but this one felt different.

There was love here.

Neither of them knew how long they could stand here like this, but neither wanted to be the first to let go.

Sky sneezed. "It's your mohair," she laughed. "Every time you wear that sports jacket, I can feel it coming on."

Jeremy laughed awkwardly, "Why haven't you ever said anything?"

"I mean, it hasn't been a real problem, I can usually keep my distance."

Jeremy pulled the coat off and threw it into the open parking spot next to them.

"That was dramatic," she said, wondering what he would do next.

He pulled her back into his arms. She whispered into his shirt, "I mean it *was* a nice jacket."

Jeremy leaned in for a kiss. His lips were soft on hers. He hoped it would be the first of many.

"Do you know how amazing you are?" he asked when he pulled back to look into her eyes. I'm giving you the first dibs on having the trophy in your office; it's mostly because of you that we won."

"Well, I think we make quite the team."

The moon twinkled at the two of them, as if it knew that they would soon be lovers. Another hug, another kiss as the cars emptied out of the lot.

"So now what?" Sky asked. "We just won the biggest wine award in the valley! What's next for the Escape Winery?"

"Well, I think the owner and the general manager need to go on a date."

he chuckled. "Sky 'Rockstar' Meadows, would my lady care to accompany me out somewhere, sometime?"

"Yes, the lady would enjoy that very much."

"Great! Look at your calendar and let me know what day works for you."

"Well, how about tomorrow? We both took it off in case we were going to be drowning our losing selves in pinot noirs."

"Yes, that's right! Let's make a day of it. We could go into Portland and check out the art museum or take a drive out to the beach. They are about the same distance away. It'll be fun!"

"The beach sounds perfect. Yes, love it!" Sky exclaimed.

"Get our feet wet in the Pacific Ocean, build a sand castle or two?"

"Should I pack an overnight bag?" Sky asked shyly.

"*Would you like to*?" Jeremy's pulse quickened.

"Yes, I would. Very much. I've been in love with you for a while now; *I can't believe you haven't noticed.*"

Honesty flooded the air, causing them both to inhale.

"I guess I had my head in the sand, stuck in business mode. How could I not have noticed the most beautiful, smart, exciting, kind and talented woman standing right in front of me?"

"I'll forgive you this time, just don't let it happen again," she smirked.

"Never." he pulled her close again and kissed her on top of her head. Sky felt her once pronounced butterflies calm and settle in until Jeremy jerked in a full body chill.

"Yes, it's cold, especially without your jacket. You go. Should I meet you at the office and we can take off from there? Around nine?"

"No, I'd like to pick you up, like a proper date. Wear comfortable clothes and bring a bag if you still feel like it, but no pressure. We can take this as slow or as fast as you want, you are already my best friend. It feels like perhaps we have time traveled through some of the usual courtship steps, but that just might be me."

"I agree. G'night, old buddy." she snickered.

"Haha, very funny. Not so fast!"

Another kiss, this one with some hunger attached to it. There would be passion, and possibilities. A learning of each other and the two of them entwined. Not just at work, but in their personal spaces, too. It was the perfect time to start a new chapter—*together.*

Another sweet kiss on the head, *another squeeze.*

"Okay, I'm freezing. I'll see you tomorrow. Your address is in the personnel file. I'll be there at nine."

Sky climbed in her car and started the engine. He knocked on the roof of the car and waved before scurrying over to his jacket on the ground and tossing it into the trunk of his car. He rushed into his front seat, rubbing his hands all over his arms and legs to warm up.

Engine on, heater blasting, he watched as Sky pulled out onto the road for home.

Luckiest Man by the Wood Brothers played prominently on the radio, and Jeremy felt every single note of it.

***

Read Sky and Jeremy's First Date Afterstory as a bonus using the code in the back of the book

Trying to Understand, and Find Love with Him Again, Me 2016

I *have been trying lately to be very aware of people and where they come from. To have some empathy and understanding about why people are the way they are. Not to be used as an excuse to let them be horrible, but to try to understand how far they have to go sometimes in learning to unwind the traumas.*

Origin family dynamics can be caustic. These original relationships are the building blocks of who we are and how we present ourselves in our relationships and in the world. We can do the work to forgive and move on, but the tendrils of dysfunction run deep. It takes real effort, hard work and time to do it, whether one has family support or not. It is often the black sheep that heals but leaves those stuck in their shit behind.

It's miraculous how any of us get along, let alone fall in love, have babies or grow old together.

As a mother, I couldn't imagine abusing a child. With so many types of abuse to be done to someone, people tend to believe that such horrible things come from strangers (in the form of sexual assault or rape) with verbal or physical abuse mostly done within a marriage or relationship. But it's the nuclear family members that are the first to set the standard of how one can and should expect to be treated.

I remember one interview I had for a nanny position in my early twenties. It was a live-in situation with a single father and his two children. I cannot remember what happened to the mother. She might have been on drugs. He had full custody. My romantic mind went directly to the movie, **The Sound of Music***- maybe the dad would fall in love with me and we could live happily ever after. I imagined settling into his house in the country and raising the kids. Dumb— yes I know.*

Anyway,

We were getting along well and he said the job was mine if I wanted it, with one requirement.

"I believe in spanking the children, so you will need to be able to do that if

they misbehave."

Before having my own children, I hadn't really thought of what punishment would be used to help keep them in line. I had been spanked a few times in my childhood, but I couldn't remember what for, or if it changed my behavior as a result. I really couldn't imagine spanking someone else's child- ever. It seemed like a pretty personal thing to do.

I refused the job and I felt good about my decision, even though it meant not moving out of my dad's house which was part of the plan.

When I had my daughters, the topic came up again. A neighbor believed in spanking her kids, as she had been as a child. I was still finding my way as a mother, so I tried it on my oldest daughter when she misbehaved (again, I can't remember what the event was), but I smacked her little butt and she ran off crying to her room.

It wasn't until weeks later that I got a call from a friend whose child asked my daughter over to play with her daughter, and she said that my daughter had hit her daughter- that made me think about it.

I hit her, and then she went and hit her friend. *That wasn't something I wanted her to do, so I had to try something else. Again as is typical in my life, an issue presents and soon after the answer or path comes my way.*

I signed up for a session of a Love and Logic parenting class and the initial class blew my mind.

The first lesson was to help a child through a hard situation that they had brought on themselves. On the screen we see a man running down the concourse of an airport trying to make his flight. The doors close in front of him and he is upset. He ran over to the desk attendant in a frantic attempt to have the plane open back up for him. They then show two scenarios.

In the first scenario, the man comes to the attendant and is greeted with like behavior: she yells back at him, saying what an idiot he is to let that happen- "How could you be so stupid?"

This reaction is very out of place and would never happen in real life. But it hit home that yelling at a child in that way does little else than to make them go on the defensive if they are old enough to stick up for themselves or perhaps degrade their feelings of self or feelings of safety and care in the relationship. This really hit home for me.

In the second scene, the same incident happens. The man misses his flight and is enraged. This time the attendant greets the man and acknowledges his agitation. She empathizes with his plight, by saying, "Oh, yes sir, I see you missed your flight. You must feel pretty upset about that."

Still upset, he rattles off why he was late for the plane, but with her commiserative energy he feels heard and calms some. She then asks- "What would

you *like to do about it?"*

She didn't fix it for him, or take the responsibility off of him, she just "felt" for him in his situation and led him to moving ahead, thereby solidifying the lesson. (Perhaps he will leave for the airport earlier next time?)

In placing the act of solving the problem back on him, there is the opportunity for him to learn a lesson rather than being more disruptive. He is now accepting of the consequences of his behavior and actions. As a further lesson-inducing step, the attendant inquires if he would like to hear some solutions that other people have used like booking another flight, or find another way to get to his destination, etcetera.

I didn't want my children to feel attacked or feel lesser about themselves for making mistakes. Making mistakes is a natural part of life, and allowing our kids to make mistakes and deal with the consequences would give them the best understanding about life and how not to make those choices again.

Throughout the class, and after, I decided I wouldn't be spanking my daughters anymore. Sitting them on the stairs to think about what they had done was good enough to drive the lesson home. I saved yelling for when they were in danger, and they never again hit their friends. Thankfully, parents can learn new tricks, too.

Not everyone had access to that class, and that knowledge. With every generation more tools and studies come out on how to best parent a child. I tried to do just a little bit better than my parents did, figuring I would make mistakes that my children could fix when parenting their own kids. There is no perfect parent. We are all doing our best. Hopefully, that is, unless other things get in the way of that.

I know from many of the conversations with my husband that his mother used to beat him. She was very verbally abusive as well. He would often take the brunt of her anger by putting himself between her and his two brothers.

Once or twice, he said, his father took his mother away to get help. He called it a "hospital." With her drinking, and her temper, they never knew which mom they would be dealing with on any given day. When she was away, his father or his Ouma was in charge. When she was home, sometimes his father would take them on boys-only car trips to the nearby wildlife parks. A sanity trip as it were. He and his two brothers were pulled out of bed very early, and placed in the car by their father.

"We are giving your mama a break, my boy." His father whispered into his ear, as he lowered him into the car along with his brothers.

Days away, complete with a few loaves of his father's handmade bread and some cured meats, and cheeses, they drove to the game park, getting there just as the gates opened for the day.

Gas was rationed in his country at the time but with his father's business of working on cars, he had an extra stash of fuel that he hid in the trunk. With it they could stay in the park for days. The boys would sleep anxiously in a tent while their father slept outside on the ground to keep watch. They were exposed enough to hear the lions, but somehow they were never attacked. It was a much different upbringing than my own.

I think his dad took them all out for more than just a fun trip in the wilderness. It must have been his way to whisk them away from the hell that they sometimes suffered at home. A crazed mother. The abuse. Constantly being told to be quiet, or be still. Don't do that, don't do this. And the ever painful, "Why couldn't one of you be a girl?"

I bet it was also a respite for his father. He didn't have to listen to it, or be the one to strongarm the alcohol away, while simultaneously dodging a flying teapot or dish.

The boys had the lifeblood of the African Bush coursing through their veins, and my husband kept his love for it alive, way after he had left his country. He'd make the animal noises for us at the dinner table, as we all sat, the four children and us. It was a marvelous and romantic dream.

Africa was a place of fantasy for me, having grown up watching Mutual of Omaha's Wild Kingdom. He had lived it in real life. I was captivated as he told of seeing the carnage of an animal caught being fed upon by the hungry pride. The predators licking their blood-drenched chins before satisfyingly laying down for a nap.

He spoke of Hippopotamuses and how they were the most dangerous animals there. More dangerous than the lions themselves, they often attacked people who were trying to cool off from the hot summer sun. He'd make the guttural grunting noises that the hippos made, capturing the sound so perfectly. I loved the way he talked about his many adventures of being out in the Bush. About the one time as a soldier he was taking a leak in the desert when he bumped into the backside of an also very surprised African Wild Dog, and the two of them ran off in opposite directions out of fright.

We were from different places. Different worlds- it seemed, and as often as I would think my life was hard, I would hear about his, and wonder how in the world had he made it out with any sense of calm, hope or the ability to love?

The wars, and living through the falling of Apartheid. Meeting Nelson Mandela. He had a front seat view of all of it. So many of the events and circumstances of which I had no knowledge from my very narrow-minded and American-focused education.

He had fought in a war and kept his military shirt and hat. Being a mere boy at the time, the sheer shock of how small his uniform was when he showed me was matched by the cloth patch marked with his blood type that was hand-sewn onto his hat for the ease of medics if he were to be shot. He shared how he and his schoolmates were handed guns at thirteen to sit on the rooftop of his school in case terrorists tried to storm the building.

To him, the era under apartheid meant many of the blacks were decently taken care of. They had jobs and money, and the whites at the time believed the curfews were for their own protection. Not being able to be out late at night meant less brawls between them, or potential murders etcetera. To me it was colonialism, run rampant.

*It is a reminder that everyone comes from a different place and time, and often our worldviews are melded out of that specific period and location, cementing our perceived role and moral stance in it. That without further reflection, the place from which we come becomes the **right** viewpoint, and all other standpoints are **wrong**.*

We are all the variably broken products of our unique upbringing and current worldly circumstances. Even children brought up by the same parents in the same house can be so different.

It feels like a miracle that people who come from such different backgrounds can fall in love and make a successful life together. With an age difference you have even less in common, and if you add a geographical difference in there, there are even more dissimilar memories.

Two people who do not share the same taste in music, wholehearted beliefs or even geographical bearings, have a harder time. Was it any wonder he and I would have tension? Did we even have a chance?

It didn't matter that I knew his history. That his mother was abusive and yelled and screamed and even hit him and his brothers when she was on a brain or alcohol bender.

It was my inability to get what I needed when I asked for it, the support I craved that was turning me into a monster.

He would arrive home from work to find an angry wife instead of the adoring honey he had dreamed I would be. My strongest outbursts were mostly from shoving my feelings inside for so long, and never feeling like I could share my innermost thoughts with him- or even be my true self in his presence.

I had stopped dancing. We listened to his music in the car to my complete annoyance. I didn't feel safe to be myself.

What I never saw coming was the level of rage that would come out of me. The cutting and horrifying statements I would say to him, even in front of the kids which made me feel even more out of control. I tried the antidepressants again, the counselor, going to the gym to push off the energy I had built up. I needed for him to have some kind of reaction in order for me to feel alive and seen in the relationship at all. I hated myself once the words were out, which felt terrible, too.

I didn't want to be like his mother, although there must have been some comfort in it for him when I acted like that. It was what he knew.

With the many roles I had taken on in this household, the forever bitchy wife wasn't supposed to be one of them. Sometimes I would storm out of the house, and go for walks trying to recenter myself and think if what I had gotten so upset about was really worth it. I'd cry, or just go window shopping, or wander in nature, to help take my mind off the situation at home.

I was becoming his latest version of his mother. Knowing his circumstances didn't stop me from yelling and spearing him with words. He was eerily comfortable with it.

To him I was a little better in that I never hit him. I never got close. My response was leaving in a huff. This seemed to hit harder on him than any of the crazed screaming I would do. He didn't want to be abandoned. Since he really never knew if his mom would come back from her days away, maybe I wouldn't come back either.

I did what I could. Taking care of all the chores, shopping, doing all the laundry, making sure everyone was fed, and resenting every bit of it.

I'd listen as he'd complain about his job. Explaining that he was over-worked, tired, and felt stuck in his position. The company didn't hire enough people, made everyone work overtime, denied vacations, this and that. He never looked around for something else. Maybe he couldn't see his way out or maybe it was his never give up attitude- a trait he had inherited from his very German father?

Sometimes I'd really crack, and say I was leaving for good. After walking out of the house a few times, and skulking back, the threat became less attention-getting.

Anymore— he doesn't react and I feel like he wouldn't care if I did.

Sometimes he'd try a bit harder in our relationship, and then pull away again. The push-me- pull-you, part of our relationship was one of the most painful parts for me.

I felt alone in a house occupied by six people at times. I felt like I'd walk towards him to love him, and he would turn away and get into something else. A hobby, or meeting up with his friends. Even with the hardness and unhappiness I know somehow he felt at home with me, he'd never ask me to leave. He held tight to the commitment he made to me, in the eyes of God and himself.

But I don't want to die here. Or have him die from the ugly, malignant state of us.

~

~3~

Many had picked up the little traveling book, lying so teasingly around the tasting room. All read some, some read all. Each was affected in some way.

They took its appearance as a sign to step over an imagined threshold they dared not step over.

Zachary Gibbon told his next door neighbor Steve that he was in love with him. He had held it inside for years. Wishing, wanting to see exactly where they might go together, the book and the idea of leading an extraordinary life stuck in him and wouldn't let up. By the following week, he had walked over to Steve's house with a plate of bacon jam-slathered brownies, fully confessing his feelings. The two had been inseparable ever since.

Having recently turned forty, Amy Higgenbottom filed the paperwork to legally change her last name to "Star" in anticipation of her foray into show business. She signed up for those acting lessons she'd been watching in the community center catalog. Since childhood she had pretended to be on screen in her regular life. She was oddly surprised when those around her didn't follow her scripted lines, so she pictured them saying them in her head. She knew she was destined for stardom.

Deandre Cooper, long-time Portland resident and activist, decided to write his memoir of escaping the streets as a young teen in the nineties after being thrown out by his grandfather. Having spent his days at the Boys and Girls Club of America, he eventually attended college and graduated with a degree in social services. He continued volunteering with the Boys and Girls Club and had risen to become a talent manager specializing in connecting unhoused youth to the resources that would help them pursue their passions into careers in art, music and food.

Countless others had perused and read, signing their name into the exclusive club that was this book. The ones who were drawn to it were often in need of a respite from whatever else was going on, or sitting patiently for more of their party to arrive. Each thought the book might be the story of the winery, but found it to be much more. They were touched by the bravery of a stranger to share who they were and how their moments had piled up inside them enough to spill over.

It was a reminder that a hidden dream, *might be worth the risk to pursue.*

After reading the pages and the invite to the experiment itself, they *could not, would not be the same.*

If only the author knew what an impact her little social experiment was having, if only the ones who had read it so far would have connected with the stories in *that knowing way.* Knew her, who she was, where she was and how to get the book back to her.

Alas, they were but strangers viewing into another person's experience. Reading, taking it in, and realizing that they also had a story to tell, if only they opened their heart enough to feel it, and their mouth or took out a pen to share it.

~

The Hints Never Stop, so Why Can't I Listen, Me 2016

A door opens, but would I walk through? I sit where I have sat for the last five years. Trying to justify, daily, a life I do not feel like I belong in.

Being afraid, not knowing the future. When I think about all that has to line up in order for me to leave it feels like a mountain I will never summit. Get a good paying job, one that will take care of me, moving expenses, a place to live. It is all new territory. When Mom moved in, the mountain got taller. When I am at the end of my own fear and ready to launch, I look at the list again and slink back into the already known hell I sit in.

Recently, at work, I have been requested to share some of my contacts in an effort to drum up more business. They want to know any real estate agents who might share access to home photos we could use for a project.

I naturally think of E. Almost my sister, I have known her forever. Well, since she was ten and I was eleven, so a while. We have been through a lot together. Although we are very different, she has always been one I admire and love. Someone who seems to have the perfect life.

I called, telling her why I was calling. She said she could help.

"So, hey, how are you doing," I said. " I love the New Year's card you sent, the kids are really growing up."

I'd always pictured her life being so much better than mine. Today she shared a dull in the shine.

"This has been hard, and that has been hard, and we are both in counseling, to the tune of about two thousand dollars a month. So— how's your relationship?"

Nailed. Over the telephone line, she knew. She always knows.

I sat spouting the usual surfacey stuff, excusing aspect after aspect of my listless life, then said, "The other day we were fighting, and I started to look for apartments."

"Whoa. That's big. Well, I have a beautiful guest house that I was going

to advertise for fifteen hours per week of help for the kids. Maybe you want to come take a look this weekend."

An escape route. Hmm.

I went.

Taking care of kids again, I mean, it was in my wheelhouse. The little unit was nice and cozy and there was even the possibility of traveling with them all some. I mean, how could I say no?

But when I got yammering on about my stupid marriage, E held a finger up to her mouth, and said, "Come with me."

She led me through her beautiful house and into her office where she had a long bookcase on the back wall, loaded with books. A block of yellow books sat paramount and she pulled one from the group and plopped it into my hand.

You are a Badass by Jen Sincero. [1]

"Stop talking about it and do something."

She walked me to the door and I felt spanked and sent outside to play. But it was perfect and maybe just what I needed. The book sat on my shelf for a few months waiting for me to feel confident enough to read it. As if that should have been a prerequisite.

I said no to her proposal and continued to bullshit myself. Sometimes the teacher comes but the student is too damn tired.

~

---

1. I later read this masterpiece and continue to read once or twice a year as maintenance. Do it. ~h

~3~

I t was another big bash at the Escape Winery. A wedding between two of the most prominent real estate agents out of Portland. This union will set them up with tens of millions of dollars of commissions each year, and it could get them multiple houses around the world. Plus they were *nauseatingly crazy about each other*, which was super annoying to the husband's broker assistant, Avel.

As the newly married couple entered the dinner hall, Vanilla Ice's song, *Ice, Ice Baby,* played as the bride held up her left hand showcasing a massive diamond wedding ring to the crowd before dinner.

Avel Novikov found the whole display obnoxious and sat back, away from the crowd. The music played on. He had been the one to pick this venue. He found its rustic elegance to be in stark contrast to the tacky, over-the-top taste of the couple but, since they had left all the details to him, he chose as he pleased.

Avel had interviewed and hired the caterer and the florist for the wedding and reception too, while his counterpart Stephania had been in charge of the cake, the decorations and the music. The entire wedding had been planned by the two assistants, while the real estate moguls made all the money to pay for it.

Avel and Stephania were given no additional pay for the wedding planning work; it was explained that it was just another *"part of the training."* Given that they were still newbies to America and traditional American weddings, it had been a steep learning curve.

Avel glanced longingly at Stephania, who was softly but firmly giving orders to the servers about getting more bread to the tables, or refilling those wine glasses. She lightly flourished her arms across the empty bread baskets like Vanna White, pointing out the lack of assortment.

They had less than a year left on their visas here in the U.S. He would probably go home and she might figure out a way to stay here. Avel wondered if she would even marry someone if she had to, in order to stay.

Even in training as assistants they made decent money. Avel spent much of it on his wardrobe, feeling most comfortable in a suit in many shades beyond gray. Going to the barber every other week kept his hair short and tight. The options here for looking good were way beyond where he came from and he loved that aspect of American life. On the outside he looked like a beast of materialism, but on the inside he was still the simple, easily-satiated, nature loving boy who loved fishing and boats and sitting by the water for hours at a time.

They got a half a percent of each of the commissions as well as their regular "intern" salary. The work was tedious but they had come to understand the processes, even the lingo had become second nature to them.

Avel regularly sent money back to his Büyük anne back in Kazan. His grandmother raised him after his parents were killed in a car accident when he was five. As a quiet teen he would often ride his bike down to the yacht club to watch the boats glide over the river when it wasn't winter and frozen over. He wanted to be a ferryman. At eighteen he got his dream, and his days were spent going back and forth between Arakchino and Kazan. Back and forth, back and forth, sometimes spending his lunches at the Volga marina.

He loved steering the boat back into Arakchino and seeing the famed Temple of All Religions in his periphery observing the many religions celebrated in Kazan and beyond. A crescent for the Islam sector, Star of David for Judaism, a few crosses for several Christian beliefs. Hinduism, Buddhism and a number of other ancient faiths were displayed.

He had been inside the temple many times, to wander the rooms, always finding something new to look at as the building seemed *forever* under construction. The exterior colors and materials were placed so perfectly it was like God's own paintbrush touched down to celebrate all of his creation in one place. The architecture, complete with minuets, domes and spires was fanciful and inspiring to the heart. The idea that multiple religions and many types of people could live together in harmony was quite a vision.

Avel loved going with his grandmother as she often brought homemade gubadia to the physician and the people being helped at the Temple. Some battled alcoholism, and that was the reason his grandmother started taking pastries there, to show gratitude for their help in ridding her own husband of his terrible penchant just prior to his death from cirrhosis.

He had watched her make the gubadia pastries many times although he never attempted to make them himself, especially here in America. The process took many hours and there were many steps. She'd start with fresh milk, which she would cook until it started to separate just before curds formed, then that product was cooked down until the small grainy curds browned. Often his Büyük anne would be up until late in the night with this step.

In the early morning, she would roll out a dough with her mother's old rolling pin, until it was thin enough to cover a pie pan. The layer of dough was covered with the grainy, browned milk curds, then cooked white rice, golden raisins and prunes were added, before shavings of hard boiled egg were sprinkled on top. A smear of butter was the final ingredient before another layer of dough was added to the top and pinched to close the edge. Finally, a crumb topping made from flour and water, with a smear of oil to brown the crust was the last step before going into the oven to bake into a golden pie.

His Büyük anne often made some into smaller individual pies to be easier to share. Just thinking about the pastry goodness of back home made his mouth water. He hadn't had a gubadia in almost two years. Even with the rich Russian immigrant culture in the Pacific Northwest of America, he hadn't found this dear culinary specialty. He wasn't sure if it was because the Tatarian people were a smaller section in the Russian demographic, or if it was because of the process involved in making it, or how little yield it ended up being for that work.

Stephania had been waitressing at the time when Brandon and Layla came through Russia on the trip that eventually brought all four of them together. She was enamored with their beautiful clothing, and their personal promise of having the American dream. The visas were fairly easy to get given that Russia had no real estate selling education program at the time. Learning the profession might be a good asset for their futures once they went back.

According to the boss's original promises, he and Stephania should have been closer to being fully-accredited brokers by now. Brandon had led him to believe he would become a partner, with dual citizenship with their sponsorship and he would go back and forth to their satellite office in Kazan. But as their time here went by, Avel noticed the excuses as to why that couldn't happen were piling up.

Brandon and Layla had planned another trip to Russia, St. Petersburg, for their honeymoon. Avel couldn't help but wonder if they were looking for the next *Avel and Stephania* to join them for the two years after they were sent home.

Avel was contemplating a lot. In the beginning he saw this opportunity as a good one, something solid he could take back with him to build his own life, but as time went on, he and Stephania worked tirelessly and felt all of the pressures of working towards success but received none of the benefits that should have come with the massive windfall they saw their employers enjoying. They were the ones up at all hours going over the thousands of documents each week; they were the ones sitting in on open houses while Brandon and Layla did their part hosting hob knob events and traveling "for business".

If he had any takeaway from this time in his life, it was the tricks he'd learned to try and replicate their success in his mother country. He felt quite confident he could get in and move effortlessly within the circles of high influencers with big rubles.

But the longer he was here, the more he wished to be home.

Waking up in the quiet of the country house in Kazan. Viewing the inlet off the Volga River as he readied for the day. Strolling among the trees on the banks by the Arakchinskoye Highway, contemplating life and what it was all about for hours, in the misty calmness of the morning before his first ferry ride.

Avel looked around the room— no one would miss him if he left for a while; things seemed under control. The heavy drinking and dancing had begun. He grabbed the book sitting innocently to his right and tucked it into his coat jacket to sneak out of the tasting room. He wanted to sit in nature and read something— something that wasn't attached to work. Something to pull his mind away from where he was at the time, and how stuck he felt in this world so different from his own.

Avel half waved at Stephania who barely made eye contact, and dashed out the side door, and the echoing music hushed instantly as the door closed behind him. Large, majestic oak trees dotted the land, almost an invitation to come and sit for a spell. He walked to the farthest row of vines and up the hill back behind one of the container cottages on the property. He peeked inside the slider door and saw the place was empty, so he planted himself in an inviting Adirondack chair on the small deck outside.

Quiet, except for the wind that swayed the branches ever so slightly. Looking out over the valley, this felt more like home. The rich green hillside across the street from the winery entrance reminded Avel of sitting on the grassy knolls by the Kremlin having a picnic with his grandparents. That one time after his grandfather was sober, but before he died. When they had laughed and laughed and believed they would have many, many more days like that.

That day the three of them walked on the overlook sidewalk built atop the stone wall of the citadel, and his grandfather told him what he knew about the land out past the walls of the Kremlin—the world outside the country that they lived in.

Avel closed his eyes and tried to remember how his grandfather's voice sounded. The husky Russian's voice had a gentle intent (In Russian) *~Everyone must seek their own future, to be able to understand and appreciate their past.*

Grandfather had stood behind Avel and reminded him how their people had rebuilt the city centuries ago, never losing hope that it could be done.

(In Russian) *~It was the people of the city's commitment to honoring the differences between all of the people instead of pitting one faith against each other that got us through.*

Avel breathed in the fresh cool air, and let go of the braggy atmosphere of the wedding. He imagined walking through the tunnel into the Kazan Kremlin fortress compound. Sidewalks of beautifully laid modern cobblestones in wavy curves, led to museums, restaurants, and art galleries. Street vendors offered souvenirs and food, while musicians filled the air with all types of music.

He hadn't realized what he had back home. Kazan was a peaceful place filled with all types of people and beliefs. There was a welcoming spirit where even the non-believers were invited into the beautiful Kul Sharif Mosque. Named for the Tartar leader who tried to save the Kazan people from Ivan the Terrible in the 16th century, the mosque's requirement was for guests to cover their knees and shoulders for both men and women. An additional condition was that women had to cover their heads with a scarf, thereby honoring the beliefs inside. The domes were painted a rich turquoise, the predominant color of Islam.

Avel had been inside the mosque a few times. He was forever fascinated with the detail and artfulness— similar in grandeur to the Annunciation Cathedral on the other side of the complex, which also commanded his attention.

The rebuilding of Kazan had taken place after Ivan the Terrible's reign. Each of the buildings had such an incredible pull of not only history but architectural beauty. The buildings he had seen in the United States lacked the depth of emotion he felt back home.

He opened the book in an effort to halt his bout of homesickness. He read quietly, pausing between each excerpt to ground himself in the now. He read on as the sun in the sky began to dip lower.

Avel was touched by this author's effort to make her life bigger by sharing her story with others. He wondered who she was and where she was, and whether she had been presented with any of her books yet. He glanced at the many signatures in the back, all witnesses to her life on the pages.

One particular passage was more alarming than the rest.

~

J.

I have left off your last initial in as much as I cannot remember your last name, nor would I want to invite your presence back into my life. I am not sure how we found each other to date back then, but I was young and impressionable and looking for answers to the forever sought question of *"what is the meaning of life."*

We went out a few times, sitting in parks mostly with you speaking new and interesting ideas all over me. Reading aloud, sharing the words and ideas from your current obsession, the wisdom of Richard Bach. In my own life I went on to read and love many of his tomes and still pick them up now and then to refresh and mull over the concepts.

As the son of a dairy farmer, you shared with me how milk is produced on the scale needed to keep us all loaded up with dairy products— I was saddened to hear that the cows are kept constantly pregnant while their babies are whisked away from them. Any milk produced will feed us rather than their babies. I also learned that a bull may attack if a menstruating woman wanders into their field. Random knowledge to carry around but it sticks.

I developed a bit of a crush on you and we eventually shared one steamy night at your house, way out in the country. It was a rustic cowhand's type dwelling on the edge of your family's property, near about a hundred miles from my home. I arrived and left again in the dark of night- winding my way through the country roads, long before cell phones had been invented. Not one of my brightest decisions, when I think back.

You telephoned me a few days later and shared that you couldn't see me again. Your ex-girlfriend had recently shown up at your door saying that she was pregnant with your child. You said you figured you'd have to marry her now, or at least you felt pressured enough to do so. I listened with empathy and understanding.

"But there is another way, " you said, scheming. "Have you seen the old movie, *Strangers on a Train,* from the 1950's?"

"No," I answered.

You went on to tell me about the film where two strangers meet randomly on a train ride. One of the men was thinking of a way to have his father killed so he could live a freestyle life with his old man's money. He hadn't offed him himself because that would surely be a motive in the eyes of the authorities. He'd spent years thinking of a perfect way to get away with the murder. The man shared his final idea with the stranger next to him- a recently jilted husband. He implored the stranger to consider taking part in a shared plot of them murdering each other's tormenter.

From the movie, you spoke the haunting words. *"We don't know each other, you see. We are two strangers, but we both have someone we want to get rid of. No one would put it together, there would be absolutely no way to tie either of us to each other's crime- it just makes sense. Get it? We swap murders. Criss Cross."* As you summarized the lines from the movie, *I felt your hidden agenda—* that if I murdered your ex, and freed you— you would murder someone *for me* in exchange.

At the time, I was only twenty years old and more than completely freaked out by the seriousness of what you proposed.

"I don't have anyone I want to murder and I could never murder anyone- ever. You better not do anything like that. God, *she is having your baby.*"

"I'm just kidding," you said, but I knew you were lying. *"But if I'm not kidding and you tell anyone what I just said, I will kill you and your family. I know where you live."*

This didn't feel like a joke, or maybe you were just testing me to see exactly how far I would go to be with you. You seemed *dead* serious. My body stiffened on the other end of the line as you waited for an answer.

"If I hear of anyone being killed in that area, someone who's pregnant in that town of yours, I'm totally going to the cops."

You hung up.

I checked your newspaper headlines daily for about a year and never saw anything close to what you had talked about.

Young, naivete I suppose. Thinking back now- *I should have gone to the cops.*

Not telling anyone about this until this very moment, I guess I had been fully afraid of you.

Sometimes I lay in bed horrified that we had slept together. With your cheap, cheesy red-colored condom that had broken inside me during our only episode, *I could have been your next victim just as easily.*

A late night drive out to your creepy, isolated house. You might have killed me and buried me in a field protected by a bull and no one would have ever found out where I was. Thankfully I was safe and never saw or heard from you again.

Maybe you found someone else to do the deed for you?

A stranger to play *Criss Cross*?

~

Again Seeking Answers at the Sea, Me 2017

*A*t the coast again visiting a friend. I seem to be running away a lot. I'm making it okay.

Like a charcoal drawing of black and white, it is where the two shades rub together that is probably the messy truth.

Our life wasn't all bad, Mr. In Between was more than kind and sweet at times, loving me the best way he knew how. We were so connected in the beginning and I had felt a wonderful love in his embrace.

He looked after me when things blew up and gave me and my daughters a place to stay, a cushion to land on. They would have been safe to stay with their father forever, but his generosity kept them near me. For that, I will always be grateful.

I think he loved me for me back then, or maybe he was just seeing the things in me that he wanted to see? Maybe he was fitting me into his life so he didn't have to be alone? I think we both changed in our seven years together, with me, maybe changing the most.

I take full responsibility for not staying the woman he married. He would have made it work regardless but I can't do it anymore. I need to leave.

When I shut the business and lost my home, he was there. I tucked my broken body into his arms at his invitation and took a breath. It had been hell. I had tried so hard to keep it together, to just keep going.

In this marriage, I became. I became the doting church wife cooking meals everyone would eat, even if they weren't healthy or pleasant to me. I let go of many of the things I loved. I didn't do art, I didn't write. I didn't even journal, which has been a lifelong habit of mine.

I didn't take care of myself, as I was always doing or looking out for someone else.

I think I could have actually written down the hundreds of preferences that I had to bob and weave around daily and, if I did, I would have been shocked to see its length. I couldn't do anything that was naturally me, I always had *to change something or do it his way. Or so I felt.*

There were things like keeping his underwear out of the dryer when I washed them, and buttering the bread of his sandwiches before the meat went on. All manageable things if told in the singular as not a big deal, but when you stack them all up, my whole life felt like walking through a sea of eggshells in the darkened night after being told to keep quiet at gunpoint.

To make it easier, I morphed myself to fit the situation, whatever it was.

The kids saw us fight, and I'm sorry about that, but maybe they needed to. So our ending would not be as jarring, surprising—as I remembered feeling when my parents split. Maybe they'd accept it, almost want it?

There were those times when I would say "Enough," and announce at the dinner table that I wanted a divorce. I think it happened twice, or maybe three times.

As much as I can't say in full fairness that it was all him and that's why it ended, I won't say it was just me either. It was just our combination that wasn't good.

His mother yelled and beat him as a child and he grew up with a loving but enabling father who was dutifully bound to his wife as well as looking after his mother-in-law as she aged.

When Mr. In Between was given the same opportunity to take my mother in after she left her husband, he did it without question. He can be protective, honorable, and kind hearted.

Just a few of the loving parts about him. And he has many friends.

In our marriage he has watched me struggle to find a good paying job. Really fight to find my place at work somewhere. He held us up.

This wasn't something that was sustainable for a lifetime, I'm sure. To live outside your authentic self is painful, depressing and chronically heart crushing. One always goes back to what one is. With constant suppression the inner spirit stops making suggestions.

Yet even then, one can bring oneself forth again, but it takes time, energy, forgiveness and love. Of ourselves, that is.

I've had to do it a few times as the doubt in me makes me wither when it comes to relationships. This is nothing new. Only another time.

I told him that I am leaving- that I cannot do this anymore. He told his daughter who lives with us the same night.

She cried, and I cried. There is hurt all around and I am sorry for that. Her brother may know now, too, I'm not sure. He lives with his mom.

My safety-seeking side tells me that I should just take it all back, and deal with this life. Skip my own happiness and cave in to attend to everyone else's needs, sign up to be some sort of devoted martyr in my own head. It's been my default for many years now. Not just with him.

No, not this time.

Everyone else will have to adjust to my need, this change. My mom will have to move again. Or I will have to find a new place for us both.

She might become my whole responsibility. I am scared, as I have never really fully taken care of myself ever, without an alimony check and child support.

And now there will be two of us.

Oddly, he is suddenly trying. Being more affectionate than he has to me in years in hopes that I will change my mind. Keep the status quo going a little bit longer.

It pisses me off. Last night he tried to rest his hand on my crotch while we were watching TV as if that was a normal resting place for his hand. And if I were to have responded, he would have taken it to mean that everything is fine and we are back to moving forward as usual.

I really need to get some news about a job.

Currently I am floating, adrift in a sea of uncertainty. With no wind in the forecast for my sails.

~

~3~

Avel heard a commotion and saw some wedding guests start to filter out into the vineyards, two staggering with their alcohol consumption. One couple was fighting, having an elevated exchange about one of them looking too long at someone else at the party. Another twosome snuck off to be romantic, the mission was obvious with their holding hands, and kissing and grabbing each other while running off deeper into the fields. *People were so stupid on alcohol.* He'd never be like that.

Avel hadn't drunk alcohol before, after years of watching his grandfather humiliate himself, over and over while he was growing up. Losing his temper at his wife, and sometimes soiling himself on the couch, there wasn't a huge draw. He would choose a different path than his grandfather, even though he did love him.

Still shaken by the J. entry in the book, he got up and tucked the book back into his jacket to smuggle it back inside the building. But not like it was.

He didn't want anyone else to stumble onto the criss-cross idea, not on his watch. If he wasn't able to make a big impact in the real estate market here in the states, the least he could do was to make America a little bit better of a place.

Walking into the men's bathroom, he quietly tore the pages describing the incident of the murder trade out of the book, wadding the excerpt up and tossing it into the toilet.

He flushed. That is where that man belonged, his idea, his evil intent. Not to be remembered and read about, not to be mimicked.

From the act, some torn paper edgings landed on the floor of the bathroom stall. He didn't feel the need to pick them up since there weren't any words on them. His work was done. He tucked the book back inside his jacket and went out to the tasting room to return it to its place.

Feeling satisfied with his good deed, he joined in on the last bit of fun before the cleanup. Even amongst the rich, snobby people here, there were some really good people here, too. This party shouldn't become his final judgment of the U.S.

Some of these people had their priorities in the right place, while others were hoarders, sucked in with the idea of more, more, more.

He watched Stephania mill around, schmoozing with the last guests before checking one last time on the limo arrival to whisk the newly marrieds off to their honeymoon.

Stephania was beautiful, her Tartarian allure was still visible even with her now layered, processed-color hair and caked-on makeup. Avel saw beneath the veil of her American display, back to the girl he had traveled from Russia with, the two of them sharing a possibility of the Great American dream.

In their scant stolen moments between deals, he had hoped to get to know her more, but that time never seemed to arrive. Living in the same apartment building they passed the halls with a polite hello rather than spending any real time together. Their employers kept them busy and on call. Once back in their respective homes, they reveled in any alone time either of them had or passed out from daily duties.

Maybe she would figure it all out, too, or maybe she hadn't had the same upbringing as he had. The same values that he had learned from his grandmother over a cup of coffee and buckwheat porridge.

He hadn't asked her what she thought of this place. Perhaps she was also biding time before going back home, learning as much as she could to give herself the full education that she came here for. They would both be leaving with enough money to start their own businesses in whatever they chose to do.

With the bosses gone they would have more work but also more time together just the two of them. Maybe he should ask her what her plans were after their time in the states was over. Maybe they could build something together, with their shared skills. He watched her rush around, she was in her element. Yes, they would have a conversation about things, but only she knew what direction she wanted to head next.

As he stacked chairs, Avel started imagining his first walk back in the woods near his house. The answers of what he might do long term could come then.

He walked over and stood beside Stephania as the happy couple jumped into the limo.

Waving goodbye to the couple, Avel felt Stephania's hand reach for his; there was a slight shock. Then he spoke in Russian.

"You did a great job, this party was such a success because of you." He squeezed her hand. *"How do you feel?"*

"I'm tired, I am glad Layla and Brandon got us rooms here, *I hope I can sleep.*"

"I hope so, too. It will be nice to wake up and see the sun coming up over the vineyards. I will walk you to your cottage. Mine is next door, and it's getting really dark."

They walked together, exhausted from the day, neither realizing they were still holding hands. Stephania opened her door and lunged at Avel, pressing her lips to his. He felt another spark. She pulled away, almost embarrassed at her behavior.

Avel stood back and smiled, looking at her as he stood in the doorway, a halo of light from the cabin interior shining around her.

"Our time here in America is almost done. I'm so scared of what is coming next. What are *you* going to do?" she asked.

" Da, I'm trying to figure it out. I feel like I have learned so much, but this place doesn't feel like home to me. I cannot see myself staying here, even if we *could* get a new visa. I've been thinking all day about home and all the beauty and the people and food there. It is so different from the forced and fake opulence we have been around since we got here. Maybe it's not like that everywhere, but I miss my forest, and walking along the Volga River. Standing at the edge while it freezes, nothing like that happens here. I miss my Büyük anne most of all, and her yummy gubadia cakes. I really want to go home. I don't fit in here."

Stephania pulled Avel inside her little living room and they plopped together onto the couch. They had been working side-by-side for nearly two years, but had never had a moment alone to talk about *real stuff*. They were always getting pulled into a deal or a drama.

"You really fooled me, I thought you liked it here, and would work to stay. Maybe you are a good actor? When we were in Kazan, I was on my way to be in the Bolshoi Ballet, but I broke my ankle when I was eighteen, I could never dance again. Waitressing was my only way to help give money to my mother and sister, until this opportunity to learn about American real estate came. I have been sending money home, and my sister is now in Kazan State Medical University. She's going to be a nurse. I don't have to worry so much about her, but I need to keep making money to help my mother. I don't want to stay here, but going back will mean starting over, finding something else."

"We could do something together?" he teased, looking into her eyes. (In Russian) " *I think we make a great team.*"

"Oh, Avel, yes, we do! We practically do everything for them— those phonies. We are really the ones selling the houses, we can do it back home.

Open an office, keep in touch with the people here, use it to our advantage."

"Yes, let's talk about it more, over breakfast in town. I saw there is a cute little Russian cafe there, maybe they have blini?"

Stephania's eyes lit up.

"Yes!" She threw her arms around him again and planted an unexpected kiss that left both of them a little breathless.

"Okay, I will see you tomorrow." Avel got up to leave and she walked him to the door.

This time together felt nice. No pressure to decide everything now, no expectations of sleeping together. He liked her— maybe even more than that, and wondered where this new partnership could go.

He kissed both of her cheeks and she closed the door.

The two of them would be handling everything: the phone calls, listing updates and inspection scheduling until the newlyweds returned. They had a few more months in the country, and would take that time to learn as much as they possibly could. Gleaning everything they could about owning and running a real estate business, but they would put it all together in a place where they felt at home.

Avel walked back to his cottage a little bit further down the hill. He looked up to Stephania's as her light turned off. He was wide awake, but dreaming.

They would sell real estate, but he might also write a book about the people he met here? Maybe in the same anonymous way as the little blue book he'd found at the winery.

Wouldn't that make for an interesting tale to share with his Büyük anne? Sharing some of the lessons he learned from his time here, while including some of the stories from the anonymous author's book as well. He would try to remember to share them with her, all except that one request of an innocent young woman, *asked by Satan himself.*

~

A Video on Instagram Changed Everything, Me 2017

I *was struggling again in a job I had taken to contribute appropriately to the household. I was a year in and had turned what had been a full-time outside sales rep position into more of the marketing position that I hoped would feed my soul and showcase my talents. My boss was pretty fine with the transition as I had taken up the gap in things that were not being handled in order for the company to grow.*

She was a tiger lady in the sales space and wanted nothing more but to go after larger commercial projects and pilfer the contracts away from others. I would never be as good as she was at that.

The business and the product itself did not align with my personal values. As a former green-business owner, my love and respect for sustainability and earth-conscious options would never be met in this position. The product we peddled was mass-produced in China under questionable environmental and labor standards. If we sold more, we'd be making the earth sicker and potentially harming those working in its manufacture. To say the least, the whole thing stuck in my craw.

Another resource at just the right time came in the form of Gary Vaynerchuk, the wonderful and no bullshit motivator/soul supporter of millions. I saw him pop up on my feed as I battled with a new way to spin our (in my opinion) reckless product for the betterment of the company's bottom line.

I was <u>literally</u> standing in the hallway at the regional distributor waiting to go into a business meeting held to determine if we wanted to step into a new arena of business when he popped onto my screen.

"Die on your own sword, not someone else's."

It was as if he and I were standing in that hallway together and he was fully sick of me playing it safe. I was living outside my integrity in more ways than one. In business and at home.

After the meeting I went and sat in my car. It was a blisteringly hot day and the rock chip crack in my windshield had exploded across to completely skewer my view. The glint from the sun shot into my eyes as I tried to watch his whole video in my car before driving home to my beyond miserable marriage.

"*Please die on your own sword,* not somebody else's. If you're gonna lose, it's much more fun to lose based on what you thought. Do you know how many of you are gonna lose on somebody else's thesis? It's gonna kill at you, it's gonna eat at you, it's going to be the worst fucking feeling, so please fuckin' pause this video right now and ask yourself, *am I doing my shit because of me?* Then you're good, whether you're winning or losing. *Or am I doing it because somebody else is telling me it's the right way?* Or I'm subconsciously pandering to please somebody or something because of the short term stability? Figure that the fuck out. "

Why do we kill ourselves for someone else's dream or goal when we should be fostering and growing our own?

It's amazing how the most appropriate blip comes across our path at just the right time. It has happened to me so many times I can't keep count. Every time I begged for an answer, it came in the most perfect package for me to receive the download.

I had turned my back on my values with this job. Was it really an even trade? Regular money and imagined security in exchange for giving up my heartfelt beliefs?

When I got home I drafted my resignation. I quit that soul-sucking job and free fell again into the unknown. Gary Vee's plea hit my personal life as well.

It was the beginning of me getting real clear of who I was and who I wasn't and never could be. It was the beginning of me fighting for myself. Of making some damn plans.

~

*H*ad another talk with Mr. In Between. I told him that I wasn't happy here. That we weren't a good match. He cried this time, like he got it, understanding that eventually I would go.

He said he would never marry again.

That is his choice. Like his declaration would sway me into staying out of pity. Guilt? Is he thinking it will stop me from leaving? To know that he would choose to be alone, as a damnation hoping to show that I will have ruined his life from here on out? I don't get it. It didn't phase me.

To stay, it feels like I will have to stop wanting anything for myself at all in this life. I'll have to become as miserable as he is and be satisfied with this garbage relationship as it is.

He said it was the woman's job to hold up the man.

Great, another thing to do.

I said, "Women are tired. We have it all now and we have to be the person caring for everyone as well as going out and—metaphorically hunting and killing for the family, too."

The dog rings the hanging bell to be let outside out the back door. She is another being needing to be cared for.

Maybe I'm in my head too much. If I let go, and surrender it over, maybe things will heal and something will change.

He says I should just, "Trust in God."

We sat in tears looking at each other. I asked him why he loved me.

"Because you're my wife. Why do you love me?" He asked.

"I asked you first."

Blah, blah, blah.

He never did answer.

~

Even Strangers Can Tell, Me 2017

A weird encounter at Applebee's. I stood with my husband and his two kids as the hostess initiated a greeting. She looked into our little group and said, "The three of you?"

I counted again- yes, I was there, in obvious closeness to the others, and yet I was invisible, not included in the ones she saw. I had become a ghost maybe, my actual being having become a mere sliver of a person.

Another reminder I did not belong. My rumination turns into an inaudible scream.

There is a quiet that comes when you decide to walk away from your life as you know it. The silence makes space for questions and answers. A calm while you wait for your next direction from the little voice that tells your heart what to do.

I see myself in a new space with no history. No expectations. The sound of silence or the new sounds that come, are different and unknown. Stability is gone. The only known is aloneness that comes with being by yourself.

The music you play is your choice, and the food you eat is your pick. No more having to cater to someone else's preferences or demands. The color of your walls is up to you. Everything.

Today I took a walk with my dog. She sniffed the ground and walked as if there was no difference with the day. Only I knew that today was different. A decision. Steps are being taken. A future to get excited about. A new job to start soon, one way past my comfort zone, yet they want me. And I will give it my all.

I look around the house and imagine packing up this and that. What was mine before I got here, or I will leave this with him. The anger and unhappiness have left and I am finding comfort in the belief that not only is this good for me, **it will be good for him**.

I try hard to avoid hurting people. Me leaving will hurt in some regards, but with time and space he will thrive and find love again. I know it.

What I know is that love isn't supposed to be this hard. Difficulties come and go but the constant feelings of misplacement are not the way life and love's supposed to be.

The time away from each other will start to heal the wounds of us both. We will feel free to be ourselves once again. The routine items on the daily checklist will be the most troublesome to some. The partner did this, the other did that. A new routine must be found.

A groove. Remembering fun times, but moving forward. I believe that he will understand. There is no hate in my heart. No ill will. I want him to be happy and I want to find my own happiness after it has been lost and forgotten for so long. It will be a process.

Sometimes, it will be scary, but those are the times when you rally your friends around to cheer you on. There will be times you depend on yourself for the first time.

I walk this house, fully believing it to be temporary. I have lost any fight and watch the daily goings-on as if watching on a screen. Safely tucked into a seat to watch the show, I am no longer bothered by what I used to be. It won't matter pretty soon.

I am saving my energy for the next adventure. There will be a packing. A moving. The paperwork of a divorce. Paying my bills for myself. The responsibility of alone.

And it will be terrifying and energizing, and bumpy. But it must be done. To find myself again. And to dance.

~

~3~

Jeremy and Sky had become an unbeatable pair. Since their first award for best wine in Oregon, they have managed to win awards for excellence in hospitality and customer service as well. *Escape* had become a national brand and was even distributed in the other family winery in Amalfi.

A large group was due to arrive tomorrow, a group from the Midwest. They were gathering to talk about organizing their shared mission, of being a political watchdog organization. They would be fact-checking *everything* that comes out of politicians' mouths.

With so many ways to gain information, and unvalidated sources rampant, people didn't know what to believe any more. This group was choosing board members, an organization name and roles would be assigned.

There would be regional fact-checking, nation and worldwide. Mostly volunteers at first, reporters would give their own time and contribute their own writing skills to pull the truth from the just plain bullshit.

The first night, many gathered in the tasting room with wine and light snacks. The lead organizers had arrived but the majority of attendees were due the next morning.

That evening was supposed to be low key, a simple get-together to introduce themselves. Name tags were a must, and along with their name, they were asked to identify a hero of theirs. It was a way to build comradery quickly, and help people to remember who that other person was.

F.Z. made his rounds around the room; he was beyond excited to be there. This concept had long been a dream of his. It was finally being realized, thanks to a few conversations with friends in high places. He had bounced around for a bit career-wise, from a corporate job to owning and running two small businesses.

His hero, he penned on his name tag, was his father.

F.Z., Sr., wasn't a large man, except in prominence; but his shoes were proving pretty hard to fill. Many adored Senior and his powerful way of getting things done with the least amount of steps and people. He had a way of motivating people that spurred them to go above and beyond. Sometimes sacrificing their families in an effort to get this man to respect them.

Now that was what F.Z. wanted most, respect and to build his empire. Again.

He scanned the room and sidled up to a group of three. They were all reporters from *Democracy Now!.*

"This will be great. We will get to dive into the stories or topics that we really need to, want to, in order to get to the truth. People *need* the truth. Not the bullshit," one said.

"Yeah, I am excited, too, to catch these assholes in the act. I can't wait to really nail some of these guys. Uh, and women." F.Z. said as he choked on his words standing next to a female colleague.

"Men aren't the only liars," she agreed.

"I know. You all can lie with the best of them." He winked at her and she rolled her eyes.

F.Z. walked away from the group to check on the schedule for the next day. He noticed that most of the people were starting to leave for their hotels in town or their onsite cabins.

Since the group was predominantly from the East Coast, many were on Eastern Standard Time. A partial day of traveling and being a full three hours ahead sleep-wise, they were pretty wiped out.

F.Z. had come to the West Coast the previous week to visit his brother and family. He had already acclimated to the time change, and would be up for a while with the excitement. There were less than ten people left in the room, and they were saying their goodbyes to be fresh in the morning for the brainstorming sessions.

He wandered around the large room taking in the architecture of the space, noticing the large beams and reclaimed wood everywhere. He saw a cozy couch in the corner with an antique wooden stand that held something. *A Bible?* he wondered.

Walking closer, he reached for the book and sat down on a large leather chair the same color as a merlot wine.

The manager, Sky, looked his way, then smiled. She was a beautiful woman *he wouldn't mind getting to know better.* He smiled back and she took off for the kitchen.

"Maybe later," he thought. He looked at the title of the blue spiral-bound book. *Find Me 3 of 5* shone in aged gold- embossed letters on the front. No author, and no more information on the back either. The first page was a prologue of sorts. An invitation. Something to do, to think about.

He watched the last person leave and the cleanup crew put trash bags near the door. They would need to get the room ready for the next day.

Again noticing the woman, Sky, buzzing around and giving orders, the place was shaping up. Two men took folding chairs off the trolley, and started setting them up in an arched shape around the front. They grabbed the stand that had held the book in the corner to use as a podium for the speeches and presentations.

Sky gave a knowing smile to the new reader of the winery's mascot book. He was unaware.

It was starting to get late, so F.Z. tucked the book under his arm to head out. He could bring it back tomorrow— he was sure no one would miss it until then.

His eyes adjusted to the night sky as he walked out the front door to find his container cabin in the vineyard above. The heavens were lit up with millions of stars. Being away from the city for a while was nice. He had spent years in the Northwest before leaving to go back to the Midwest.

Back then, his father had gotten him a job in his home city, and at the time he was working as a waiter, so he decided to give the new opportunity a shot.

F.Z. opened the sliding door on the side of the container and took a seat on the Eames leather chair in the corner. Each cabin was decorated with a certain era in mind, and his just happened to be mid century which he loved.

A ball-lamp hung over the chair and he reached over to turn it on at the base. The lamp lit up the whole room and the light filtered outside so that the first few rows of neighboring grapevines could be seen.

Pulling his reading glasses out of the breast pocket of his blue-striped, button up oxford shirt, he settled in for a read. As someone who thought of himself as an academic, the pages flew quickly and he was surprised to come to an excerpt with his very own initials. *There weren't many people with initials like his.*

~

A Mom Knows- They Always Know, Me, 2017-18

*W*hile looking for work, I had a lot of time at home with Mom. When she lived far away, I could share just enough of my life to have others believe that I was fine, and that things were okay in my marriage. That we were managing.

But having Mom live with us, she was a non-stop visitor who knew me to my core, and I was suddenly challenged in my compromised position much more than I was ready to be.

Here she was, a very loving, but helpless spectator to my intense, and never-ending unhappiness.

She would talk to me about it when we were alone. I remember she asked me, while we sat in my colorful office, the only room in the house I felt was of my own design,

"Do you trust yourself to make the decision to leave?"

I wept then, and she held me.

"No, I don't trust myself to make this big of a decision. I probably made the wrong decision last time, and I can't leave now, not when I am so low and have nothing going for myself. I am miserable here, yes, but we have a roof over our heads. What if I am totally wrong?"

When I left my first marriage, I was going towards someone else, so I hadn't felt alone in my leaving. This time, there was no one, only me. Going this time would be on the merits of my own opinion and desires for my life. I had spent most of my life doing for others, being in help or service, of whatever dream they had. Was finding me worth it?

Again I am safe in the scheme of things. The bills are paid, we are housed, he looks after me as well as my mother and my oldest daughter who was attending her last year of college in the big city. I couldn't take on all of us with no job.

I kept waiting for something to happen, to come along and radically change our lives so that I would be able to smile and feel like myself again.

We'd just gone through a presidential election. While I knew that he and I were opposite in our political standings, the candidate that he was rooting for was someone that I was real worried about. We had managed to just agree to disagree for the most part- in previous elections, each of us knew our votes would cancel out the other's, but this time—it was different.

As the political temperature in the house rose, I listened to him spout off his conservative zealot talking points to his children over dinner, hoping to indoctrinate the next generation into his mindset.

He didn't seem to see that his kids were more empathetic and shared, like me, a more worldly point of view. They didn't make other people wrong for being or thinking a certain way, and they didn't judge based on looks or status the way he did.

When he tampered with the TV so my mother couldn't watch her news channel, that was the last straw for me. Censorship in my own home? His young son had timidly tattled on his father for changing the controls.

I could no longer be with this man.

That day, I completely lost my shit. I texted him and asked him to come out of the store and talk to me. We stood in the parking lot, him having no idea why I had called him outside.

"I was in there, buying your Christmas gift," he said, then he saw my eyes flash yellow with anger, a sight he had seen many times before.

I proceeded to completely rip off his head in the mall parking lot- verbally, that is. I didn't care who was around, I didn't care who heard me. I was not going to let him bully us and censor our existence. I would not stay silent anymore.

Over dinner that night, around a full table, I announced my intent to divorce him. It hadn't been the first time I had uttered these words in front of the children, but I meant it this time.

Fuck this!

I was still unemployed, my mom was living with us, and it was Christmas. The prenup I'd signed meant I had no financial parachute whatsoever.

I spent my days looking for work. He spent this time trying to get me to change my mind about the whole thing.

While I waited for my chance to escape, I took every chance to get back to what I loved: I painted, walked out in nature and reconnected with friends in my old city, all outside of his view—in secret. I would be strong enough to find my way to myself again, I just needed a break!

The job search was still ghastly. Jobs I would have totally rocked disappeared with no call backs. Weeks passed.

"When are you going to leave?" my daughters would ask from the safety of their father's house. I told them I needed a job and would get out as soon *as I could. Would the universe's timing be in time for me?*

The election happened, and to our shock the dangerous man won. This world was about to change, and not in a good way.

My eldest was in her room, studying for her senior year college finals, when the announcement came over the TV. I went up and told her the results. We cried and held each other and I said, "People will die."

The next day, I vomited from the shock of this soon to be world, and the pure stress of my life. Christmas was close, and no one was hiring. Employers didn't want to have to deal with extra payroll for maybe a couple of days of employment before the new year, and that had tabled all hiring efforts. Many were on vacation.

"Try back after the first of the year."

My husband was still trying to make it work with us. At times, I really wanted it to, too. Financially, it would've been easier. But I was seriously unhappy. A sadness, a hollow I had never known before.

I had wanted to believe that we could find our way back to each other. That something could change in one of us that might magically fix it. I tried remembering the good times. But the togetherness was gone, corroded away by the years, the differences, and the lack of love.

My daughters gave me a gift that Christmas which was absolutely perfect.

It was a silver bracelet with the word FEARLESS engraved in capital letters. What I couldn't understand was that even with all of my fail-ures-somehow they believed I could and would do better. Somehow they knew that this marriage wouldn't be a life sentence for me. It wasn't the spot for me- or any of us.

So many times in the coming months that bracelet would be the talisman, the sentiment, that would hold me together on my worst days. It showed that they believed in me. Maybe I could, too.

*Christmas finally passed and I secretly shuffled away all of my pre-mar-riage Christmas decorations from our once shared boxes, and handed them off to my daughters for safe keeping to keep at their Dad's. **I knew I would not have another holiday season there**.*

The bracelet meant to me that they believed that I was strong enough to start over and find a better place for myself. It was a gift I could never repay.

New Years. Valentine's Day. No job. No prospects.

March finally came. Spring.

A time of rebirth. I had been waiting as patiently as I could, chasing a job that might give me the financial security to actually leave and be okay. In the end that job offer didn't come.

Another opportunity came, but the interviewer was away on vacation and couldn't meet me for a few weeks. Waiting again.

With no certainty in place, but with a caring friend and a room up for rent, I jumped anyway, and did a free fall into the biggest, scariest uncertainty of my life.

Hoping, and praying that my wings would pop out on the way down.

I couldn't stay there another day, another minute.

I was dying here. Suppressing, every day, my thoughts, feelings, my beliefs and who I was as a person. How long could I go on like this? Something must go my way.

There must be enough scraps left of me to put my life back together.

This can't be the end of my story.

~

F.Z.

Always knowing everything, using your big fancy words, testing me. Even handing me a box of your college vocabulary words just so I could keep up with you. Frankly, you didn't turn me on when I saw you in the pages of the binder at the dating service I'd signed up for in the early nineties, but running into you downstairs at the restaurant where you worked, I had a second thought.

More like, why the hell not? What have I got to lose, my membership was almost up, and maybe you had something to teach me. Teach me you did, but not in the way you wanted to maybe. You were a brainiac, and I was, at first, in awe of your knowledge.

I guess I did need to grow up and become more adventurous, see what the world really had to offer. You pushed me, and I intrigued you enough to keep me around as a little side-project. Like Eliza in *My Fair Lady* with Audrey Hepburn. *You* could make me into the kind of woman worthy of you.

We went along for a while, then you became bored of me, deciding to move back to your native state to a job your father helped you get.

I showed interest in your road trip back East, and even though we had broken up, you agreed to take me along. You planned a great trip for us, and I saw many of the things some only see on postcards.

It was under the redwoods camped out in a tent that we got together again, in the biblical sense. Not because either of us had talked about getting back together but because things happen in a tent between two people sometimes. As I lie in your arms, you told me that a friend of yours had bet you a hundred dollars that you'd sleep with me on the trip which apparently you hoped to win.

In Vegas, we even toyed with getting married, just for the hell of it.

Thank God, we didn't.

Before we reached our final destination, you explained to me that since your mother didn't have any daughters— *any girls, women* who were brought home by her son's would be the recipients of a shopping trip. Your brother's girlfriends' had been showered with things but since I was the only one you'd brought around, this time it would be me. The whole idea was weird. I didn't know her at all, but now I would go shopping with her and had to let her buy me stuff? Clothing, shoes? I guess it was my people pleasing nature that let it happen.

At the end of a long shopping day, I sat up in your parents' guest room beautifully coiffed by your mom. I stood over the suitcase, packing, as I was leaving the next day. Voices drew me to the open window. I could hear you and your father as you had stepped outside to talk. I crouched lower to listen. Senior queried your thoughts about me. You stated that *I wasn't what you had in mind,* that *you couldn't imagine being with someone as plain and boring as me. That I wasn't smart enough for you*.

I consider that moment and overhearing you— a gift. The closure I needed.

The next day was my solo train trip back home. I was out of money completely and had resolved myself that I wouldn't eat for the two days it took to get home.

You knew my plight and handed me a hundred dollar bill. I took it and said goodbye, got on the train, and never looked back at you as the train pulled out of the station. You noticed that, and asked me about it later on the phone.

I told you then that I had overheard you tell your father about me. Everything you said and thought of me. You felt bad.

The miles between us were a good thing, and I found love and made a family soon after.

My mechanical engineer husband never hesitated to have a technical conversation with me. I reveled in the deep topics we would get into.

I think sometimes about that hundred dollars.

I guess I had *earned* it.

Sometimes you can meet people who teach you without making you feel stupid. That's the kind of folks I like to be with.

~

The story was familiar. Too familiar. A girl he had known and actually traveled back to the Midwest with must have written this. ***It must be her***.

"My God, this is what she says about me after our time and trip together?"

His ears got red, and he felt his blood start to boil.

"How could she air our dirty laundry like this? How many people have read this?"

He flipped to the pages in the back, hundreds- maybe thousands- of anger-blurred signatures lined the back pages. ***People he knew could have read this!*** They might have even thought it was him!

"How dare she! She was never good enough for me. I had tried to teach her about world events. I gave her those vocabulary words so she would be able to keep up with my friends. I tried to make her into someone, dammit!"

He steamed inside. *She had the gall, the nerve to put this out into the world. About me! People from this group might see it and ask me about it, or start a joke about it being me.*

"She will never see this book again," he spit as he ripped the cover off the book in fury. The pages behind went airborne in pieces soon after. He got to the names in the back and tore each page into hundreds of pieces. Those containing their shared story were ripped so small til his fingernails bled. His blood pressure beat into his skull.

"Who does she think she is? She is a nobody and this is the end of this dream. *Right here and right now!*"

F.Z. dropped to the ground, pulling towards him all of the scattered shreds of paper from the corners of the container cottage, like a rat hoarding its last crumbs. He shoved them into the plastic bag that was supposed to hold his dirty laundry. He stormed out of the dwelling and headed out towards the dumpster behind the tasting room. Full garbage bags waited nearby. A lock on the lid was visible and ample. The cleanup crew was bringing trash out and placing it by the bin.

Hiding his bag inside another bag, he would be sure that it was disposed of.

He wasn't going to give *her* the satisfaction of seeing *this* book again. He skulked away, aggressively rubbing his hands on his pants, as if cleaning up a murder scene. His eyes darted back and forth in a frenzy to see if anyone had seen him, then locked the latch on the door of his container home. Finally he was safe, *but was he*?

F.Z. lay awake that night, crazed, obsessing about what had become of the other four copies. Were they all the same, who had read those ones? Would he be found out?

Dawn teased and as the staff started to take to their posts, he saw Sky and realized that she had last seen him with the book.

Oh no! He couldn't risk an encounter or questions. He packed his bags, and threw them into the back of his rental car.

This fact-checking empire had been his dream, but right now he had to leave. He could catch up with the team later, and make an excuse about a family emergency.

This was a family emergency. He felt threatened. He had taken care of his business though, and he felt justified. He smiled with the idea that part of her dream had been crushed by him.

"How dare she!" he murmured over and over as sweat beaded on his brow. He punched the gas pedal. "This was supposed to be my moment! My time, finally! And she ruined it! Over twenty years ago I left her behind, but now she pops up?"

That boring, dumb girl from his past had him on the run.

Maybe he would look her up again. Just to rattle her cage a little. See if any of the other books had reached her. He knew he had been a jerk to her, telling his father that she wasn't good enough, as it turned out, within earshot.

Not pretty enough, not nearly smart enough. To overhear him say all that from the bedroom window must have hurt. But she had gotten her revenge. They were even.

The destroyed remains of Find Me 3 of 5 sat soiled amongst the rubbish left by the Fact- Checking Brigade, *covered in the deceit of a man who had sworn to bring truth to the masses.*

3 of 5 is lost.*

However...

Copies of Book Three sit in a banker's box on a shelf high up in a guest room closet in Laramie, Wyoming, awaiting a second chance. ;)

Book Club Discussion Questions

1. What would you do/think if you received a package in the mail with such a quest?

2. Who was your favorite character and why?

3. When the author married again, did you think it would work out?

4. What is a dream you've always had but something held you back from trying?

5. Have you ever felt you had to be someone else to get along?

6. What character's plight did you most relate to?

7. Did you feel any big emotions in this book? Sad, happy, angry? Why?

8. If you were a friend of the author during this time in her life, what advice would you share with her?

9. Did you learn about anything in the pages of this book that made you want to dive deeper into the topic?

10. If you found a book like this, where would you put it or what would you do with it?

11. What do you think took the author so long to figure out this relationship was not good for her?

12. Will this book inspire you to take any chances in your own life?

If you would like me to zoom in on your meetings, send me a note! I would probably love to~ <3

Mentions and Places Listed in this Book

Colin Firth-*https://www.imdb.com/name/nm0000147/*

Understanding Men, Celebrating Women course and workshops-*https://www.alisonarmstrong.com/*

A Gift from the Sea- Anne Morrow Lindbergh (available all over)

Boni Lynn Drive up-*https://chanceencounters.weebly.com/my-blog/memories-of-boni-lynn*

Mediumship- Many sources

Turkey Rama Festival of McMinnville OR-Defunct-*https://www.oregonencyclopedia.org/articles/turkey_rama/*

Craigslist Missed Connections-*https://en.wikipedia.org/wiki/Missed_Connections:_An_Exploration_into_the_Online_Postings_of_Desperate_Romantics*

Atrani Italy-*https://www.youtube.com/watch?v=4twZHSmdvXs* (I have no relationship with this source-just looked fun)

Amalfi Lemons-*https://amalfilemon.com/our-story/*

Sacajawea- Shoshone @Wind River preferred references:

https://jacksonholehistory.org/learn/archives-research/wind-river-treaty-documents/

https://jacksonholehistory.org/learn/archives-research/through-the-eyes-of-tsutukwanah-photo-exhibit/

https://www.wyohistory.org/

https://www.sacajaweacenter.org/

http://www.easternshoshone.org/

New website for Museum-*http://www.easternshoshonemuseum.com/*

Dentalium Shells-*https://www.lakotatimes.com/articles/pankeska-pestola-dentalium-shell/*

Shoshone Love Poem- *https://www.ya-native.com/Culture_GreatBasin/Shoshone/ShoshoneLoveSong.html#google_vignette*

Babette's Feast Movie-*https://www.imdb.com/title/tt0092603/?ref_=nv_sr_srsg_6_tt_2_nm_6_in_0_q_Babette*

The Five People you meet in Heaven-*https://www.imdb.com/title/tt0400435/* Book by Mitch Albom

East Indian Wedding traditions-*https://julianribinikweddings.com/everything-you-need-to-know-about-indian-wedding-traditions*

Autism Experts- *https://www.aspergerexperts.com/* and *https://autismexperts.pro*

Love Marriage or Arranged Marriage

Lyme Disease- *https://www.mayoclinic.org/diseases-conditions/lyme-disease/symptoms-causes/syc-20374651*

You Can Heal your Life- Louise Hay-*https://www.youtube.com/watch?v=gYNpw0gkifI*

Penelope the One Upper- Saturday Night Live-*https://snl.fandom.com/wiki/Penelope* also check out Youtube

Under the Tuscan Sun- Movie-*https://www.imdb.com/title/tt0328589/* Book by Frances Mayes

Bread and Tulips- Movie-*https://www.imdb.com/title/tt0237539/* Book by Pane E. Tulipani

Wild- Movie- *https://www.imdb.com/title/tt2305051/* Book by Cheryl Strayed

Luckiest Man- Song by the Wood Brothers

You are a Badass By Jen Sincero-*https://jensincero.com/* I did end up reading this book and listen to it 1-2x a year since! LOVE!

Kazan Kremlin- *https://whc.unesco.org/en/list/980/*

Temple of All Religions-*https://www.atlasobscura.com/places/temple-of-all-religions*

Kul Sharif Mosque-*https://www.youtube.com/watch?v=eAolmlDyxto*

Richard Bach Books-*https://richardbach.com/*

Strangers on a Train movie- *https://www.imdb.com/title/tt0044079/?ref_=fn_all_ttl_1* Book by Patricia Highsmith

Love and Logic Classes-*https://www.loveandlogic.com*

Gary Vaynerchuk-*https://garyvaynerchuk.com/* & *https://www.youtube.com/watch?app=desktop&v=hVoXNXZvDRo&t=0s*

My Fair Lady Movie-*https://www.imdb.com/title/tt0058385/* Play by George Bernard Shaw

Author's note

It occurred to me recently that this story may bring people closer to stepping a toe into feeling like someone else. ***Since*** we are only able to see life through our own lens, having placed one experience on top of the next to see the whole picture, we miss out on what others may see and experience.

It is my hope that this series spurs you into a different view, an understanding that each of us becomes who we are— over time. People affect us, along with the daily things that happen, and how we navigate through them.

Reconciling our early years and how we either continue with or break the generational binds we share is a forever accessible choice. ***We can decide to grow and change*** or we can decide to stay stuck, it is up to us.

There is no such thing as too late.

It is my ultimate goal to convey that every single person on this planet has a story to tell. There are thousands/millions/billions of lessons to be shared. Ultimately it is in the power of collective sharing that lessens the hurt, guilt and overall loneliness that plagues.

To bring us together.

Still a huge believer ***in humanity and love***,

H

Newsletter, updates and more

*W*hy an After-story?

I know, I miss them, too. If you want to hear more bits about the characters in this book who left too soon, sign up for my newsletters to hear more about them and other pondering thoughts.

It's been a pleasure.

Sincerely,

H.H. Rune

Free After-story of Sky and Jeremy from Book Three here:

For news and the latest from the Extraordinary Life Seeker series…
and to watch the travels of the limited edition trackable versions of Find
Me
please visit

hhrune.com

Stay Tuned for the next book in the Extraordinary Life Seeker series, Find
Me, Book Four, out late 2025 or early 2026.
H.H. Rune's books are brought forth by:

If you choose to pass this book along

Date	Name	Location

hhrune.com

Date	Name	Location

Date	Name	Location

Date	Name	Location